Wiley Royce
Versus
The Martians

LM Foster

This is a work of fiction. Names, characters, places and incidents are products of the author's imagination. Any resemblance to actual events, locales, organizations, or persons, either living or dead, is entirely coincidental.

ISBN-10: 0692638849
ISBN-13: 978-0692638842

Back cover photo: NASA

9th Street Press
www.9thstreetpress.com

Whenever you do a thing, act as if all the world were watching.
Thomas Jefferson

ONE

Tom Bastion glanced at that part of the sky where he knew he would find the star Sirius. It was cloudy tonight, so he couldn't see it, and he smiled to himself for looking anyway. He'd lived in California for decades and wondered exactly how many times he'd reconnoitered the position of the home sun in the night sky in all that time.

Tom had first arrived in Mexico, as those of his kind did for this landmass. It was the closest portal to his destination: there used to be one on the Great Plains, but it had closed long ago. From Mapimi, he'd journeyed through Southern California to the Inland Empire, where his Uncle Morry owned a bookstore in Riverside.

When Morry returned home, Tom had taken over ownership. It wasn't like he had to make a living from it; bookstores make about as much money as blacksmiths anymore. As he was fond of telling his friends, "My extended family has been turning a tidy profit on this rock for a long time. *Centuries,* to be exact. I am what you would call independently wealthy, and I'm the last one left, that I know of."

But running a bookstore was a lot of fun, and it allowed Tom to indulge in his passion for literature, as well as his other passion, that of meeting and interacting with the people of his adopted planet. Where he was from, there was no strife, so some of the more adventuresome types came to Earth to see what was up. It was like a trip to Vegas for them. Some eventually went back home – like Uncle Morry. Most stayed.

Not too long after his arrival, Tom had been fortunate enough to meet a young woman named Maxine. She was sweet and kind, an old soul, and she would've become Tom's girlfriend had he wished her to be. But she was just too young. He was in his early forties then; he'd done a lot of living already, and desired to explore all the myriad things that this planet had to offer which the homeworld did not. But Maxine still had her own living to do, so Tom settled on having her for his best friend.

On Maxine's twenty-second birthday, December 22, 2012, on that night that the world was supposed to end, but of course did not, she introduced Tom to Liz, a woman closer to his age. He knew that he'd found the only woman for him the moment they met. And if one is lucky enough to find one's other half, one discloses, eventually, where one is from, and all the strangeness therein entailed. Eventually. They married and traveled the world together, but only for ten short years.

Cancer claimed the love of his life at the age of forty-eight.

Tom's existence was solitary after that, his only real friends being Maxine and the man she'd married, and their child, Janae. Janae had been eight years old when Liz passed, and in the years that followed, as she grew, she frequently tried to fix her beloved Tommy up with the various schoolteachers she admired, or anyone that she thought might be deserving.

But Tom was steadfast in his grief. He remained alone. It took a young man named Wiley Royce to show him his selfishness.

There was a customer that frequented the bookstore, an end-of-the-world prepper named Dionne. It was obvious that she had quite the crush on Tom, and Wiley wanted to know why he wouldn't give her a tumble.

"It wouldn't be fair to Dionne, Wiley. I love someone else. Liz – she's waiting for me. I believe that. I have to believe it."

Wiley shook his head. "If you believe it, I'm happy for you. But all I see is a miserable, lonely old man. Even if she is waiting for you – do you think that she'd want you to be unhappy and lonely for the rest of your life, until the time comes for you to join her? I'm sure she was a wonderful woman – I get that just from your sorrow at her loss. So I'm sure she wouldn't want you to be the way you are. I'm sure she'd like to see you have someone like Dionne for . . . company."

Tom shook his head, and Wiley laughed harshly. "You're ridiculous. It wouldn't be fair to Dionne that you've decided that you're gonna meet Liz after you *die?* Listen to yourself."

"Still–"

"Why don't you explain it to Dionne and let her decide? I don't think she's as metaphysical as all that. I don't think she cares about who you want to be with after you're dead. I think she cares about who you want to be with *now*. And she wants it to be her."

The young man had a point, one that Tom, in his despondency, had never considered. "Liz wouldn't want me to be lonely . . ."

So the bookstore owner had taken up with Dionne. They didn't marry; Dionne liked to keep her name out of the public record as much as possible. She loved him, and Tom discovered that Wiley was right. Liz would've wanted him to be happy, and whatever waited after death – Dionne didn't care about any of that.

Tom was grateful for Dionne's company, and he loved her as much as was possible for him. But sadness still visited him sometimes: Dionne was not Liz, and she had her own views of the world, some of which struck Tom as a little bit off-kilter, if not downright nuts. His new woman whole-heartedly believed in a myriad of conspiracy theories; she believed the world was on the brink of collapse, that the end was due as surely as was the sunrise. That it hadn't yet happened made no difference to her. It was coming.

Tom did not tell Dionne that he was from another planet.

TWO

Not unlike Tom himself, sound investments on the part of past family members had left Dionne quite well-off. In the city (Tom liked the city best), the two of them shared the house that had belonged to Liz, so that he could be close to the bookstore. In the mountains, Dionne had another house, complete with HEPA-filtered bomb-shelter and stores of dehydrated food. When the end came, she aimed to survive it.

Most of the time, Dionne stayed in town with the man she loved, however. A selective bit of rationalization on her part had convinced her that there would always be time to flee to her stronghold when disaster finally struck, and she relished sleeping beside Tom more than she relished the smug knowledge that she would survive in the mountains because she was prepared.

Tonight, when he walked in the door after work, he found her watching Netflix, learning another chapter in the canon of All Things Are Not What They Seem.

Dionne paused the screen and gave him an effusive hug and kiss. Even though she loved him, to Dionne, her man was too complacent, unwilling to accept all the ways and means by which a shadowy *them* attempted to shape their destinies. He would see, though. Soon enough.

"Did you know that our world is positively lousy with aliens, Tom?"

His eyebrows went up in surprise, although he knew he shouldn't really be surprised. MK-ULTRA, we didn't really land on the moon, JFK was set up, Bush knew about 9/11, the presidential election of 2028 was fixed. Dionne believed all of those, as well as a hundred others. It was only a matter of time before she got into the whole aliens-are-amongst-us thing. The fact that it was true concerned Tom not in the least. Whatever she was watching on Netflix hadn't revealed the secret to her. No one here knew the truth.

Dionne pushed a button on the remote, and a deep voice intoned, *Alien Archives. Exposing the biggest secret on Planet Earth.*

This oughta be good, Tom thought indulgently, and plopped down beside her on the couch.

This episode of *Alien Archives* preached to the already suspicious choir about the existence of *The Blue Planet Project,* a secret but conveniently leaked U.S. government document which outlined the existence of *alien races visiting Earth, their technology, experimentation, and underground installations, all pointing to a massive government cover-up.*

Tourism. Tom smiled to himself. If the U.S. or any other government knew anything – and Tom was sure that they did not – then that's all they'd be covering up. His people came here like a bunch of clean-living folk from Des Moines on that tour bus to Vegas: to have fun, to indulge in a little anonymous decadence, maybe, the type they didn't have back home.

To those of his race, Earth was, as Tom had once told Liz: "This unapologetic den of iniquity, this carnival of strange. I fucking love it here! Tobacco, liquor. Bacon. T-bones and fast cars. The best music in the universe. Gambling. Movies. *Dirty movies.* Art. Literature. Architecture. Machinery."

There was none of that on the homeworld.

Tom didn't pay a lot of attention to the parade of "experts" that spoke of how the Earth's entire philosophy would change, once everybody realized that *The Blue Planet Project* was indeed gospel. But when they started to describe the aliens amongst us, his attention was arrested.

They showed a picture of something called a *Reptiloid,* and Tom experienced an uncomfortable recognition. It was just a flash – a lizard-like creature, but humanoid in shape, green and scaly, with big black eyes and lots of teeth.

"Rewind that," Tom requested before he realized that he'd even done so. Dionne raised an eyebrow in surprise. Tom was never interested in the conspiracies. The *truths.*

"I want to see the Reptiloid again. I think I . . . dreamed of him once."

Dionne did as she was asked, and paused the screen on the lizard-man. The creature resembled a member of the race that had once threatened to destroy Tom's own people on the homeworld. There had been a war, in the dim reaches of time. Every child learned the history. The enemy had been called, perhaps without a lot of imagination, the *Dino People.*

Tom nodded and Dionne pressed the button. Next up, *Alien Archives* showed renderings of the more familiar Grays. Tom knew all about them. They were a servant class on his planet, the only remnants of the conquered Dino People, biologically engineered down from those ferocious forebears until they were harmless. The only thing that looked even remotely like a Dino on his planet anymore were those Grays. There were illustrations of the old enemy, of course – everyone on the homeworld knew what their fearsome adversary had once looked like. But they didn't exist anymore.

Yet *Alien Archives* had flashed an accurate representation of one of them onscreen. Tom wondered if one of his fellows worked for the show, and if this quick picture of a Dino was intended as some kind of inside joke for any off-worlders that had decided to make themselves a batch of popcorn and have a good laugh at what the Earthlings thought they knew. He'd always reckoned that such a trick was how humanity knew about the Grays – a playful homeworlder had started the story. There were no Grays visiting Earth. They were simply maids and cooks; *the help.*

But seeing a Dino on Netflix had been a little jarring for Tom, not really funny. These beings had threatened his entire race at one time.

The episode trotted out an author for *The Blue Planet Project,* a top government scientist with the highest of clearances, who had jotted down all these notes about the whys and wherefores of the alien visitations – *Where did they come from and what do they want?*

Mud wrestling, Tom thought and grinned to himself. *Drag racing. Disneyland.*

Unfortunately, but not surprisingly, the blabbermouth scientist had disappeared. The wages of talking about the visitors was death, apparently. But his notes, compiled as *The Blue Planet Project,* were a genie not to be put back in the bottle, according to *Alien Archives.*

Now the Reptiloids took center stage in the narrative, blinking their black eyes and looking nightmarish. Thanks to *The Blue Planet Project,* details of underground hybridization experiments – humans combined with Reptiloids – were now on the internet, for all to see.

Again, Tom smiled to himself. There had to be a homeworlder on the *Alien Archives'* staff. Because here was another inside joke – hybridization between Earthlings and aliens had indeed occurred, eons ago. But it hadn't been the Dinos that had done the cross-breeding with humanity. It had been the hominid species, or at least the closest thing the homeworld had to it.

Yet here was one of Dionne's aluminum-foil hat crazy conspiracy shows, talking about shadowy pacts – the government was allowing alien abductions in order that there might be Reptiloid-human hybridization. They had even presented a damn accurate, blinking illustration of a Dino.

The show ended on an appropriately chilling note. The 18,000 inhabitant underground city of the Reptiloids, somewhere in New Mexico, which had been built for the aliens' use by the government, was currently turning out hybrids and secreting them in all walks of life, in many North and South American cities. It was an experiment to see if they could assimilate, to see if they could avoid detection. Your co-worker, your kids' teacher, your minister, the guy behind you in line at the supermarket – were they really human, or were they a reptile in disguise, trying to blend?

There was no way to tell.

Once the aliens were convinced that the hybridization was working, the infiltration would be stepped up; the invasion would begin. Perhaps it had begun already.

"You don't really believe that there are Dinos–" Tom quickly corrected himself – *"Reptiloids* walking around on Earth? Masquerading as people?"

"There are more things in heaven and earth, as they say. For all I know, Wiley could be an alien. He sure knows a lot about technology."

"Wiley's no alien," Tom assured her. "He's just a quick-witted, smart-assed monkey, born and bred right here in River City."

The next episode of *Alien Archives* would commence in twenty seconds, but Dionne had lost interest in the fate of mankind at the hands of lizards from another world. She clicked off the television and turned her full attention to the guy that ran the bookstore.

THREE

Wiley Royce was dreaming of the glorious future. Perched on a hill, he viewed the smooth, flowing freeway below, the glittering city filled with self-driving cars. Their digital screens glowed colorfully. Ah, the automated future, already halfway arrived!

Wiley took a deep, satisfied sigh. He looked down at his hand and found contained therein an electromagnetic pulse apparatus of his own devising. He sighed, again with satisfaction, and pointed the EMP at the efficiently running city. He grinned in his sleep and pushed the button. The cacophony of screeching metal which followed woke him from his dream.

Wiley smiled in the darkness. He'd never disrupt self-driving cars, would never kill his fellow man, never destroy their property. Just the knowledge that he could, and effortlessly, was enough for Wiley. That any number of others also could, served as a cautionary tale. No one would ever find Wiley Royce inside a car that drove itself.

Brendee stirred in her sleep and he kissed her on the neck. She opened her eyes and smiled at him. "Why are you awake?"

"I dreamt that I set the freeway back a few years." His grin widened. "A simple thing, really, just a little electronic disruption."

"That's you, Wiley." Brendee enfolded him in her arms. "Always smarter than everyone else."

"Jack of all trades . . ."

"Master of all you survey."

"If the shoe fits."

FOUR

Making love with her husband was the chief joy in Brendee's life. It had been that way from their first moments together, and she considered herself fortunate that this cornerstone of marriage was so awesomely rock solid in hers. Wiley – sexy, secretive, sometimes infuriatingly superior Wiley – always knew what she wanted. Beyond satisfied, as always, she returned to dreamland.

Across the valley from Dionne's stronghold, Wiley and Brendee had their own cabin, were staying there for the weekend. Wiley arose, threw on a set of sweats and padded, silently barefoot, out into the living room. He reveled in the silence, the simplicity of the feel of the wooden floor beneath his seldom shod feet. He waved his hand in front of a switch and the curtains rolled back with a grand swish, revealing the September sunrise. He waved his hand again, and through the seeming magic of proximity technology, two of the glass panels also folded back.

Wiley walked out onto the deck and took in a lungful of the crisp air. He stood with his feet together for a heartbeat, and then began the slow, balanced, intricately graceful movements of Tai Chi. Brendee tried to catch this daily performance as often as possible: she found Wiley's interpretation of the ancient Chinese martial art to be incredibly, sinuously arousing.

"You need to get out more," he'd tell her with his sly smile.

Wiley had learned Tai Chi and yoga as part of an unorthodox course of physical therapy after a broken leg as a teenager. As always, he ended his routine with a handstand, pointed his toes and stretched his legs out to his sides until they were almost parallel with the deck. He held the pose for quite some time – Wiley was very strong, and prided himself on being exceptionally fit – then he hopped upright again. Snatching a basket off of a deck chair, he descended the steps to the garden below to pick some peppers and maybe a little spinach (if there was any left), dig up a couple onions, to put into omelets for his family for breakfast.

The eggs were from chickens that Tom kept in his backyard in the city. Wiley had always tried to eat as healthy as possible, and the discovery not long ago of the evils of the additives in our food had driven him to annoy friends and family alike with strictures and strident admonitions about what they simply *should not eat*. But there was nothing as ridiculous as raw milk in Wiley's fridge. There was absolutely nothing wrong with pasteurization, and modern milk was fortified with Vitamin D. Just because germs were natural didn't mean that Wiley didn't want them boiled out of his milk. He wasn't a hippie, after all.

He danced around in the kitchen whilst he made breakfast, singing some ancient song that his wife would not have recognized. He wished idly that they could spend more time at the cabin, because the air and the veggies were fresh and he was away from the endlessly simple-minded peccadillos of his forever-following-the-latest-thing fellow man. When they were up here, it was as if no one else existed, and that was the way Wiley liked it best. He'd been a loner all his life, and while he couldn't live without Brendee and their son and their small circle of friends, Wiley could live without his fellow man. They were all such sheep.

Wiley wasn't into roughing it; escaping from the city didn't mean giving up any of the comforts of home, just the ignorant baaing sheep and the poisoned food and unrecycled filth that they heaped around themselves. And of course, he could always amuse himself with their tragedies and foibles and stupidities, just by taking out his phone, logging onto the internet, or turning on one of the big TVs in the cabin. Even though the place was solar powered, completely off the grid, Wiley had no desire to withdraw from the world. He still liked to know what was going on, if for no other reasons than to make fun of it. He just didn't want to mingle with the unwashed masses if he didn't have to.

Although a simple internal combustion engine flummoxed him, he was a genius with all things electronic. All the appliances in the cabin were state of the art, all controllable from his phone. The place was completely wired for security, for entertainment, for communication with that outside world. But still, Wiley thought that he would be amenable to giving up some comforts – read technologies – if he could also give up having to return to the city, if he could just stay here. They stocked any foodstuffs he couldn't grow at the local market; they could definitely get rid of one car.

Wiley Royce had it made, and he felt his good fortune the keenest when he was in Big Bear at this fully functional modern outpost, far from the madding crowds. He spent as much time up here as possible with his bride and his kid and his best friends, and the rest of his time he spent in town, not working too hard but still making plenty of money, repairing all those expensive little electronic devices with which modern man could not live without. He was so good at it that he could no doubt make a living from it up in the mountains – *I could conduct my business by mail-order,* he sometimes thought stubbornly. But his wife worked in town, as did his friends; eventually his boy would have to go to school. These were part of the trade-offs of *having the world by the ass,* as his grandfather liked to say. Wiley loved his people, and so he lived in Riverside when they lived there.

And his friend Tom liked the city best. He tried to eat only chemical-free food, but he backslid on that sometimes – even though there was no *International House of Pancakes* in Big Bear – and he loved the noise and the stink and the people in town. Wiley owed most of the best things he enjoyed to the old guy's largesse: Tom had given him the space in the bookstore from which to run his repair shop, and Tom helped him do his taxes. For a smart guy, Wiley loathed anything to do with math. If it hadn't been for Tom, Wiley wouldn't have his sanctuary in the mountains.

But beyond all his fiduciary helps, Wiley respected Tom for his incredibly keen intellect. He possessed a vast knowledge of literature and history and art, old movies and old music; an enjoyment of which Wiley had always found lacking in his peers. It had been Tom that had clued Wiley to the dangerous chemicals lurking in our food, and if Wiley had gone completely around the bend about it, Tom hadn't chided him too much.

Sometimes Wiley wished that he'd known Tom before the death of his beloved Liz, because it was obvious that the tragedy of that had mellowed him considerably. He was still the most kicked-back, relaxed person that Wiley had ever known, however; brilliant, irrepressible, with a dead-on, killer wit; a disrespectful, know-it-all of an old goat. The bookstore owner reminded the electronics genius of himself in many ways, and Wiley encompassed no higher compliment than that.

And Tom was a storyteller, and his stories were intriguing, thought-provoking, much more so than today's celebrity Twitter comment and the online outrage it engendered, or tomorrow's political scandal, or the tempests-in-a-teapot at work with which Wiley's wife and friends bored him.

If the old dog barks, he gives counsel. Tom made Wiley *think.*

FIVE

He was sitting behind the counter at *Morry's Books,* with his bare feet up. From his phone, he was reading something entitled, *50 Simple Things You Can Do to Save the Earth.*

"Use one less paper napkin. How 'bout no paper napkins at all?"

"You're a hippie." Tom bid farewell to the one book-buying customer he'd had for several days.

"Use both sides of paper," Wiley read. "How about not printing it at all? It's all on your device. Isn't that good enough? I am not a hippie. People are just—"

"Baaa," Tom finished for him.

"Here's another one. *Recycle newspaper.* Seriously? Who reads newspapers anymore?"

Tom glanced around his store. *Who reads books anymore?* He was glad that Wiley was there to keep him company, even if he was on a hippie jag this morning.

Tom had never for a moment regretted offering the kid the space in the bookstore for his repair business. Because of his education, entirely self-sought, and his genius for electronics, Wiley considered himself several steps above his fellow man. It made him an amusing and sometimes exasperating companion.

"Go vegetarian once a week. How about *go vegetarian all the time, you fat slob?"*

"That reminds me. T-Bones for dinner tonight. Are you in?"

"Of course." Wiley was a vegetarian most of the time, but the unkind fates of the cows and the pigs and the chickens concerned him not at all. He was a vegetarian for his own health, unless Tom was broiling T-bones.

"Turn off your computer at night. You can save $14 a year. Oh, for Christ's sake!"

"Energy conservation, my son. The key to saving the planet."

"Right. What did you tell me once? *I'm not here to save the planet. I can't even save myself?"*

Tom gestured at Wiley's phone. "You started it."

"It was on my feed."

"Because you're a hippie."

"I'm not here to save the planet, either. It's too far gone."

"That's what Dionne says."

Wiley quoted her. *"We can only save our own.* Ain't that the truth?"

The old-fashioned bell above the door tinkled, and Wiley looked up from his castigation of world-saving as the arena of sheep to see who had arrived. A trim young man of about twenty-three smiled mildly at him. He had dark hair and large, clear blue eyes. He was accompanied by a beautiful young woman of about the same age, of similar coloring, except that her eyes were gray. She blinked expressionlessly at Wiley.

The young man turned his smile to the store's proprietor. "I'm looking for Tom Bastion."

"You've found him." Tom offered his hand.

"And glad I am!" The young man pumped Tom's hand enthusiastically. "I'm sure you received our message."

Tom glanced at Wiley, who shook his head. "What kind of–"

"My name is Byron."

"Like the poet?" Wiley suggested.

No comprehension showed in Byron's eyes. He had not heard of the poet.

"And this is my sister, Viktoria. With a *k.* " Byron paused to see if some comment would be made upon his sister's unusually spelled name. When the seated stranger remained silent, Bryon told Tom, "We're your grandniece and nephew. You didn't receive our message? We didn't expect a reply, communications being what they are, but we were assured that you would receive it."

Tom's mouth fell open and Wiley stood up abruptly. "So you're from . . ."

"Out of town, yes," Byron said quickly. Tom remained speechless, so the young man explained further. "We're Alba's grandchildren."

"Who's–"

"My sister." Tom had finally found his voice.

"Your sister, from–"

"Yes, Wiley. My sister, from . . ."

Tom suddenly recalled the night he'd first broached the truth of his origins to Liz. He'd known her about a year, had been in love with her from the second they'd met. He'd wanted to tell her earlier, but the opportunity had not presented itself. Then the perfect moment arrived.

13

Maxine was not a conspiracy theorist like Dionne; she didn't believe that we'd never landed on the moon, nor did she believe that aliens currently stalked the earth. But she did enjoy the aliens-built-the-pyramids concept, that other-worlders had visited in the distant past. She was a big fan of *Ancient Aliens,* the show, and was disappointed on that Christmas Eve, because the cable was on the fritz, and she was going to miss the marathon.

Tom was inspired. The time had at last arrived, and he knew just how to couch his revelations.

"All might not be lost, Max. I have a little story that I've been thinking of – about all this *Ancient Aliens* crap."

Liz and Maxine both loved to listen to Tom talk, so they settled in to hear his story. He asked them to picture a planet similar to Earth. "No need to stretch the imagination too much – it's a place a lot like this one: same kind of atmosphere, same gravity, stuff like that. A little warmer maybe."

"Does this other planet have a name?" Liz asked.

"Let's call it Sirius, shall we?"

"Oh, no, Tom, not Sirius. Every alien story ever told starts with Sirius. Think up some other planet, some other name. Besides, Sirius is a star."

"Yes, Sirius is a star, the brightest star in the night sky. There are actually two stars, a binary system, Sirius A and Sirius B. Sirius, the Dog Star, *Sopdet, Tishtrya.* What's in a name?"

"But it's not a planet," Liz insisted.

"This is a long story, and there are a lot of names. I'm trying to make things as simple as possible. Let's just say the planet of which we speak is in the Sirius star system, so we'll call it Sirius, *just like in every alien story ever told.* Agreed?"

Had that really been so long ago?

Now Tom said, "My sister Alba. From . . . Sirius."

Byron and Viktoria's mouths fell open. They looked from Tom to Wiley and then back to Tom again. Like Fight Club, the first rule about being from Sirius was that one didn't talk about being from Sirius. Not to the local monkeys, anyway. They had only just arrived in their cousin's adopted town today, and this simplest and most important of commandments had already been broken.

To ease the incredibly awkward silence, Wiley came around the counter and shook hands with them. "Wiley Royce . . . Earthling. Welcome. I've never met anyone else from–"

"He knows about . . . ?" Viktoria asked incredulously.

"Vaguely," Wiley supplied. "It came up in conversation once."

"Yes, Wiley knows that I'm from . . . that I'm not from around here." At the continued shocked expressions on the faces of . . . *my relatives,* Tom added, "No one else knows."

"Nate knows."

"Yes, well . . . Yes. Nate knows, but he doesn't believe it. But no one else knows."

But that wasn't exactly correct, either, was it?

Tom didn't want to go into the explanation of why Wiley and his friend Nate knew he was *not from around here* with . . . There was that word again: *my relatives. Byron and Viktoria. My relatives from Sirius. I guess I'm not the last one in the family that wanted to come here, after all.*

But the circumstances surrounding Wiley and Nate's knowledge played through Tom's mind anyway, because here were his grandniece and grandnephew, newly arrived from the homeworld, and Tom had lied to them already. There were two others who knew where Tom was from, although, like Nate, neither of them believed it.

On that long-ago Christmas Eve, when Maxine was prevented from watching the *Ancient Aliens* marathon because of a malfunctioning DirecTV dish, Tom had told her and Liz the entire history of his planet, as if it was just a tall tale that he was making up as he went along.

He told his lady-love and his best friend about the Dino war, that the lizards had finally been overthrown after a long and bloody conflict, wiped out, in fact. And afterward, the Sirians that had come to Earth eventually went home. "But the more adventuresome people still visit."

"People like . . . you?" Maxine had asked.

"Maybe."

Liz would eventually come to believe that Tom was indeed from Sirius, but Maxine always thought that the whole panoramic yarn was just a whimsical fantasy that her clever friend had concocted to amuse them on a television-less Christmas Eve.

Until the fantasy turned dark. And the dark part had been Wiley and Nate's introduction to Tom's origin story.

Sol's third planet being a small world after all, and the city of Riverside even smaller, after becoming friends with the bookstore owner, Wiley and Nate had discovered that they'd gone to high school with his friend Maxine's daughter, Janae. They learned that because he was such pals with her mom, Tom had been like an extra grandpa to Janae.

When Janae introduced Wiley and Nate to her father, Sam, it was he who laid out the awful truth for them.

"Tom's crazy. He's delusional. Maybe even schizophrenic. We got him to talk to a professional once, after . . . They tried to give him anti-psychotics, but he wouldn't take them. He wouldn't talk to the shrink again, either."

"I'm not gonna sit here and listen to you bad-mouth Tommy, Dad." Janae rose. "There is not one thing crazy about him. I'm the second door on the left, Wiley. Come get me when my dad's done smearing my grandfather."

"He's not your grandfather, Janae." But she'd already left the room. Sam waited for the door to slam, then continued. "Tom's delusional. He thinks he's–"

"Napoleon?" Wiley looked down the empty hall after Janae.

Sam shook his head. "I said he was crazy, not illogical. Napoleon is dead. Tom's delusion goes beyond thinking he's some historical figure, whose life and death could be demonstrated to him. It's much worse than that. The Federales–"

"Federales?" Wiley ceased peering down the hall and looked back at Sam.

He nodded, his eyes full of pain. "About two months before she died, Tom took his wife to Mapimi, Mexico. He got into an argument with an old man that lived on a ranch there – an actual fist fight, essentially. Details are sketchy, but I guess they restrained Tom on the ranch and called the law. Apparently Tom knew this old guy that he attempted to assault – Martin – and he took pity on him. He figured that this irrational behavior was all over Liz's illness.

"Martin and the Federales got in touch with us – my wife speaks a little Spanish – and the upshot of it was that they escorted Tom and Liz to the border and we took possession of them in San Diego. Martin refused to press charges, even though I guess the assault was pretty bad. He didn't want to see Tom thrown in a Mexican jail when his wife was dying."

"What was the fight about?"

"Like I say, details are sketchy, but it shakes out like this. Tom attacked his old friend, burned his barn to the ground, because Martin refused to help him return to his *homeworld. To the planet Sirius.* If he could get Liz back to Sirius – that's *where he's from,* you see – then they'd cure her cancer."

16

"So you're telling us that Tom thinks he's–" Nate began.

"An alien. An extraterrestrial. From the planet Sirius."

"Your tale, sir, would cure deafness." Wiley raised his eyebrows mildly. "Is that all? There are worse things to believe you are than an alien. A righteous man. Your brother's keeper." Tom's delusion didn't bother Wiley overly. He surely wasn't shocked by it.

Frowning, Sam glared at him. "Liz was *dying,* and Tom dragged her all the way to the middle of Mexico for nothing. Through twelve hundred miles of heat and dust. *For nothing.* He dragged her all the way to Mapimi, because *he's nuts."*

Wiley remained unconvinced of Tom's madness. Eventually, he asked for his friend's side of the story. In typical Wiley fashion, he pulled no punches.

"Are you from Sirius, Tom? Sam said you got in a fist fight with some guy in Mexico, because he wouldn't help you get back to–"

"I was misled on that. Forget about Sirius for a minute – let's just say that I'm not from around here, okay? Let's just say that, in order to get back to where I'm from, I had to get in touch with Martin, there in Mexico. So I did. There'd never been any trouble with going back before. He'd sent Morry back.

"It took about a month for Martin to get back to me. Communication is not the best between here and Mapimi – I had to talk to one guy, then he had to talk to another guy, then they had to go out to the ranch and talk to Martin. It's still the third world down there, for Christ's sake. But eventually the messages were exchanged: I said I wanted to go back to . . . to go back *home,* and he said he'd make the proper arrangements. I knew that they could cure Liz there.

"But when we arrived, Martin said that he hadn't realized that I wanted to take Liz with me. *'Usted ha dicho nada acerca de traer a esta mujer extranjera. Ninguna persona que haya nacido aquí es bienvenida allí,'* he told me indignantly. *'You said nothing about bringing this foreign woman. No person who is born here is welcome there.'*

"Like he knew what the fuck he was talking about. He's never been there. He's nothing but a meet-and-greet, someone who plucks us out of the desert, gives us some clothes, some money, then sends us on our way. Out of gratitude for his simple services, I put his fucking granddaughter through college, for Christ's sake." Tom looked guiltily at Nate and Wiley for a moment, as if he'd said too much.

"I insisted. Martin felt sorry for me, sorry for Liz. He sent another message to . . . He sent another message *home*. Communications are slow–"

"It's some distance," Wiley opined.

Tom grinned humorlessly. "Indeed. We stayed at the ranch for a week. But the answer came back the same. *Nadie que nació aquí. No one who was born here.*"

"So you assaulted Martin–"

"Is that what Sam told you?"

Wiley nodded.

"No. That's not what happened. Something must've gotten lost in translation. I just . . . threatened him. The communication device was in his barn with the . . . *apparatus* for sending us back."

When his young friends looked dubious, Tom said, "It wasn't a transporter, like from *Star Trek,* gentlemen, at least not to anyone looking at it. It just looked like one of those big, old-fashioned satellite dishes, with a bunch of car batteries hooked up to it in some kind of sequence. Very third world-looking. We're not too big on electrical contrivances . . . where I'm from, and there's not exactly a spring-break-in-Cancun rush to go back. They don't use it very often. Once we're here, we tend to stay here. It's great here."

"How exactly does this transporter work?"

"I don't know how it works; only how it *goes.*" Tom smiled wryly. "The, for lack of a better word, *operator* hooks up the leads on the batteries. Then you take off your clothes. There's a big, Frankenstein's-lab-looking switch–"

"Why do you have to take off your clothes?" Nate offered Wiley an *Is he for real?* look.

"The thing to be transported has to be at least eighty-five percent organic. Alive, in other words."

"So if you've got fillings in your teeth–"

"Or pins and screws . . ." Wiley touched his left leg. "You can't go?"

"You'd be okay, my son. A few nuts and bolts wouldn't make any difference. I don't think you're twenty percent metal.

"You just do it naked because that lowers the percentage of possible non-organic material. The set-up is different on the other side." Tom grinned. "No car batteries, but we start off in the buff there, too. Something about the process, regardless of the direction.

18

"You stand in front of the dish and the operator hooks up the leads, flips the switch. There is an energization . . ."

"Can you feel it?" Nate suddenly pictured flashing, red, yellow and blue electrocution.

"No. You *spread yourself upon the wind, thinner and thinner, until only the wind remains.*" Tom smiled and Wiley smiled back. Nate didn't recognize the reference.

Tom heaved a sad sigh. "But I'm no engineer – I didn't know exactly how it worked. Holding Martin at gunpoint," he looked guiltily down at the counter, "I tried to hook it up. But I didn't know what I was doing. There was a little humming noise, then the thing burst into flames. The hay and the old wood caught immediately. My car was in there, too. When we fled the barn, some of the ranch hands were waiting for us. They jumped me, tied me up, dragged me back to the house.

"Martin said he was sorry, over and over again. There was nothing he could do, nothing I could do. So I gave up. I can never go home again, my friends, but it really doesn't matter. This place is my home now.

"Since I no longer had a car, I told Martin how to get in touch with Maxine, and he had the authorities take us all the way back to the border. Martin had the official tell Maxine and Sam that I'd lost my mind, that I believed I could return to Sirius from Mapimi. The official was stern, telling her that they didn't like gringos coming down there, disturbing the peace, setting fires, riling up the locals, talking about aliens. They'd give us back, seeing how Liz was sick . . . Seeing how she was dying, and they knew she could get better treatment back in the States, blah, blah, blah. Martin said he was sorry, the official said he was sorry, and they delivered us at the border to Sam and Max, like some kind of hostage exchange.

"Sam didn't say a word to me all the way home. He didn't say a word, in fact, until after Liz died. Then he screamed at me, telling me that I was nuts, that I'd hastened her death with my insanity. Max just cried.

"She begged me to go see a shrink, so I did, for her. I told this doctor that it was all simply a big misunderstanding. I told him I'd heard about healing springs in Mexico, or some such bullshit. There aren't any springs in Mapimi. It's the fucking desert.

"But there was no official report from Mexico; I hadn't hurt anyone. Liz was gone. I passed all the *are-you-a-nutball?* tests the shrink administered, so he had no choice but to let me go on my merry way. With a prescription for scopolamine. Or lithium, or Prozac, or something. I didn't even get it filled."

Tom sighed. "That was pretty much the end of my friendship with Sam." He considered his young friends for a minute, then smiled. "Believe whatever you want on that score, gentlemen. Believe I'm an alien, believe I'm delusional. You can't prove it one way or another, any more than I can. Our DNA is indistinguishable."

How convenient, Nate said to himself.

SIX

Wiley had never asked Tom for too many details about Sirius. After telling him that it was a machinery and pollution-free natural paradise, that because of these amenities, its inhabitants lived for decades longer that the people on Earth, Tom had let the subject drop. Wiley had not picked it up again.

All that's gonna change, now that my relatives *are here.* Tom tried desperately to think up something to say, but for several seconds was at a loss. He knew that his fellows came to this planet all the time; it had been going on since – *since the* Ancient Aliens *days,* he thought wryly. And despite a world full of UFO experts, Tom knew that none of them had even an inkling that it was still going on.

But except for his Uncle Morry, Tom had never met another tourist from Sirius. He'd often speculated that it might be because of that little incident with Martin in Mexico – he knew he wasn't exactly welcome back home any more. But Tom considered that it was more likely that he hadn't met any fellow tourists because they were just that. Tourists. When you went to Vegas, you wanted to interact with the natives. You didn't waste your time looking for other travelers from Des Moines.

"So you . . . arrived . . . in Mexico?" Tom asked at last.

Viktoria continued to eye Wiley with distrust. "We arrived the same way you did." Her tone held a certain finality, indicating that she didn't want to discuss it further.

Wiley caught the tension, but continued on blithely. "You're here on vacation?"

Byron smiled at him. "But of course."

"For how long?" Tom asked, then seemed embarrassed that he'd asked it.

"For as long as it takes," Viktoria replied mysteriously.

"For as long as what takes?"

Tom didn't like mysteries. He discovered that he was unsure just how he felt about this sudden appearance of Alba's grandchildren. He hadn't seen Alba since his teens; she'd never expressed an interest in Earth, so why should –

"Oh, you know." Again Byron smiled winningly. "Taking in the sights. Visiting the museums. Enjoying the local color."

"Where are you staying?" Wiley asked, as if they had indeed just breezed in from Des Moines.

The young Sirians looked at Tom expectantly. *Just what he needs,* Wiley thought. *Alien visitors sleeping in the house he shares with the conspiracy nut.*

When Tom didn't immediately offer up his spare bedrooms, Wiley said, "I'm sure there's a unit in my building, if you're gonna be here awhile."

Now Tom remembered himself. "That's okay, Wiley. They can stay with me. They're family, after all."

"Great! I can't wait to hear all about what life is like on another–"

"It's not something that is discussed," Viktoria snapped imperiously.

"It's okay, Vikky." Wiley winked at her seriousness. "I'm not gonna tell anybody."

"Wiley is your friend, Tom?"

"He is."

"Then it would be my pleasure to inform him about . . . *where we're from.*" Byron glanced at his sister, dismissed her pique. "If you're my cousin's friend, then he must trust you to keep this most important of secrets. So will I."

The bell above the door sounded again, this time admitting a tall, sturdy, blonde man, carrying an adorable, bald-headed baby boy.

"Nate!" Wiley cried. "We were just talking about you."

Wiley took the baby from his friend's grasp. "Hiya, Eric, my son! What wonders have you seen today?" Eric, who was not Wiley's son but Nate's, and unsure of what wonders he had seen because he was not much more than a year old, gurgled and kicked in delight, nonetheless.

Nate just had time to wonder what Wiley was saying about him to two complete strangers, when Tom introduced them. Byron offered his hand and Nate shook it, and Viktoria's as well, told them his name.

Wiley tickled Eric. "Byron and Viktoria are Tom's relatives. So that means they're from . . . Let's just say they're a long way from home."

Nonplussed, Nate looked at Tom; Viktoria frowned.

Byron smiled again. "Wiley told us that you, too, are aware of Tom's origins."

"He told us he was from–"

"And that's where they're from, too. Isn't that right, Eric?" Wiley bounced Nate's boy. "A whole raft of aliens, right here in River City. A veritable inva–"

Viktoria interrupted Wiley before he could say *invasion.* "We'd rather that you not mention it to anyone, Nate."

"Of course not. Who would I–"

"Who would believe you?" Tom thought of his lost friendship with Maxine's husband.

"With that in mind – you guys got a backstory?"

The Sirians blinked stupidly at Wiley. Nate thought there was something odd about the way they blinked, but then told himself that he was imagining it. He'd just been informed that these strangers were strange indeed, visitors from another world. So of course he would imagine something different about them.

But it was ridiculous.

He didn't believe that they were from another planet, any more than he believed Tom was from another planet. He'd always figured that it was just a story Tom told; Nate didn't know the real reason why he'd dragged his dying wife to Mexico. Maybe he *had* thought that there were healing springs. But Nate was pretty sure that it wasn't because Tom was from Sirius and wanted to return there. He was *pretty sure.*

When nobody spoke, Wiley explained what he meant by a *backstory.* "You guys just blew into town, claiming to be Tom's long-lost kin. His girlfriend tends to be suspicious. She's gonna wanna know where you're from, how you got here . . . Or, have you already told her about *your origins* by now?"

"Dionne believes that there are Dinos amongst us, so, no, I haven't told her." When Byron and Viktoria glanced sharply at him, he smiled for the first time since they'd walked in. "Surely you were debriefed? In my time, there were classes you had to take before you left . . ."

"Not so much anymore. Things have changed since you were last home."

For some reason, Viktoria's statement made Tom feel uneasy, and his smile fled. But then he chided himself, as Nate had done. Surely, things had to have changed back home since he'd been there.

23

He'd been gone a long time. Things had changed everywhere. It was just the natural progression of time.

In his day, there'd been a waiting list to come to Earth; that was why, even though he was jumped to the front of the line because he had a relative waiting for him, he hadn't made it until he was past forty. That had definitely changed: these new relatives appeared to be in their early-twenties.

And apparently they didn't teach 'em much about the planet they were visiting, either. Byron had not a clue about the poet with whom he shared a name; they didn't know what a *backstory* was. Their diction was odd. The way they blinked . . . *No, I'm imagining that.*

"There are rumors about alien visitation here. They started about the same time as the Atomic Age."

No recognition. Apparently they didn't teach them any Earth history *at all* anymore.

Tom tried again. "There are shows on television . . ."

Still the blank stares. Surely they knew about television?

"About all these theories about aliens. My girlfriend . . . We sat through one the other night." Tom grinned at Wiley and Nate, mostly so he wouldn't have to look at the Sirians' blank expressions anymore. "The government's in it up to their eyeballs, gentlemen. Full collaboration."

"That is untrue." Viktoria shook her head. "No one here has any knowledge of our presence."

"But they *think* they know." Tom discovered that he was just the tiniest bit annoyed with her take-me-to-your-leader *alienness.* At least the kid was a little bit more laid back. But not much.

"And Dionne thinks she knows more than most," Nate commented.

Tom nodded. "Wiley's right. You need a backstory. Even if she doesn't think you're aliens–" *which you so obviously are–* "Dionne might think you're foreign spies or something."

"From whence does this paranoia spring?" Viktoria demanded. "Aren't all this area's inhabitants happy and oblivious?"

"Like sheep," Wiley agreed.

"Dionne believes that the ranchers are out to do her in. She sees threats around every corner."

"We are no threat. We are here simply to–"

"We're here on vacation. We don't want to alarm your woman, Tom. What should our backstory be?"

24

Wiley snapped his fingers. "How about – you're from Estonia. Like in *Encino Man.*" He smirked at Nate's baffled expression, now the same as the Sirians'. "It was a movie. From a long, long time ago."

Nate rolled his eyes. "Christ, Wiley. You and your old movies."

"And not hardly a classic, either," Tom said.

"But you've seen it."

"Of course, Wiley."

"No bad movies on Sirius, huh?"

"No movies at all."

Nate gritted his teeth in exasperation. He was supposed to believe that Tom was from another planet, and once again, as he had done so many times since he'd first met Wiley in high school, he found himself waiting for an explanation of some ancient movie, probably from decades before he was born. Tom was allegedly from where they didn't have movies, and Wiley was into all the old ones, as well as literature, art, philosophy. The classics. That's why Wiley thought he was smarter than everyone else. That's why he and Tom were such good friends.

"It went like this. There's an earthquake, and it coughs up this frozen caveman. These two guys thaw him out and take him to high school with them."

"That's an impossibility."

It occurred to Nate that Viktoria was definitely Tom's relative, even if she wasn't from Sirius. She was another know-it-all, just like he was. Like Wiley was.

"The human body cannot withstand freezing–"

"It was a movie, Viktoria. Fiction. They're big on that here. Didn't they tell you anything at all about Earth culture?"

"They told us how to locate you. We understood that you would help us assimilate."

A heartbeat of silence passed at that statement, then Wiley continued. "Anyway, the guys in this movie, their situation was similar to ours. They had this caveman. He needed to *assimilate*. He needed a backstory. So they told everyone that he was an exchange student from Estonia. So I thought we could use that."

Byron smiled. "All right. That will be our backstory. We're Tom's relatives. From Estonia."

"You guys can read and write English, right?"

25

"Of course. Our educational methods are superior to yours. They involve . . . They're quite advanced. We speak several languages. We're not backwater monkeys like . . ." Viktoria let the thought die.

Like you are. Wiley ignored Viktoria's outrage, self-censored. "Here on the backwater monkey planet, we have a thing called a smartphone." He picked his own up off the counter where he'd left it, typed, scrolled. He went to hand it to Byron, then changed his mind. "My phone's a little different than most. It's *quite advanced.* Hold on just a second."

He disappeared into the office behind the counter, then returned after a moment with two cellphones. "Here ya go, kiddies. This world is now at your fingertips." He handed one to Viktoria. "I'm sure the action will be child's play to someone of your advanced education, Vikky, but if you need any help, just ask."

He scrolled on the other phone. "Here ya, go, Byron. The Wikipedia page on Estonia."

"What do we owe you, Wiley?"

Wiley grinned in surprise. "I see you're aware of that charming colloquialism. If you know that nothing's free on Planet Earth, you'll fit right in. Eventually."

"We were assured that we would have access to currency?" Vikky smiled brightly at Tom.

"But of course. You're family, after all. I'll get you a couple of ATM cards."

When the siblings again blinked blankly, Tom added, "For access to the family fortune."

Wiley was a little amazed at this largesse, but on the other hand, he knew Tom had plenty of money. Feeling generous himself, he told Byron, "The phones are my gift."

"They're not—"

"Actually, they are, my son. Of that special variety. Monthly-payment-free." Wiley winked at Nate, then suddenly endeavored to look serious. "But don't tell anyone you've got free cellphone service. Exactly how we here at *Morry's Books* and *Wiley's Electronics* are able to provide such a . . . non-traditional thing . . . That's one of my little secrets."

Byron read, *"A developed country with an advanced, high-income economy and high living standards, Estonia ranks very high in the Human Development Index, and performs favorably in measurements of economic freedom, civil liberties, education, and press freedom. Estonia is often described as one of the most wired countries in Europe.* A great place to be from!"

"Just don't be quoting the gross national product to Dionne," Wiley advised. "That might seem a little . . . artificial." He shared a glance with Tom. "You guys don't want to come off as artificial, do ya?"

SEVEN

Dinner that evening was the Meeting of the Tribes.

At least once a month, Tom and Dionne feted all of their friends (whom they considered family) to a big get-together. Maxine and Sam rarely showed up anymore, but their daughter Janae and her girlfriend Tisha were almost always the first to arrive, although they were not present this evening. Tonight it was Wiley and Brendee and their son Bo, Nate and his wife Deneen and Eric, and Tom's newly arrived cousins from overseas.

During the meal, Wiley brought the full force of his inestimable imagination to bear on the Estonian backstory. For Dionne's benefit, as well as for Brendee and Deneen, he weaved a stirring tale of pathos and triumph, relating it, he said, as Tom had related it to him.

Tom's sister Alba – long lost, as they had been separated by divorce as children – had immigrated to Europe with her father. Something to do with his line of work: he'd been some stripe of low-level diplomat. They had eventually settled in Estonia.

The years passed, and Alba married a native; a child was born. That child matured, married, and produced Byron and Viktoria. They had American names, sort of, because their mom remembered *her* mom's tales of America, tales she in turn related to her children.

Byron grew, studied hard in college. Viktoria, on the other hand, had attended . . . Wiley wanted his womenfolk to believe that Vikky had been sheltered all her life; he suddenly pictured the quiet seclusion of the abbey in *The Sound of Music* as a place that would produce the stilted-speech oddball that she appeared to be.

"Viktoria attended convent school." Not being religious, Wiley didn't realize that this was a term that applied to Catholics, a faith to which Viktoria surely couldn't pretend membership.

Eventually, Byron graduated from Estonia U., and never having forgotten his dreams of America, he had snatched his sibling from the hands of the sisters, and had looked up his grandmother's brother. And here they were!

"What did you study in school?" Brendee asked.

Wiley's wife had once intended to become a lawyer, but the arrival of their son had changed her mind. She worked as a paralegal these days, regular nine-to-five hours. She didn't miss the scintillating courtroom drama that she'd once imagined for herself as a litigator, however. Life with Wiley and their boy was quite exciting enough.

Bo was almost three now, and his mother considered him a handful, although his father took all his toddler antics in stride. Besides making his customers' electronic devices *all better,* besides providing free cellphone service to his friend's out-of-town guests, besides believing he was smarter than everyone else, Brendee knew that nothing amused and delighted her husband more than his son. It was one more thing for which she loved him, another thing for which she felt fortunate.

Byron paused, smiled. Brendee thought she caught the family resemblance then: he and Tom had the same smile. Of course, Bryon also had the same blue eyes as Tom, and the black hair that he must've possessed in his youth, but for all that, he could've been Wiley's younger brother, Bo's uncle. Both of Brendee's men also had black hair and blue eyes.

It was Byron's smile that reminded her of Tom: happy, welcoming, infinitely friendly. Wiley's smile, on the other hand, often showed a wry tinge of superiority; it could be off-putting. Vaguely predatory.

Brendee noticed that Tom wasn't smiling now. His expression was of nervous anticipation, like that of someone who might not necessarily be expecting good news. Apparently Byron's college studies were unknown to him, also.

"Archaeology was my major," the young man said at last. "Mesoamerican cultures in general, and the city of Teotihuacan in particular."

Brendee couldn't tell if this was good news to Tom or not. He asked, *"Usted habla Nahuatl, hijo mío?"*

Nate frowned in annoyance. Not only was Tom a know-it-all, he was a know-it-all in other languages, too. In this he surpassed Wiley, and now Nate chuckled to himself: Wiley would have to wait for a translation, just like the rest of them. He'd never turned his ever-clicking mind to a study of foreign tongues.

"But of course. Nahuatl was a required course," Byron replied.

Wiley took out his phone, but, to Nate's surprise, Deneen beat him to the Google search. "You speak Aztec, Byron?"

"Not conversationally. But it helps in my studies of the great city."

Not to be outdone, Wiley read from his phone. *"The name Teotihuacan was given by the Nahuatl-speaking Aztecs centuries after the fall of the city. Nahuatl scholars have interpreted the name as 'place of those who have the road of the gods,' because the Aztecs believed that the gods created the universe at that site.* So the Aztecs didn't build all those pyramids and stuff down there?"

Byron met Tom's eyes. "No one is sure exactly who built them."

"Hence the need for continuing studies. More veggie-lasagna, anyone?" Tom sensed that his Riverside-native friends were not into a rousing discussion of paleo-Mesoamerican cultures over dinner.

Veggie-lasagna was a recipe of Tom's devising, and one of Wiley's favorites. Made with homegrown vegetables and homemade noodles, the two of them considered it to be the perfect companion dish to Tom's excellent T-bones. It was a little bland to everyone else. But it was all-natural, and that suited Tom and Wiley just fine.

Wiley said he would take another helping, but he wasn't through with Teotihuacan quite yet, no matter how much he might be boring the table.

"Listen to this." He again read from his phone. *"A new exhibit will open on Saturday, October 5th in the San Bernardino County Museum's Hall of History, entitled 'River of Mercury – Artifacts from Teotihuacan's Temple of the Feathered Serpent.'*

"In 2015, a large quantity of liquid mercury was discovered in a tunnel beneath the pyramid. At the time, researchers said that the metal may have been placed there to symbolize an underworld river or lake, and it could be a sign that the first royal tomb ever found in Teotihuacan was nearby. By 2020, the chamber had been located and excavated. Grave goods and a large stone, box-like structure, which researchers believe may have been a sarcophagus, were found, but the remains of Teotihuacan's first kings have continued to elude archaeologists, leaving future generations to unravel the centuries of mystery surrounding the leadership of the once powerful city.

"On display at the Museum will be many of the thousands of other articles discovered in the chamber, however, including jaguar and lizard remains, perfectly preserved in the low oxygen environment. Four anthropomorphic stone sculptures made of greenstone greet the visitor upon entering the exhibit, as well as many more figures wrought in Guatemalan jade.

"There are rubber balls, beads, complete necklaces, amber and dozens of obsidian blades and arrow heads, and elaborately carved conch shells. There is the famous wooden box and the golden disc it contained, covered with raised markings in a yet undeciphered language.

"Also on display will be several of the clay spheres discovered beneath the Temple in 2013. The spheres are believed to have originally been covered in pyrite, a yellow-colored mineral known as 'Fool's Gold.' Their use and/or significance is unknown.

"An interactive kiosk at the end of the exhibit invites visitors to speculate on the spheres' purpose and offers them an opportunity to try their hands at translating the disk."

This announcement was met with silence: as Tom had guessed, all this talk of a long-vanished civilization was mind-numbing to his dinner guests.

Finally, Deneen said with mild sarcasm, "It sounds like fun."

"It does, actually," Wiley countered. "Especially if you've got an archaeologist for a guide. You and me – we're going to this next month, aren't we, Byron?"

"But of course," the student of antiquities replied. "It's–"

His sister cut him off. "It's one of the reasons for our visit here."

EIGHT

The conversation around the table turned to subjects more germane to the Tribes.

Deneen mentioned that Eric was cutting a new tooth. "It makes him drool a lot." She demonstrated that such was the case by wiping his chin.

"I remember when Bo was teething. He always wanted to chew on my phone."

"Teething," Bo said sagely from his mother's lap, mimicking his dad. "Teething-phone."

"Janae had these rubber things that looked like Oreo cookies," Tom reminisced. "A pink one and a black one. I think it amused Max to have people think that she was so ignorant as to be feeding her baby cookies."

Wiley made a face. "People *do* feed their babies cookies, the goddamned sheep. The industrialization of the palate begins in childhood–"

"Not now, Wiley," Dionne said gently, but with a little bit of an edge. "We have company."

Wiley climbed down off of his high-horse of the industrialization of the palate and what-one-should-feed-one's-offspring, for the benefit of Bryon and Viktoria. He asked Tom, "Where is Janae, anyway?"

"She texted her regrets earlier. Some school function, not to be missed."

Now Dionne frowned. "When is she ever gonna be finished with school? Maybe if you would stop paying for it . . ."

Tom refused to frown. "It's only money, Dionne."

Brendee shared a brief glance with Deneen. With it, they commiserated that they knew why Dionne was so down on the young woman that considered herself to be Tom's granddaughter. Janae worshipped the old guy; he was her mother's best friend, and Janae had grown up in the bookstore. She loved and respected Sam, of course, but throughout her life, it was her beloved Tommy from whom she'd always sought advice, with whom she'd always shared her secrets.

Janae had let Brendee and Deneen know that she thought Tom had taken quite the step down in associating with Dionne, after his beautiful and intelligent first wife. Brendee and Deneen suspected that the truth was simpler: Janae was jealous of the time Tom spent with his current companion, time she thought would be better spent buddying around with her.

Dionne was only aware of the fact that Janae had always been cool to her, if not downright cold. But she was very fond of Tisha, because Janae's girlfriend always listened patiently to Dionne's conspiracy theories, responded with thoughtful, interested questions. Dionne believed her to be a fellow believer, or almost.

Brendee thought about Janae. There had been a time, after their son was born, during which Brendee had felt tired, restless, out of sync with herself and with her husband. Wiley gave her all the space she needed, but into that space had sashayed a beautiful and fearless woman who had flirted with him, and Wiley, perennial student of women, had flirted back: Janae. Brendee was never sure if it had been Wiley's own nature or her temporary distractedness that had led him to this flirtation, but he had frankly admitted that he'd enjoyed the attention.

Wiley had not strayed any farther than words – of this Brendee was sure, beyond a shadow of a doubt – and their marriage had returned to its glorious heights: Wiley had quoted some boring old black and white movie: *We'll always have Paris. We didn't have it before, we'd lost it until you came to Casablanca. We got it back last night.*

Whatever. Brendee was just glad to have her awesome love-life back.

Wiley had declined Janae's invitations, but by making them, she'd shown herself down to be a homewrecker, and Brendee had never quite lost the suspicion that Janae might again make a play for her husband someday. So she was relieved when Janae had declared herself to be in love with black-haired, blue-eyed, utterly beautiful Tisha. Janae thenceforth only had eyes for her.

Thinking of Tisha, Brendee scanned the table and once again marveled at all the similar genes present. Tom and his good-looking young cousin, Wiley and Bo, all raven-haired and blue-eyed. Brendee reflected, not or the first time, that she and Janae both favored the same type of men. And in Janae's case, the other gender, too: Wiley and Tisha looked so much alike that they could've been brother and sister. More so than Byron and Viktoria, Brendee thought, as Viktoria's eyes were gray, and her hair more dark brown than black.

Brendee was sure that there was more to Janae's affection for Tisha than her resemblance to Wiley, but she couldn't help wondering what Janae was going to think of Byron. Here was a man not much younger than herself, with the same coloring, the same smile as her beloved Tommy . . .

Nate's wife had brown hair, but Wiley and Tom each preferred blondes, Brendee realized as she considered her dinner companions. She was blonde, as was Janae. She'd seen pictures of Tom's first wife; she'd also been blonde. Dionne . . . Well, Dionne was as gray as Tom himself, now, but she'd also been fair-haired in her youth. Brendee wondered idly what shade of women Byron liked . . .

NINE

After the meal concluded, a tradition as old as time commenced: the voluntary segregation of the genders. Still too young to accompany their fathers – they were sleepy, anyway – Bo and Eric soon napped together on the couch, whilst Brendee and Deneen settled in beside them to enjoy a little girl-talk with Dionne and Viktoria.

"I was raised Catholic, too," Dionne told her guests. "Went to parochial school, wore the little uniform." She smiled craftily at Brendee's surprised expression. "But I went to regular public high school after that. Dad wanted me to get a little bit more of a secular education. Something based more in the real world. 'She needs to learn science. The theory of evolution and all that,' he said. And after I found out how the world really works . . . A higher power isn't gonna save us, so you might say that I've lapsed in my devotions. But I always wondered how I would've turned out had I stayed and studied with the sisters."

Dionne looked expectantly at Viktoria, and Viktoria looked back expressionlessly.

"What's convent school like?" Dionne prompted at last. "In Estonia?"

"Oh! Of course! Our back – you want to hear about . . . *where we're from.*"

Viktoria had listened carefully to Wiley's fiction about Europe, including the quick mention of her *studies with the sisters.* She'd learned a little about the major religions of Earth before coming to it, and she'd realized that Wiley had been trying to offer a rationale as to why she seemed so . . . *different.* Viktoria was indeed different, but convent school as an explanation just wouldn't do. It was silly.

"Wiley was incorrect. I am not of the Catholic faith. When he referred to convent school – it must've been Tom's expression. What he meant was that I was raised apart from more traditional communities. My mother and grandmother, and Tom, too, at one point – we were members of a group . . . Let's just say that we believe in . . . the laws of nature more than a specific deity."

Wiley had wanted to make her out to be a blushing, virginal Catholic schoolgirl to explain why she was dissimilar to these Earth women. How ridiculous was that? But a religious sect was still a good cover. Viktoria would tell them about Sirius, disguising the different lifestyle as a little-known Earth religious faith. She complimented herself on her cleverness.

"We consider ourselves to be masters of our environment. All these electronic contrivances . . ." She gestured at the ladies' cellphones on the coffee table, at the dark television. "And other machinery. We make do without them. We mostly eschew what you call marriage, also, although we're free to choose a life-mate if we so desire." Viktoria giggled. "It's not common, however."

Eric awakened, and Viktoria wiggled her fingers at him. The baby smiled. "Our children are raised at centers, by those that love children the most." Eric stretched out his chubby arms, and Deneen handed him to Viktoria.

"Aren't you simply precious?" she cooed. "The parents come to visit them, and when they are of age, they join the rest of our society. I thought about this as a . . . *career choice,* myself, for a time, caring for the children. Then Byron suggested that we come here.

"He, too, was also raised thus, but he left to attend a secular college."

Viktoria couldn't know that Tom's first wife had suspected for a time that he might be from some off-the-wall religious cult, too. He'd seemed quite odd to Liz in the first months of their relationship, just like Viktoria was odd. He'd also mentioned a lack of machinery where he was from, that it was a big agricultural environment. Liz had figured that maybe he was Amish.

When Brendee and Deneen and Dionne looked nonplussed, Viktoria added, "Because of this upbringing, I'm sure I seem strange to you."

"Not at all, Vikky!" Brendee exclaimed, attempting to politely deny the obvious.

"You're kind. But it's true. I even *feel* strange. But so far, I enjoy your culture immensely, and would very much appreciate your advice on assimila – on blending in."

"Of course!" Deneen cried. "We'll go shopping!"

"The first thing you have to know about life in these United States, honey, is that there are a bunch of different factions out to get you."

"For example, don't ask Wiley about what's in our food," Brendee warned with a grin.

Viktoria grinned back, then addressed Dionne. "Tom mentioned something – he said the two of you recently watched a television program about rumors of alien visitation?"

Dionne waved her hand dismissively. "Aliens are the least of our problems in this country, Vikky." Deneen rolled her eyes, so the older woman added, "But we don't have to get into all that right now. After all, you've just arrived. No need to make you paranoid. Even if they are out to get you."

TEN

Wiley had suggested something about teaching the young man from Estonia about the finer points of poker, so the men retired outside to the garage. Long ago, Tom and Sam had spent many a happy hour out there, talking about women, building and rebuilding engines. Most never saw spark or fuel: Tom just liked to take them apart to see how they meshed, and Sam liked to put them back together again. Once upon a time, Sam had just enjoyed being friends with Tom.

But their friendship had evaporated after Liz passed, and Tom had seen enough engines. Now he used the garage as a place where he could smoke a cigarette and hang out with Wiley and Nate, as a man-cave where he could escape from Dionne occasionally. There was a card table, and a shelf full of glasses and liquor, and a mini-fridge stocked with beer and limes from the tree Tom had planted in the backyard when he'd first met Liz.

"So this game – what's it called?"

"Poker." Wiley grinned like a shark, showing all his teeth. "Have you hit that ATM yet? How much money you got, my son?"

Byron reached for his wallet, but he stopped when Nate shook his head. "Forget about it, Byron, at least for right now. You don't want to learn to play cards from Wiley."

"He cheats," Tom advised.

"Who told you that?" Wiley responded with mock offense.

Tom and Nate in unison: "You did."

"Allow me to make you a drink, then, Byron," Wiley proposed.

"All right. It will be my first."

Wiley selected a bottle of gin from the shelf and four glasses. He dropped in ice from a bucket in the fridge, then declared to no one in particular, "Sometimes, the best thing about being married is that your wife can be designated driver."

"That's called *sexism*, my son." Tom cut up a lime.

"The drink?"

"The attitude," Nate supplied. "Few men in this world love their wives more than Wiley Royce. Don't for a moment think otherwise, even though he seems disrespectful about her when she's not around."

Byron smiled at Wiley, took a glass from him. "Loyalty to a woman is an admirable quality, I suppose. Where I come from, the women are—"

"Yes. I want to hear all about that." Wiley handed Nate and Tom a glass and sat down across the table from Byron. "I've been a student of women for my entire adult life. I'd love to hear what ones from another planet are like."

Tom poured generous shots, added tonic, dropped in lime wedges. *"To absent friends,"* he toasted, and he and the Earthlings clinked glasses. Byron copied them. Then he took a too hearty swig and Wiley chortled when he coughed.

"Slowly, my son."

Byron watched the three of them sip, then looked dubiously at his glass. "This is not some kind of . . . poison?"

Wiley picked up the bottle of No. 3 London Dry again. "Of the finest variety."

"It doesn't kill you as smoothly as a good Kentucky bourbon, however," Tom opined.

"Why would you choose to consume something that will kill you?"

"You've really never had a drink before, Byron?" Nate asked in disbelief.

"There's no liquor on—"

"Right." Nate drained his glass. He wasn't buying that Byron was from another planet. He couldn't be. The whole idea was just nuts.

"This is all part of the fun of Earth," Tom said. "It's not *actually* going to kill you."

"Not tonight, anyway." Wiley emptied his glass.

He was not generally much of a drinker, but he'd learned to appreciate gin and the drunkenness it provided from Tom. It was Friday night, the monthly Meeting of the Tribes, as good an excuse as any to get sloshed.

"Drink up, Byron," he encouraged. "It'll expand your perceptions."

"If the doors of perception were cleansed, everything would appear to man as it is, infinite. For man has closed himself up, till he sees all things through narrow chinks of his cavern." Tom winked at Wiley. "We'll save the mescaline for another day."

"Have you done mescaline, Tom?" Though he'd come to enjoy his gin, Wiley had never sampled any drugs, not even pot. He believed that they'd take the edge off of his intellect, perhaps permanently.

"I've done a lot of things, Wiley."

That's not really an answer. Before Tom could start in on any real or made-up tales of drug trips, Nate pre-empted him. "Tell us about your women, Byron." He didn't believe that Byron was from Sirius, but he was curious to hear what Mr. I-Never-Had-A-Drink had to say about the opposite sex. What else hadn't he done?

Wiley affected a fake accent. *"How much for the little girl? The women . . . How much for the women?"*

Tom giggled. He sounded Russian: *"You! How much for your wife?"*

He and Wiley dissolved into laughter. Nate wasn't much of a drinker either, but he always had a hard time keeping up with Wiley and Tom when they decided that the sun was far enough over the yardarm. It was obvious that tonight's consumption was going to go straight to their heads, just the way they liked it.

Byron stared blankly at them.

"It's from a–"

"I know, Tom." Nate sighed. "It's from a movie." He looked to Byron to save him from more cinematic quotations.

"The women on Sirius are–"

"Beautiful. Plentiful." Tom spread his hands in an all-encompassing gesture and giggled again. "But generally, they can take us or leave us. Not a lot of what you'd call *true love* on the homeworld."

"I'd be lost without my true love," Wiley intoned with some seriousness. Nate wasn't sure if he was kidding or not.

"Indeed," Tom agreed. "Before I met Liz–"

"Just like Viktoria said, it's been a long time since you've been . . . home," Nate interrupted. "Maybe we should let the newbie to our shores tell the story." Nate felt unkind, but he didn't want to listen to Tom talk about his lost wife at the moment. Such remembrances always made the younger man feel sad about inevitabilities that he didn't want to consider.

"But Tom's right, Nate. The women are both beautiful and plentiful on Sirius, and they really do mostly take us or leave us. Children are cared for by the community. If a woman wants to have a baby, she does. If she doesn't, she doesn't. They pretty much run our planet, at least as far as reproduction is concerned."

Nate nodded. "They pretty much run our planet, too. Reproduction and otherwise."

Wiley affected astonishment. "You've got to be kidding. Maybe in your household."

Nate ignored him. He didn't want to listen to Wiley rehash his vaunted theories about what women wanted. He'd been hearing them since high school. Just because his machinations had worked on Brendee . . . Nate knew that there'd been a lot of factors at play there, and just because Wiley had controlled them . . . Nate thought that there'd been a lot of luck involved, too.

"A woman who's chosen to reproduce can keep the baby with her until he's about five, or she can give him to the caretakers right after he's born. If she wants to have another one, with another man . . . It's all up to her."

"You don't know who your parents are?" Wiley asked incredulously.

"It's not so *Brave New World* as all that," Tom said. "Mom and Dad come to the centers to visit. The children just don't live with them."

"Leaving Mom and Dad to resume the swinging single life . . ." Wiley opined.

"Something like that."

"Do you have any kids, Tom? Back . . . back home?" Nate inquired.

Tom shook his head. "I never took the fatherhood plunge."

"It was offered?" Wiley winked. Tom was attractive for his age; more than a few of the matronly visitors to the bookstore attempted to pick him up on a regular basis. And some of the younger ones, too.

"Once or twice. I even had a right-handed partnership once."

"Did you?" Byron asked in genuine surprise. "What was that like?"

Tom smiled at Wiley and Nate, patiently waiting for explanation. "Watch."

He uncapped the gin, and carelessly tossed the cap to Byron, who caught it in his left hand. Tom gestured for him to throw it back, and then also caught it in *his* left hand. He looked at his friends.

"So?" Nate took the opportunity of the bottle's being open to pour another shot into his glass. "And?"

"You're both left-handed," Wiley, ever-attentive, observed.

41

"And so is Viktoria, and about ninety-eight percent of the population on Sirius. So you might say that righties are a rarity there." Tom took the bottle from Nate, poured himself another generous portion, then recapped it.

"Now love may be a many-splendored thing, as you gentlemen can attest, but there ain't a whole lot of it on the homeworld. Isn't that correct, Byron?"

He shrugged, nodded. "I never missed it." He finished his drink with another little cough and held it out to Tom to replenish.

"At least not love, in the monogamous sense." Tom made Byron a proper drink, with tonic and a fresh wedge of lime, but still with perhaps a little too much gin.

"No yearning for completion with that one and only soul mate. But some people do stay together monogamously for a week or a month or a year or forever. But they're rare. Like righties. That's why it's referred to as *a right-handed partnership.*"

"And how did that work out for you?" Byron's curiosity was palpable. He was amazed.

"Ah, she got tired of me. Before I got tired of her."

Wiley blinked. "That's it?"

"It was a season in my life." Tom paused, studied Byron closely. "You say you've never been in love? Never chose a partner of the right-hand, with whom to remain–"

Byron snorted. "Not hardly. Nor has anyone ever suggested such a thing to me."

Tom laughed at Wiley's look of astonishment. "That's how it is on Sirius, my son. We come. We go. We reproduce sometimes. We grow things. There's no jealousy, no heartbreak. Just one big, happy, healthy, boring-ass, agricultural planet."

"So you came to Earth to look for love?"

Tom grinned wickedly. "In all the wrong places. No, Nate, I didn't come here looking for love. I didn't really even know about love." He reached over onto a workbench behind him and found a pack of cigarettes and a lighter. "Another form of poison," he told Byron.

"And one that'll definitely kill you," Wiley warned.

"It says so, right here on the label." Tom smiled. "The ability to kill yourself with any number of selected poisons – that's one of the draws to this place, gentlemen. Wine, women, song – I came here to have a good time. And I did, for long enough.

"But then it came time to take my Uncle Morry to Mapimi. He wanted to go back home because his wife had passed on. They'd been married for fifty-three years, a most enduring right-handed partnership. They'd had a little girl that died in infancy, and a son that died in the war. I never did know which war. It was always just *The War* when Morry mentioned it. There was nothing left for him here after his beloved Belle died, so he decided to go back.

"On the way to Mexico, Morry told me that a good time was all right, but this planet had another thing to offer, much more easily come by than on Sirius. And that thing was love – *true love*. The possibility of living one's long life out on this glorious rock with someone who's your soul mate. The possibility of sharing your life, *yourself*, with the one perfect individual that loves you just as much as you love her. The possibility of finding the other half that makes you whole." Tom smiled at Wiley and Nate, happily married both, because he knew they understood.

"I came looking for a good time, but I found so much more."

Again Byron snorted derisively. "If you say so."

Nate thought that the gin was going to his head, too, regardless of where he was from. "So why did you come here, Byron?"

"I didn't come here to find true love, and I didn't come here to find a good time."

From the slightly unfocussed quality in his eyes, Nate was now convinced that Byron had a nice little buzz going, allegedly his first.

"Quite simply, my friends – I've come here to save your planet."

ELEVEN

"Do you have a boyfriend in Estonia?" Deneen asked.

"Many of my friends are boys."

Deneen shared a glance with Brendee. Apparently the English courses at the commune had been a little lacking. "I mean – a special boy. Someone that you're involved with. Someone that you–"

"Someone that you love," Brendee suggested.

"Oh, a right-handed – such as you have with your men! A monogamous, exclusive–"

"You're not monogamous in Estonia?" Dionne's eyebrows rose.

"I'm unfamiliar with most of their customs, as I am of yours. As I said, we lived in a separate community. Among my people, monogamous pairing is sometimes achieved, but it doesn't often last."

"Nor does it often last here." Dionne chuckled. "The three of us – we're probably what you'd call a statistical improbability. Most marriages fail within–"

"So you don't have a boyfriend?" Deneen repeated. If Dionne started talking about marriage failure rates, then it would just lead her to a discussion of all the other reasons why modern American society was circling the drain, and Deneen had heard her tell it all before. It depressed her.

"I have many friends that are boys. But none of them are *special* to me, as are yours. I've always been more interested in community matters; the direction in which my people are headed. Is it good for all, or should changes be made? Like I say, I once considered caring for children."

"So you're a social worker." Dionne frowned.

"Something like that."

TWELVE

There was a moment of silence at Byron's declaration, then Wiley guffawed. He brayed like a donkey. Tom and Nate were more polite; they only showed amused smiles.

Wiley at last got his giggles under control. "And just how do you propose to save our planet? The sheep don't want to be saved, Byron, my son. Trust me on that. Nor, as Dionne says, do most of them deserve saving."

Byron wasn't offended. "How much have they heard about the history of Sirius, Tom?"

Tom blew a smoke ring to indicate that they'd heard nothing, then followed it up with the word. "Zero."

"Perhaps my goal to save their world would not seem so laughable if they knew how much they have in common with us. Perhaps—"

"Tom once told us that our DNA is indistinguishable from . . . people from your planet." Nate also recalled how convenient that little tidbit had seemed at the time. No DNA test to prove Tom's purported other-worldliness, because what d'ya know, Sirian DNA is the same as human DNA.

"But did he tell you *why?*" Byron asked with drunken emphasis. "How it came to be that way? Perhaps you should tell 'em, Tom. Perhaps then they'd understand why I want to save mankind."

"Perhaps *you* should tell 'em, Byron," Tom replied with a trace of irritation. "I can't imagine why you'd even think mankind needs saving. And Wiley . . ." Tom nudged Wiley's elbow and his chin dropped off of his hand. He'd been staring studiously at Byron. "Wiley's not going to believe anything about world-saving from me, even if I suddenly formulated a plan. We've been friends for too long."

"All right." Byron smoothed out his shirt, ran a hand through his black hair. "I *will* tell them. Harken, gentlemen, whilst I relate to you the story of two mighty peoples."

"Wait, Byron. I think we all need another drink first." Tom doled out more gin, and studied his friends while he did so. It was clear that Wiley had just decided to go along with the whole thing, but Nate wasn't buying any of it. He never had.

"Feel free to raise your hands if you have any questions, gentlemen. Proceed, my son."

THIRTEEN

Deneen cared as little for social work as did Dionne, and thereby immediately changed the subject.

"What would you like to shop for first, Vikky? Clothes, make-up? Jewelry?"

Consumption of unnecessary baubles. Viktoria had been instructed that such was a major preoccupation on this planet. She reckoned that Tom would've said that it was all part of the fun here.

"Whatever you think I need."

"How about a nice chic cover for your phone?" Deneen picked it up from the coffee table. "It's so boring like this, don't you think? It looks naked."

"An amazing device."

"But it could be so much prettier," Deneen insisted.

"If you say so. Brendee's mate gifted these to us. He said that they are of a special variety."

"Wiley needs to give me a free phone," Deneen pouted.

"He said that such was his little secret. He doesn't share this secret with his friends?"

"Wiley doesn't share too many secrets." Brendee smiled wryly. "And free cellphones . . . That's one he definitely doesn't want getting out."

"An admirable quality," Viktoria opined, thinking that she was glad of Wiley's ability to keep his mouth shut. "I'm grateful for this gift. My brother says it's invaluable. He's been consulting his constantly, all afternoon, but I – could you teach me more about its use?"

"First, I'll put our numbers in for you." Denny began to type. "Then you can call us, anytime."

Brendee recalled Vikky's proclaimed fondness for children. "If you'd like to babysit sometime."

"I would be delighted."

"I'll babysit," Dionne volunteered. "You guys go to the mall tomorrow. Teach Vikky how to be a girlish American."

FOURTEEN

Byron began his recitation of the history of Sirius.

"Eons ago, there existed on the homeworld, two mighty peoples. On one hemisphere dwelt the Dinos, evolved to a man-like shape and form from dinosaur-like creatures."

Tom took out his phone. His grin was a little lopsided – Nate saw that he was getting drunk, too. He showed his friends a photo of a scaly, green reptile-man with huge black eyes.

"What is that?"

"I wouldn't expect Nate to have seen one of these, but you surprise me, Wiley. There's clearly a hole in your knowledge of oldie-time, popular entertainment. This ugly fellow is a Sleestak, which first began giving children nightmares in the 1970s. They were the bad guys on a Saturday-morning television show called *The Land of the Lost–*"

"Hell, Tom. The 70's were sixty-some-odd years ago." Nate surprised himself by defending Wiley's usually encyclopedic knowledge of worthless old junk that no one else had either heard of or cared about. "You can't expect him to know about every ancient thing that was ever broadcast."

"How ancient is *Casablanca?* He's seen that one." Tom looked at the Sleestak on his phone. "But on the other hand, *Land of Lost* wasn't exactly Bogart and Bergman, I guess."

"You're saying that these Dino People on Sirius, they're really these . . ." The gin was confusing Nate, too. "What are you saying?"

"I'm saying that the Dinos *looked* a great deal like the fictional Sleestaks, but they were much faster, more . . . *graceful,* if you will," Tom said begrudgingly. "They also looked a lot like the Reptiloids on Dionne's alien show. I gotta play that one for ya, Byron. Gave me quite a shock. A fairly good rendering of a Dino, as if they were still walking around, slaughtering mermaids."

"Mermaids?"

Tom smiled at Wiley and Nate apologetically. "I am, as the man said, getting ahead in the story." He gestured at Byron with his cigarette, repeated, "Proceed, my son."

"The Dinos were a reptilian race. Across the ocean from them lived the hominid race, which was amphibious, in that they possessed lungs and thereby breathed air, but they were aquatic. They were mammals, of course. They lounged around in the shallows, occasionally on the beach . . ."

Byron stopped, because Tom was offering further visual aids via his cellphone. "This is how the Assyrians depicted them."

The stone carving in the picture showed a man with long hair and a great beard, wearing a tall, rounded hat. Below the waist, he had the scales and tailfin of a fish.

"That's most definitely a mermaid," Nate agreed.

"The Assyrians *saw* these mermaids from Sirius?" Wiley asked suspiciously.

"According to their mythology, my son."

Byron went on. "So you have these two races, on separate continents, unknown to each other."

Tom shook his head. "The Mermaid People knew about the Dinos."

"They swam across the ocean and checked them out," Wiley offered.

Again Tom shook his head. "That's why I always disliked that term. *Mermaid People.* It confuses the monkeys. The Mermaid People were a freshwater race–"

"What would you call them, then? Naiads? They supposedly lived in freshwater."

"They Naiads were nymphs, Wiley. All women. Some god's daughters. Like the Nereids and Oceanids, who were sea nymphs." Tom watched Nate glance in exasperation at Byron. His blonde friend knew nothing of earthly mythology, and his expression communicated that he was pretty sure that the young Sirian didn't, either. "I guess we'll just go with the *Mermaid People.*"

"It's the common translation."

"Whatever. Just remember. They were a freshwater species."

Nate thought he detected a slight slur in Tom's voice already, a little *sch* sound that didn't exactly exist in *species*. But maybe he was imagining it, because Tom again sounded sober and scholarly when he said, "Their civilization had arisen in a great inland lake. It was vast, millions of square miles. The oceans that surrounded their continent, that separated their side of the world from that of the Dinos, were filled with predators and had an almost toxic level of salinity."

"So if they didn't swim across the ocean, how did they know about the Dino people?" Nate asked.

"They flew," Byron supplied.

"They had wings, too?"

"No, Wiley, they had aircraft. Spaceships."

"So . . . Let me make sure I'm following this. Here's Sirius, and it's got mermaids and lizards, flying around in spaceships?"

Tom shook his head again. "No. The Mermaid People were a race of intelligent beings who had developed the capacity for space travel." He gestured to one side of the table. "On the other continent, you had the Dino People, who were primitive–"

"Noble savages," Byron suggested. "Isn't that what they used to call your indigenous–"

"Yeah, nobody calls them that anymore." Wiley expressed embarrassment at the visitor's faux pas. "It's considered an insult, so–"

"But the Dino People *were* savages, and there was nothing noble about them." Tom tilted his head and looked curiously at his cousin. Was Byron just trying to make the story more interesting to his listeners, or was there actually a hint of *admiration* in his voice when he spoke of the Dinos? *Noble savages?*

"I'm sorry for interrupting, Byron. This is your story." *Your interpretation of it, anyway.*

Byron nodded. "The Dino People eventually arrived at the brink of seafaring. As Tom said, the Mermaids had possessed the capacity of interstellar travel for some time. When they saw that the Dinos would soon discover their marshy continent across the sea – they came to a decision."

"A planet-altering decision."

The ensuing silence lengthened. "Christ, Byron. Don't leave us hanging. What did the Mermaids decide to do?"

Byron sighed and again Tom was struck with his odd attitude. This was a point of triumph in the history of Sirius, the moment when his forebears had taken the initial step that would lead them to eventual world domination, to the peaceful, successful, happy society they enjoyed today. Why did his young cousin seem almost *depressed* by it?

"The Mermaid People came to the conclusion that the bipedal Dinos were a threat to them. Once the Dinos crossed the ocean, the Mermaids were sure that they'd then be in mortal danger. There was never any consideration of attempting to live in harmony with the less advanced civilization."

"So what did they do?" Nate wished that the kid would just get to the point of this fiction. He reckoned that he liked a good interstellar yarn as much as the next guy, but Byron was just dragging it all out.

"They decided that, in order to combat what they deemed the imminent Dino Menace, they would have to embrace bipedalism. So they gathered an armada–"

"Wait a minute," Wiley interrupted. "How does one *embrace* bipedalism? Surely you're not gonna try to tell us that simple wishing made it so? We haven't even been able to embrace flying cars yet, and God knows I've wished for that enough."

"He's getting to it, Wiley," Tom chided. "Have another drink. Stop interrupting. All will be revealed."

"The Mermaid People had been looking into the idea of acquiring legs, if you will, for quite some time, actually. They had sent various expeditions to Earth, to monitor the development of a similar hominid species here."

"We had mermaids here?" Nate asked. That was just too much.

"Aquatile Mensch," Tom murmured.

"What?"

Tom smiled, shook his head.

"No, Nate," Wiley said. "I get it – you're talking about us. The Sirians were monitoring *us.*"

Byron grinned. "Precisely. And now that they felt that the need to modify their physiology was at hand, they assembled an armada. They came to Earth, appropriated necessary cells and tissues; eggs and sperms and gametes. Sirian/human zygotes were manufactured and surgically inserted into brave female crew member volunteers. During the nine months that the new beings were gestating, their mothers swam, ate, relaxed, and meditated upon the future in a large freshwater pool constructed for them in Bolivia–"

"Hold on." Now it was Nate's turn to interrupt. "If they were mermaids, how did they construct anything on land?"

"The Grays," Tom supplied. "The *Igigi.*" He smiled, and there was a trace of wistfulness in it. *"Ah, distinctly I remember, it was in the bleak December."*

Wiley smiled in recognition and Nate frowned. If it wasn't old movies, it was poetry. It was irritating. What the hell was Tom talking about now?

Tom caught his annoyance. "I was just remembering that the last time I trotted out this story, it was at Christmastime, *in the bleak December*. Before you were born."

Ah, Liz. How I miss you!

The elder Sirian put out his cigarette and continued. "Anyway, the Mermaids that came to Earth didn't come alone. They brought with them two classes of servants, bioengineered from Dino captives. The first were a group of harmless, small creatures – they looked like the familiar Gray Alien of popular mythos. In fact, I've always figured that all the stories about the Grays – it must be some kind of Sirian inside joke, a rumor started to scare the modern monkeys on dark and stormy nights."

"But you're saying they're real." Nate didn't believe he was going along with this bullshit.

"They *are* real," Byron replied. "But there aren't any of them here."

"Not anymore," Wiley said slowly.

"No. Not anymore. The other group the Mermaids brought with them, which I referred to as the *Igigi* – after the rebellious servants of the Annunaki in Sumerian mythology – they were the workhorse slaves, huge, bioengineered past even the brutish prime of their Dino forebears. Although they were all sprung from the same genetic base, they were as different from the Grays as a Clydesdale is from a pony. Genetic manipulation is kind of a Sirian specialty, as you'll soon hear.

"The big fellas were necessary for the heavy lifting; even with the assistance of the anti-gravity methodologies which the Sirians had also brought along with them, it would've been difficult for the big-headed, spindly-limbed Grays to fit all of those massive blocks of stone for the pool together by themselves. There aren't any Igigi anymore, even on Sirius, and certainly not here. Not unless you count . . ."

Byron looked at him questioningly.

"*Sásq'ets.*"

Byron nodded in understanding, and Wiley said, "I don't think I want to know."

"You don't." Tom nodded at his cousin to continue the tale.

"The combining of human and Sirian DNA occurred not only in Bolivia–"

"That's just the only pool left," Tom interrupted again. He wiggled his eyebrows. "Puma Punku, gentlemen."

Wiley and Nate looked at him blankly.

"I forget. You guys don't know about all the ancient sites here, purportedly built by aliens. I know Dionne's heard of it. She and the aluminum-foil hat crew just happen to be correct in this particular case. Puma Punku – one hundred percent Sirian built." Tom grinned at Byron. "But it's so shot to hell that they've never figured out that it was just a big holding tank."

He paused and again his memories of his first wife assailed him. "I've been there. There's not much left, but it feels good to kind of pay your respects."

Byron shrugged indifferently and Tom noticed once more that the young Sirian seemed to possess very little esteem for the brave explorers that had made him what he was today. He continued his recitation of their story clinically, with no pride or admiration. It was strange to Tom. Apparently things *had* changed back home.

"The Sirian mermaid women carried their hybrid babies to term. Then the babies grew up and mingled with the natives, passing the hybrid genes on. Everyone on Earth today–"

"So you're saying I have mermaid genes?"

"You don't think so, Nate?" Tom lit another cigarette. "You were taught that mankind evolved from apelike creatures, correct? *Australopithecus* and such? But science has always been looking for that missing link, because you don't look anything like a monkey, do you? Wiley maybe . . ." Tom nudged his friend again.

"You're hairless, compared to other hominids; your nostrils face downward, unlike theirs. As a species, you're quite adept at holding your breath, like that other aquatic mammal, the whale. The skin on your fingers and toes – and only on your fingers and toes – becomes wrinkled in the water, allowing you to maintain your ability to grip the railing and rungs of that pool ladder, hold onto the handle of that water-ski rope.

"There were a few scientists, decades ago, that almost got it right. Their theory was called the *Aquatic Ape Hypothesis.* All these mermaid-y characteristics, they proposed, appeared in man because . . ." Tom referred to his phone. *"Primitive ape-stock was forced by competition from life in the trees to feed on the seashores and to hunt for food, shell fish, sea-urchins etc., in the shallow waters off the coast.*

"Of course, they were laughed out of the groves of academe, mostly for numerous inconsistencies in their theory. But they weren't far off the mark. Mankind didn't *evolve* all these traits that just happened to be suitable to an aquatic existence. You don't look like a monkey because of some hairless missing link yet to be discovered, Nate. These traits were bioengineered into you when your ancestors' genes were melded with those of Sirian mermaids.

"Like Eric inherited blonde hair from you, but he's got his mother's beautiful green eyes – humanity got downturned noses and hairlessness, and a host of psychological behaviors that are immaterial at this juncture. And Sirians got legs."

Byron waited to see if Tom would elaborate further, but his cousin didn't continue. "Once the hybridization was completed here, the mermaid Sirians returned home."

"And they took spaceships-full of the new crossbreeds with them," Tom again interrupted. "The new hybrid peoples, you see, had just been press-ganged into the fight against the Dinos." Byron opened his mouth, but Tom continued. "The first crossbreeds adapted immediately. Though they were vastly outnumbered, they drove the Dino People back into the highlands of the Eastern Continent, away from the shores of the inland sea. At least temporarily.

"The Mermaid People lined up to have their embryos bioengineered so that the next generation would be born with legs. It was a bittersweet choice; they were deciding to let their way of life die out. They were deciding to embrace an entirely *new* way of life. The offspring would mostly be created out of their own genetic stock, plus some of the new material from Earth; they would thereby have this rather major mutation. But basically, the only difference between the new babies and the old babies was that the new babies had legs instead of tails. An unexpected offshoot was that they were almost all left-handed.

"There was a brief period of relative peace, after the Dinos were first repelled. On the Eastern Continent, you had Mermaid People, bipedal crossbreed imports from Earth, new bipedal Sirians, and Dino interlopers in the highlands. More bipeds were born every day, and they were loved and cherished by their amphibious parents.

"Then the Dinos started to raid again. Once again they slaughtered and ate any hominids they could catch, whether amphibious or terrestrial."

Wiley blanched. "They . . . *ate them?*"

Tom nodded, became grim. "When the Dinos made landfall on the Eastern Continent, when they first discovered the inland lake and its inhabitants . . . The Mermaids were an amphibious people; their cities came right up to the shallows. Like Byron said, they even occasionally lounged on the beach.

"The Dinos slaughtered thousands in those first days, harpooning them, dragging their wriggling, not-yet dead bodies onto the shore. Filleting and eating them right there, as if they were so many bluefin."

Wiley turned even paler and slammed his latest drink. He liked to eat healthy, but like everyone else in the first world, he was far removed from the business end of his food supply. He didn't like to think about *filleting* anything.

"The crossbreeds had pushed the Dinos to higher ground for a time, but now they started to raid again. And there was still that whole giant continent of Dinos across the sea, billions of them. The Mermaids didn't want to sacrifice their new and precious bipedal offspring to the toothy maw of further confrontation with the lizards, yet this problem couldn't be ignored. The Dino People already outnumbered the Mermaids and their new terrestrial children by a staggering amount, worldwide.

"They didn't lay eggs like some reptilian species, but were live bearers, like some snakes. And, like snakes, but unlike people, they usually gave birth to no fewer than three or four young at a time, with a shorter gestation period. So the hominids were outnumbered, and would continue to be outnumbered, unless something was done.

"So the Sirians, now walking on legs of their own, came back here and crossbred more soldiers. They expanded all the original centers begun by their Mermaid predecessors, and started others. In South America, in the American Southwest, in the British Isles, in Egypt, in Greece, in Turkey, in the Middle East."

Tom paused to let the ramifications of all that sink in. Wiley and Nate weren't rabid followers of alien theories like Dionne was, but neither did they live in a vacuum. The stubborn, utterly unsubstantiated proposition that *Homo sapiens* was not alone in the universe – and that cultures such as the Egyptians and the Aztecs had in fact been quite chummy with out-worlders in the pyramid-building days – Wiley and Nate didn't have to watch *Alien Archives* to know about these ideas. Like Santa Claus and the Easter Bunny, they'd heard the stories all their lives. They were a part of their culture.

And now Tom and his young cousin were telling them that it was all true, that aliens had visited Earth in the past, that humanity was actually the product of a global science experiment, Sirians tinkering with human genetics, like Mendel with his pea plants.

"Eventually the Dino threat was eliminated. Completely. The lizards were wiped out, as thoroughly as that asteroid had wiped them out on Earth."

"Wasn't that a little extreme? Like Byron said, couldn't there have been some kind of . . . I dunno, acceptance of their differences? They'd shared the planet at one time, unknown to each other. Couldn't there have been some kind of . . . détente?"

Tom laughed. "The people of Sirius had been in danger of being subjugated by a race that really consisted of nothing more than smarter than average lizards, Wiley. They'd been in danger of being wiped out entirely, themselves. So they acted to protect their species. The Dinos were a brutal enemy, a mermaid and biped-eating abomination. You wouldn't give komodo dragons the vote, would you? The better species prevailed. Its evolution. Isn't that right, Byron?"

"One of your Earth philosophers observed that history is written by the victors. Things are what they are." Byron avoided Tom's gaze and contemplated the bottom of his glass, then drained it slowly.

After a moment, he smiled once more. "But now that you've heard the intertwined histories of our planets, surely you can see why I'd take the opportunity to save mankind, now that it has presented itself? Why, we're practically brothers!" Byron put his arm around Wiley's shoulders and gave him a squeeze.

"That's great, Byron. I always wanted a brother," Wiley lied. He'd always cherished being an only child. He thought it made him more intelligent. "But how are you gonna save us? What opportunity has presented itself?"

"I'll explain everything when we go to the Feathered Serpent Exhibit. One of the artifacts they have is key. I'm afraid that this poison–?"

"Gin."

"I'm afraid that this gin has muddled my thoughts – I think I'll ramble incoherently if I try to explain it all now." He giggled, put his hand over his mouth like a schoolgirl. "How long does this effect last?"

"It'll be gone by the morning," Nate told him.

"You'll have a headache," Wiley promised, "but Tom's got a cure for it. You oughta bottle that shit, Tom. You'd make a fortune."

"It doesn't have any shelf life, Wiley. It oxidizes right away. They'd have to put preservatives into it–"

56

"And we can't be havin' that." Wiley slapped Tom on the back, then considered Byron inquisitively. "You can't just give us a little hint? I mean, saving the world, that's a pretty big deal – you couldn't just give us a general outline?"

Byron opened his mouth, then knuckles rapped on the door, followed by Deneen's anxious voice: "Wiley! You gotta come in the house! Vikky dropped her phone in the sink!"

Tom opened the door and Nate's wife rushed in. "The water was running. I turned her phone off right away, like you said to do, but . . . Can you fix it?"

"But of course." Wiley gestured toward the house. "After you."

When Deneen was out of earshot, he told Byron, "I don't care if you are descended from mermaids, my son. You have to make your sister understand that *technology here isn't waterproof.*"

FIFTEEN

The ladies had decided to cut up some fruit for a little dessert. Viktoria had observed that they each carried their phones with them out to the kitchen, so she followed suit. She couldn't imagine why they felt the need to bring the communicators along – their people were all within shouting distance – but while they'd left their children behind, asleep on the couch, they'd brought their cellphones with them, so Viktoria did the same.

What she failed to notice was that the other ladies put their phones down on the kitchen table. Viktoria set hers beside the sink, and when Deneen exclaimed over something: "This blouse would look so cute on you, Vikky!" Viktoria turned from the orange-colored melon she was slicing up and knocked her phone into the sink, beneath the running tap.

She looked down at it, appreciating the play of the water splashing off the multi-colored, patterned background that Deneen had installed for her.

Deneen heard the clatter, and practically leapt across the room. "Quick, turn it off!" When Viktoria didn't move, she looked incredulously at the strange girl and immediately retrieved the phone from its bath.

Apparently admiring one's phone underwater is not done, Viktoria told herself.

"Maybe it'll be all right. I'm sure his Electronics Majesty can fix it." Deneen pushed the power button until the phone winked off, then went out the back door to fetch Wiley.

When they all came back into the house, Tom instructed Deneen to ask Dionne where the beads were. "I know there's some around here somewhere," he called after her. He smiled at Viktoria. "Gotta save those cellphones."

"Beads?"

"It's a desiccant." Tom continued to look at her; for the first time since she and Byron had arrived, he thought he caught a ghost of a resemblance to his sister, Alba.

Wiley took the dripping cellphone from her hand. "Just like I told your brother, Ariel, this is one thingamabob you can't get wet."

Wiley shook the droplets off of it, over the sink. "It's *delicate.* Strictly a . . . *terrestrial* device."

Viktoria felt foolish, but noticed that Wiley didn't seem overly concerned. "Can it be repaired?"

"I've never lost a wet patient yet."

She felt an upwelling of – could it be *respect?* – at his utter confidence.

Viktoria had been led to believe that the people here were basically ignorant of their technology. They were slaves to the brightly lit screens with which they surrounded themselves, without the vaguest clue as to how they operated. If she had indeed ruined the little thing by exposing it to moisture – in a crisis such as this, she believed that the average person would be helpless.

That's what happened to their forebears, Viktoria knew. Once the Sirians returned home, the technology that they had so carelessly left behind began to run down. Being the descendants of water-borne creatures, they'd never had a whole lot of use for electricity, and their bioluminescent lighting, which had received their fuels from Sirian sources, eventually ran out of them and went dark. The energy that had once made the ley stones that they had installed around the globe seem as though they were almost alive, dissipated into the atmosphere. The various, formerly Sirian-run cultures across the world lost touch with each other.

It had been impossible for the basically very primitive populations to maintain the sophisticated civilizations that the Sirians had set up for them. These were societies and technologies that humanity had not earned, had not discovered, had not struggled to produce on their own. They didn't understand them, and as such, couldn't hope to reproduce or even maintain them. As the years passed, the empires that the Sirians had installed here fell apart.

The monkeys had been forced to start all over again. They'd had to relearn everything that a superior culture and technology had once just handed to them.

And they had indeed done so. Even though she'd told her new friends that they got along without electronics and machinery in *her community* – Brendee and Dionne and Denny would never have guessed how much they got along without them – Viktoria was already fascinated with the screens all around her, large and small. Wiley's gifted cellphone had hooked her.

Viktoria knew that there had to be keepers of the knowledge, if it was true as she had learned, that the rank and file were ignorant of how things worked. She'd imagined some kind of priestly class – hadn't she been told that they worshipped these *delicate, terrestrial* devices? When her ancestors had left here, hadn't the ones that had worked closely with them, the ones that had attempted to keep their worlds together after their benefactors decamped – hadn't these people considered themselves priests?

Viktoria had known that someone who knew how things worked had to exist. She'd just never expected to meet any of them. And Wiley was certainly no priest. He was just an arrogant monkey, precisely the type of creature she'd expected to find here. But he was apparently also one of the technologically initiated, and that gave Viktoria a new interest in him.

After their goals were accomplished, after the new status quo had been established, Viktoria thought she might have a use for Wiley Royce.

SIXTEEN

He sat on the sofa between the two sleeping boys and rapidly, expertly, disassembled Viktoria's phone. She watched him closely, while the others remained in the kitchen, eating fruit and talking. They'd all seen Wiley take apart a phone at one time or another.

He dropped the components into a plastic bag filled with small, cloudy beads, sealed it, then looked up and was surprised to find Viktoria staring steadily at him. "Now we wait. It should be okay, though. They're a lot more water-resistant than they used to be. It'll be as dry as it's gonna get by the morning and then I'll put it back to—"

"Who is Ariel?"

"What?"

"You called me Ariel."

"Oh. Yeah." Wiley was warmed by the fact that Viktoria continued to stare at him. "Ariel's a mermaid. It's a story we tell to our children. Mermaids are fictional here. She was rather obsessed with . . . *terrestrial culture.* She collected things that fell off ships. She wound up selling her voice to the sea witch in exchange for legs."

Viktoria blinked – somewhat owlishly, Wiley thought – and he explained further. "Byron had just finished telling us the history of Sirius, so I thought it was a fitting—"

"I am no more nor less mermaid than you are. Our DNA is—"

"Indistinguishable. Yeah, I've heard that one." Wiley watched her for a moment. "But Byron told us that your culture is quite a bit different than ours. He said he'd never been in love."

Viktoria's gray eyes never left his, and Wiley found that he enjoyed her unwavering stare. As he'd told Byron, he'd studied women for all of his adult life. Watched them. He hadn't actually been with very many, but then field study had never been necessary for him, because a few secrets dropped in his ear and observation had told him all he'd needed to know.

Wiley believed that he knew exactly what was going on behind Viktoria's lovely gray eyes. The dilated pupils, the slightly parted lips . . . His wife often stared at him in the same manner – it was one of Wiley's chief joys in life. And Janae had looked at him the same way – and Janae had been quite forthcoming about what she'd wanted from him.

"Have you ever been in love, Vikky?"

Viktoria smiled coyly. "It is as my brother undoubtedly said. We have affection, passion; but we have very little of what you call love, here. The desire to stay with the same individual. I've never felt that desire, so I guess you could say, no. I've never been in love."

"But you have . . . I'm sure you've . . ."

Her smiled widened. "Yes, Wiley. Since I was about seventeen."

"Me, too, as a matter of fact," he replied, mostly just for something to say. Then he changed the subject a little bit. "What do you think of the men here, so far?"

"I find some of them quite intriguing."

Her smile told Wiley that he was one of them, and he would've been surprised had it been any other way. He found women transparent; they couldn't disguise that look in their eyes. He knew precisely what they wanted when they looked at him like that. And with Brendee and Janae, he'd been correct. That he was wrong about what Vikky wanted would've astonished him.

Brendee and Deneen returned to the living room and began gathering up their sleeping boys. Wiley threw Bo's diaper bag over one shoulder; Nate did the same with Eric's.

"Dinner was great, as always, Dionne," Brendee proclaimed. "And it was so nice meeting you guys."

"I'll call you tomorrow, Vikky," Deneen promised. "So we can go to the mall."

Dionne reiterated that she would babysit for the boys. Wiley picked up the bag of beads containing Viktoria's cellphone, and Tom suddenly mimicked a little girl's voice.

"Santie Claus, why? Why are you taking our Christmas tree? Why?"

"There's a light on this tree that won't light on one side," Wiley replied. *"So I'm taking it home to my workshop, my dear. I'll fix it up there, then I'll bring it back here."*

The two of them giggled uproariously; they only stopped when they noticed that no one had joined them.

"You guys are drunk," Dionne observed. She narrowed her eyes at Nate and Byron. "All four of you are drunk!"

"It's–"

"I know, Wiley." Byron winked at Nate. "It's from a movie."

SEVENTEEN

On the drive over to Tom's house the next morning, Deneen asked her friend, "Do you think Vikky's a tramp, Brendee?"

"A tramp!" Bo repeated.

Brendee glanced at her son in the rearview mirror. "Hopefully, he'll forget that one." She eyed Deneen balefully. "If you don't say it again."

"Sorry, Brend. He's getting to the age when we're gonna have to start using code-words. I remember when my sister was little. Kids repeat everything you say."

Brendee nodded. She knew how it was. She had a younger brother and sister, also, so Brendee and her older brother had developed quite an extensive code-language.

"We had to start using – what does Wiley call 'em? Something with a *u.*"

Brendee was at a complete loss for several seconds, then she realized what term her friend sought. "A *euphemism." With a u.*

"Yeah. That's it. But do you, though? Think that Vikky's a . . ." Deneen searched for a kid-friendly alternative to the common word; all the other expressions that came to her mind wouldn't be good for Bo to hear and inevitably repeat, either. "A T-R-A–"

"Why would you say that, Denny? We don't even know her!"

"All that talk about *having lots of friends that are boys.* About how nobody's monogamous among her people. Tra – there's a name for girls that aren't *monogamous."* Denny rolled the word off of her tongue. She liked it – it sounded like what it meant. Not like *euphemism.* That could mean anything.

"You were quite the not-monogamous girl yourself in high school."

"Not mogamus!" Bo declared.

Denny smiled at him. She was not offended at being *euphemistically* labeled a tramp by the toddler nor his mother. What Brendee said was accurate. She'd had her share of adventures with the opposite sex in high school, and had not cared what they, or Brendee, or anybody else had thought about it.

"Until I found the right man." Now she offered Brendee a knowing smile. "At least I had a little fun beforehand. Not like you."

"Dave was fun. He was fun enough. But Wiley . . ."

"Christ, I remember! You never stopped talking about Wiley from the very moment – *I think he's awesome, Deneen. I want to eat him.*"

"Wiley *is* awesome, Deneen." Brendee would forever think so. Wiley always knew exactly what she wanted.

Another crafty smile. "Janae sure thought so."

"Seriously," Brendee agreed. "Thank God for Tisha."

"I was wondering . . . Janae's got that weird crush thing going on for Grandpa Tom . . ."

"Yeah, I was wondering the same thing. What's she gonna think of Byron?"

"You people and your skinny, black-haired guys." Denny shook her head. "Not my type."

"Wiley's not skinny. He's . . . *lean.* Like a swimmer."

"And Byron could be his brother. Or a much younger Tom. Janae might just lose her hillbilly mind. It's not like she's actually related to them. Byron's fair game."

"She's got Tisha," Brendee said primly. "I'm sure she wouldn't just throw her over for–"

"God only knows what Janae's liable to do," Denny opined. "I'm not sure about all that lesbian stuff. Maybe she just hasn't found the right man–"

"You're ridiculous, Den. You sound like something out of 1952. Janae likes women–"

"She likes men, too. She likes men that look like Wiley, and Tom, and Byron. I'm just saying . . . I wanna see the look on her face when she meets him."

They pictured how Janae might react to this younger version of her beloved Tommy in silence for a moment, then Denny added, "And Vikky. Maybe that's all she needs, too."

"What?"

"Maybe all she needs is to find the right man. Like we did. Maybe all Vikky needs to be *monogamous* is an American boyfriend."

EIGHTEEN

Brendee was not surprised to see Janae's car parked in Tom's driveway. It was Saturday, there was no school, and it wasn't like Tom's for-all-intents-and-purposes granddaughter had anything as prosaic and commonplace as a job.

Someday, she'd once told Brendee. After she got tired of school and decided what she wanted to be. *Or if Tom ever gets tired of paying for it,* Brendee had thought.

Dionne already had the playpen set up in the living room. She'd never had children of her own, and after Eric's birth, she'd gone right out and bought all the baby accoutrements, just so they would be on hand, so she could babysit if Denny needed a sitter.

Dionne considered herself the luckiest person in this dying world. Once she'd been just a lonely old woman, waiting for the collapse; then she'd somehow snared the attractive, intelligent bookstore owner, and he'd brought with him into her life these young men and women that she'd come to think of as family. Children, and grandchildren, too. Had she believed in God, Dionne would've thanked Him daily for her good fortune.

Deneen set Eric in the playpen, but Bo held out his arms to Grandma Dionne, so she smiled and took him from his mother, covered his face with ticklish kisses until he giggled.

"You just missed Tommy," Janae said absently from the couch. She gazed at Deneen and Brendee with an expression of slightly dazed wonderment. "Have you guys met Byron?"

The man himself sat on the other couch, smiling placidly, as always.

"We have." Deneen removed a glass baby bottle from Eric's diaper bag and handed it to him.

"Thanks, Mom," Janae spoke for him, then arose and snatched him from the playpen.

Brendee was reminded of Viktoria's words: *Our children are raised by those that love children the most,* and considered that it was that way for their boys. Neither Bo nor Eric had ever seen the inside of a daycare facility. While Brendee and Deneen and Nate worked, Wiley watched his son at the shop during the day – there was a playpen there, too – and Dionne looked after Eric.

The boys never wanted for attention at Tom's house. If not Dionne, it was Janae, or Tisha; there was always another joyful woman on hand to hold them, a happy man to toss them into the air. As if to underline this idea, Viktoria came into the room and took Bo from Dionne, gave him a delighted squeeze.

Denny glanced over at Janae. She had reseated herself on the couch with Eric on her lap, but uncharacteristically, she was more or less ignoring him. She was staring at Byron, listening attentively, as if he was revealing the secrets of the universe.

"Wiley said he would teach me about Shakespeare today."

Janae's eyes sparkled. "I could do that for you, Byron."

Denny frowned. It was true. Janae had learned the classics at her grandfather's knee, and was just as apt to drop a couplet as Tom was. Or Wiley, for that matter. The three of them shared a knowledge and enjoyment of all that strange old boring stuff, plays and poetry, stories and ancient movies and old music, stuff that she and Brendee had never heard of.

Denny had often wondered if it annoyed Brendee when they would start quoting things at each other, grinning and laughing as if it was all some private joke. It certainly annoyed her. Tom and Janae, and especially Wiley, ever since high school – they sometimes made Denny feel stupid. She was glad that Nate wasn't into such things.

"Wouldn't you rather go to the mall with us?" she asked Janae.

"How nice of you to ask, Denny!" She turned a happy smile back to Byron. "Would you like to go?"

"Maybe some other time," he replied apologetically, as if she'd asked him something of great import. "Wiley and Tom are expecting me."

There was a moment of silence whilst Janae stared at him again, and Brendee and Deneen shared a we-were-right glance. Dionne rolled her eyes at whatever this new intrigue might be.

"Well," Brendee said at last, "Let's get this show on the road, then."

NINETEEN

Wiley smiled expansively when Byron entered *Morry's Books*. He had stacked up several weighty editions of *The Collected Works of William Shakespeare* on the counter, as well as copies of individual plays in paperback form.

"What would you like to consider first, my illiterate friend?" Wiley chose *Hamlet* from the top of the stack, thumbed through it. *"Tragedy, comedy, history, pastoral, pastoral-comical, historical-pastoral, tragical-historical, tragical-comical-historical-pastoral, scene individable, or poem unlimited?"*

Byron offered his serene smile. "Whichever pleases you, Wiley."

"Hamlet's as good as any, I guess."

Tom idly glanced through another copy of the story of the melancholy Dane. "What did Olivier say in the movie version? *This is the tragedy of a man who could not make up his mind.* Hamlet's told of a grave injustice and is bade to avenge it."

Wiley had noticed that Tom frequently stared pointedly at Byron, as if he had questions to ask, but wasn't quite sure how to phrase them yet. Now he seemed to've made up his mind.

"I can't help thinking about how you told our history last night, Byron . . . You seemed to feel some . . . I don't know . . . You seemed to feel some pity for our ancient enemy. Almost as if, like Hamlet, you couldn't make up your mind about how you feel about what you seem to perceive as an injustice."

Byron looked surprised. "What has that to do with . . ." He gestured at Wiley and his books.

"It just struck me as strange, that's all." Tom noted that Wiley was also surprised, but he'd started down this road and aimed to continue upon it. "You referred to the Dinos as *noble savages,* as if you held some kind of *respect* for–"

"What possible difference could it make? They're long gone now."

Byron's voice had an edge that Wiley hadn't heard before, a harshness, and it riveted his attention. He said quietly, "Maybe Byron just feels that genocide is wrong."

Tom laughed. He looked at his phone for a moment. "Webster's defines *genocide* as *the deliberate killing of people who belong to a particular racial, political, or cultural group.* The operative word there is *people,* my son. The Dinos weren't people; they were–"

"They were people of a different species. They had beliefs and a culture, history . . ." Wiley looked to Byron for confirmation and he nodded. "I can see how someone could be sad about the loss of such a thing, like when the last elder of some rainforest tribe dies, and their language and way of life dies with him."

Tom shook his head. "Cultures pass on, Wiley. *Latin is a dead language, dead as it can be. First it killed the Romans, and now it's killing me.* Other cultures rise. It's part of the panorama of history here. But that's not what happened on Sirius. You, and Byron, too, I suspect, are missing the point entirely.

"Our Italian friends . . . The blood of the Caesars still flows in their veins. The Romans are long gone, but their descendants remain. You come from European stock yourself – perhaps your several generations' removed great grandfather was a Spaniard that was wrecked with the Armada, who swam ashore and met a blue-eyed Irish lass . . .

"My point is this, Wiley. Genocide *is* wrong. One group of people trying to wipe out another group, when beneath the skin, we're all still *people.* The same, biologically compatible species. There's no ideological philosophy that can erase that most basic of truths, no matter how many Hitlers and Mussolinis, Ho Chi Minhs and Maos try to deny it.

"But there are no green-eyed, hominid-reptile descendants on Sirius, for the simple and inescapable reason that the two species cannot interbreed. You whine about the loss of the Dino *culture,* a *people* irrevocably destroyed. They weren't people, Wiley. They were a different species, alien–"

"You're an alien, Tom."

"But I'm the same species as you, my brother and only friend. The Dinos were not. The war was not over a clash of cultures or beliefs." Tom laughed without humor. "Their belief was that they were the superior species, and they were proved wrong."

"A superior species might've made allowances for their differences."

"I do believe you're becoming a hippie, Wiley. A fucking social worker, as Dionne would say." Tom smiled at last, and when Wiley just shrugged, his smile fled. "No. There could be no allowances for the conquered enemy; the differences were too great. The Dinos *ate* my ancestors, Wiley. You can't expect me to mourn their fate."

"Perhaps they would've stopped that, had they been allowed to—"

"You know the one about tigers changing their stripes? It has a literal application here. You're not going to put Bo in with the tigers, no matter what kind of training or conditioning they've had – if they get hungry enough, they're gonna eat him." Tom paused. "Don't cry too much, though, Wiley. Remember? There are still Dinos on Sirius, after a fashion. The Grays – they're Dinos—"

"Like a Chihuahua is a wolf," Byron said emotionlessly.

Now Wiley smiled. "Maybe the Grays get together and tell stories about their ancestors, when none of the Sirians are around. Maybe they talk about a glorious future – if they were bioengineered one way, they could be bioengineered back, right? *The South shall rise again . . ."*

"Right." Tom was not amused. "It's not like they're told romantic stories about their forebears. You have no idea what you're suggesting, Wiley. It's not even remotely funny."

Tom frowned severely. It was an expression that Wiley had rarely seen from him, and he quickly moved to alleviate the suddenly dark mood. "Look, Tom, I don't really know anything about—"

"No, you don't."

"You don't really know, either," Byron stated quietly. "The Dinos have been gone for millennia. No one knows what they were truly like."

"They ate their enemies. That's all I need to know."

Another heartbeat of antagonistic silence passed, then Tom clapped Wiley on the shoulder. "I'm gonna go over to the Farmer's Market, so I can make a batch of that hangover cure. Scare up the blender for me, will ya? I think it might put us all in a better mood."

TWENTY

In the car, Denny chattered happily about all the things that her new friend was going to see at the mall. Vikky listened attentively, giggled prettily in anticipation, asked questions. Brendee was silent; she watched Janae gaze out the car window, and wondered what might be going on in the devious little mind behind the preoccupied expression.

Vikky embraced the mood of discovery. She didn't really care all that much about clothes and perfume and jewelry and make-up, but it *was* all different to her, and Denny took such delight in holding things up in front of her, in waiting while she tried them on, in adjusting them, in pronouncing thumbs-up or thumbs-down on the looks. Denny's enthusiasm for this activity was infectious.

After *Pacsun* and *Wet Seal, Windsor* and *Nordstrom's,* Janae needed a break, however. She and Brendee sat outside of *Forever 21,* while Denny and Vikky kept up the good fight and continued to shop.

Brendee decided to bring up the topic foremost in her mind, but Janae beat her to it. She grinned conspiratorially and asked the exact question that Brendee was thinking of asking her: "So what do you think of Byron?"

"You first." Brendee smirked. *I've already got a blue-eyed, black-haired mate. I kinda thought you did, too . . .*

"He looks a lot like Wiley."

You get right to the point, I gotta give you that, Brendee thought.

"You think so?" she replied ingenuously. "I dunno, Janae. They're the same type, I guess. But Byron reminds me more of Tom."

Janae let that comparison go by without comment. "Wiley and Byron are the same type, yeah. But Byron . . . He just seems so . . ." Janae searched for the right word, found it at last. *"Innocent.* Wiley looks at you like he knows what you're thinking . . ."

Janae realized that she was speaking to Wiley's wife; what Janae had once thought about Wiley and the fact that he'd known it was probably not the best subject for her to bring up with Brendee.

Now or ever. So she quickly returned the conversation to Tom's cousin.

"But this kid . . . He just blinks at me with those big blue eyes . . . He seems so . . . *boyish.*" She grinned again.

Brendee returned her grin. She recalled that Wiley had struck her as simply a watchful, shy *boy,* when she'd first met him, as apparently Byron seemed to Janae. It wasn't until later that Brendee discovered to her delight that Wiley was anything but shy, and she thought that perhaps Byron, after the things that Viktoria had told them . . .

"Did you hear anything about his upbringing? Did he say anything about–"

"I just met him this morning, Brendee. I haven't talked to him that much. I've mostly just looked at him." That off-color grin again. "He makes me feel like a bad ol' cougar."

"Hell, Janae. We can't be more than two or three years older than him."

"I know, right? But still. He seems so innocent."

Brendee considered. Byron did seem . . . She wasn't sure about *innocent,* but maybe a little shy. Bookish, with his mention of being a student of ancient cultures. But Viktoria had said that there was little monogamy in the community in which they'd been raised, and Wiley had also seemed shy at first. She'd been so wrong in that impression . . .

"The things I'd like to do to him," Janae was saying. "Just to see the look of surprise on his face."

"What about Tisha?" Brendee blurted out.

"This is hetero talk, Brendee. Just girl talk, if you will, about men." Janae paused, frowned. "And I guess you're gonna find out eventually. Tisha and I are . . . *on a break.*"

"On a – what?"

"Wiley never showed you that one?"

Brendee blinked as if slapped. What had her husband shown Janae that he hadn't – what was she talking about?

"It was from an old television show. I know he's seen it. This couple . . . They have an argument. The girl says, *We need a break from each other.* So the guy thinks they're broken up. He goes ahead and sleeps with some other girl. His girlfriend finds out about it – she didn't think they'd broken up – but now she breaks up with him for real, because she figures he cheated on her. He says it wasn't cheating because *We were on a break!* Hilarity ensues."

Brendee was still dumbstruck. Was Janae trying to tell her that Tisha had cheated on her? That she'd cheated on Tisha? What did Wiley have to do with – *Oh, yeah.* Brendee relaxed a little bit. It had been Wiley who had failed to tell her about *ye olde television programme,* from whence this comedic expression for heartbreak had originated. Wiley was in the clear.

But Brendee was still not quite sure what Janae was trying to communicate to her. "So you and Tisha are on a break? You broke up?"

Janae shrugged.

"Permanently?"

Janae shrugged again. "Maybe. Maybe not." She smiled. "Don't look so sad, Brendee. These things happen. *Que sera, sera* and all."

"But I thought . . ." *I thought I didn't have to worry about you chasing after my husband anymore.* "I thought you and Tisha were in love!"

Janae sighed. "Shall I offer you clichés? We'll always love each other, but we're no longer in love. Does that make sense to you?"

"I'm . . . I'm sorry to hear that, Janae. I liked Tisha very much."

"Like I say, these things happen. I'll live." Janae burst into song, just to prove that she wasn't too upset. *"It ain't the first time, baby. Ba-a-a-y-by, it won't be the last. I better get the boys 'round, and do some drinkin' fast."* When Brendee continued to look confused, Janae smiled. "A really old song. Tommy used to put it on for me whenever I told him I'd ended another relationship. *I don't know if I'll cry, I don't know if I'll die laughin'."*

Brendee frowned. Janae and Tom *and Wiley* and their old movies and TV shows and songs. It didn't really bother her, but at times like this, she could understand why it annoyed Denny so much. *It's like the three of them belong to a club from which the rest of us have been excluded . . .*

"So, are you gonna make a play for . . ." *Christ, did I say that out loud?*

Janae didn't look at her. "Maybe. I dunno. Maybe I should just coast for a while. Wouldn't want to break the boy's heart because I'm on the rebound, right?"

"Of course. But it *is* fun to talk about." There was no harm in thinking about it, sharing a little giggle about another good-looking, blue-eyed, black-haired man with Janae. Such were their type, after all.

With a suddenness that surprised her, Wes Thomerville strolled into Brendee's mind. He was another of her and Janae's type, the best looking black-haired, blue-eyed man Brendee had ever seen, in fact. Wes was Brendee's little secret, the only secret she had, really, the one she'd kept from her husband and her friends, her parents, her brothers and sister.

Ah, Wes! Brendee allowed the memories to course through her as she sat there beside contemplative, suddenly silent Janae. Brendee had been obsessed with him in high school, had thought about him first upon waking, last before closing her eyes to slumber. Once she'd beheld tall and lean Wes and his black guitar, she'd immediately begun to become annoyed with her stocky, red-headed, brown-eyed boyfriend, Dave. Wes was the reason that Brendee hadn't needed the kind of adventures that Denny had enjoyed in high school.

But no one knew about Brendee's obsession with him, because he wasn't even real.

That's not exactly correct, Brendee amended. She supposed that Wes was probably still walking around in Riverside somewhere, probably had a wife and kids, maybe even grandkids by now. But she'd always thought of him as not real because the only glimpse of him she'd ever seen – it was all her mother's fault – was a music video he'd done way back in 2011 or 2012, long before Brendee was even a twinkle in her father's eye.

The story went like this: Wes Thomerville had been lead singer for a band called Rolling Blackout; Brendee's mom – Darlene – had had a hellacious crush on him when she was in her early twenties. Darlene and her friends had gone to see his band every weekend at some now long defunct bar. The band had put out only one CD – it was actually a short documentary, entitled *Rolling Blackout's Hometown Debut.*

Darlene had never actually known Wes, past gazing affectionately at him at his shows, and asking for his autograph. He was happily married, several years older than her – he'd paid no attention to his small group of adoring young fans. The band had never made it out of Riverside; Darlene had matured, married Brendee's father, produced four children. She'd forgotten all about Wes Thomerville.

And Brendee never would've known of his existence if it hadn't been for Darlene's desire to take a walk down Memory Lane one afternoon when her daughter was seventeen.

73

"I want to show you what passed for sexy when I was about your age," Darlene had quipped, and then she'd shown Brendee a music video, a cut from *Rolling Blackout's Hometown Debut*. A stupid, whiny song about revenge, by a band that had never become famous, sung by some guy that Brendee had never heard of.

Wesley Francis Thomerville. Although Brendee would never know his middle name.

The corny little video, only three minutes and thirty-five seconds long, was the sexiest thing she'd ever seen.

Of course she couldn't say as much to her mom. It just wouldn't do to let Darlene know that for once they agreed on something – *Wes Thomerville was awesome.* Brendee feigned indifference, but later covertly copied the video to her computer, and soon made a ritual out of watching it, every Friday night. It wasn't real – the man himself had to be into his mid-fifties at the time. The real Wes never interested Brendee in the slightest. But that three minutes and thirty-five seconds of video from before she was born thrilled her to the bone.

Not too long after she'd discovered Wes and his awesome video, Brendee had just happened to have a conversation with her friend Nate Osbourne. He'd asked her if she would tutor some guy named Wiley in math. Brendee agreed.

She would later decide that it had been one of the best decisions she'd ever made.

Because, by some fluke of fate, because of all those black-haired, blue-eyed genes floating around Riverside – Brendee discovered to her utter and enduring delight that Nate's shy friend bore a striking and uncanny resemblance to Wes Thomerville.

After the initial shock of meeting Wiley, one of the first thoughts Brendee had encompassed was: *Wait till Mom sees him.* Darlene's mouth had indeed dropped open when she'd beheld Brendee's new boyfriend. To this day, Brendee knew that Darlene had a little bit of what could only be termed a *crush* on her son-in-law. *Everyone* knew about that, just like everyone knew that Darlene had been smitten with a dark-haired singer in her youth.

At a family barbeque, Brendee's dad had even asked, "Have you ever wanted to learn how to play the guitar, Wiley?" Bo Comstock had been a musician once, just like Wes. But he didn't *look* anything like Wes . . .

"Not really, Mr. Comstock. Why do you ask?"

"Oh, no reason. If you ever want lessons, just let me know. I'm sure Darlene would love to watch you play."

Darlene had put her hand over her face and blushed like a schoolgirl. Her parents' friends burst out laughing. Brendee wasn't the only one who'd (secretly) noticed Wiley's resemblance to Wes Thomerville – and Darlene's friends and her own husband were making fun of her about it.

Wiley had looked at Brendee and asked, "What's that all about?"

"I'm sure I don't know," she replied innocently. "I think they all might be drunk."

No one knew about Brendee's one-time obsession with the old singer, nor that it had caused her to immediately notice seemingly shy Wiley, that it had led her to fall in love with him. It was Brendee's secret.

Except that Wiley knew. He'd known all along. He was quite proficient at getting into the phones and computers of his unsuspecting friends and neighbors, because he was a self-taught, exceptionally capable hacker, and quite by chance he'd happened upon the path into Brendee's computer, before they'd even met. Such snooping was a pastime in which he'd frequently engaged in high school, for no other reason than to amuse himself.

Wiley had viddied the short, ancient clip that got the cute blonde's motor running so much, had noted his own resemblance to its singer. When Nate suggested her as a math tutor, Wiley had already known that Brendee would fall for him, and once Nate watched the song, he had known it, too. That was *their* little secret.

TWENTY-ONE

Byron picked up the copy of *Hamlet* from the counter where Tom had set it and began reading. *"You come most carefully upon your hour.* I like that."

Wiley had been staring at the door to *Morry's Books,* contemplating Tom's hasty, angry departure. Now he turned and considered Byron again. "We'll get to Elsinore in a minute. Tell me about Sirius. Tom says it's a paradise. He says you all live for a very long time. No pollution, no plastic. That sounds so incredible. I want to hear all about it."

"Everything is grown on Sirius. Tools, clothing, dwellings. Once upon a time, even spacecraft. All through bioengineering." Byron smiled at Wiley's look of wonder. "So there's never been any need for concrete or steel or plastic. There are small metal and stone tools, of course, but everything else is grown.

"Great trees, like your sequoias, are made to mature in a certain, rapid fashion, with appropriate voids and downturned branches, and voila! We have buildings that would put your most famous architects to shame. And when the buildings – the trees – die, they're turned into compost to feed newly growing structures. Various undersea creatures have been modified to provide propulsion – once for spaceships, now only for small watercraft – and their bioluminescent traits are utilized for light."

Wiley thought of *The Flintstones,* and the birds and mammoths and dinosaurs that acted as car horns and shower heads and elevators.

"The climate – have you been anywhere else on Earth, Wiley?"

"Only in books, my friend. On the internet. That's always been enough for me." Wiley had always believed that the world was at his fingertips through these means, so he'd never felt the slightest inclination to actually travel to visit any particular part of it. Everywhere, there were just too many sheep.

"The climate on Sirius is similar to here in Southern California, though wetter. We have enough rain; we don't need to irrigate."

"How do you get around? How do you ship? Harvest?"

Wiley unconsciously touched the scar on his left thigh. He'd fallen off of a combine on his grandfather's farm when he was a teenager, had broken all three bones in his leg. It was during his convalescence that he'd discovered books, and through them, art and literature, philosophy. All the knowledge that made him feel superior to his ignorant fellow man.

"Food is grown locally, so there's no need to ship it, nor to harvest it on the massive scales known here. People just gather what they need from the fields. Roads aren't paved. Transportation is accomplished by small wheeled vehicles, similar to bicycles. Or we walk."

Byron paused, and Wiley imagined the unsullied wonder of Sirius: smog-less, car-less cities, near enough to the fields, where people walked to gather their food. How awesome that would be!

"No livestock?"

"The major source of animal-based protein has always been fish. There are some small mammals, similar to your . . . What is the word? Vermin? Like raccoons, opossums. A few birds. We don't eat any of them, however. And the closest thing to a pet – there is a fairly large aquatic mammal, similar to your harbor seal. Once upon a time, they were like dogs to the mermaids of old. They still congregate on the shorelines. They're tame; people feed them and pet them."

A world of vegetarians that had never shared their lives with cats and dogs or cows or horses or sheep. Or elephants or lions or tigers or bears. Wiley wasn't sure how he felt about that part; he couldn't imagine the forest without the bird calls and the peepings of all the other creatures out in the darkness. But on the other hand, he'd never been what you'd call a natural history buff, either. He thought he could live without animals and not miss them.

"Tom says–"

The man himself re-entered the bookstore, to the accompaniment of the jingling bell. He carried a small cloth bag; stalks of celery poked from the top.

"What, were they out of plastic bags?"

Tom shook his head. "I didn't want to hear you bitch, Wiley, so I went earth-friendly."

"You can't build on those landfills, my son. Plastic is choking this planet."

Byron smiled blankly at this exchange, and Wiley added, "Speaking of a paradise sans plastic, your cousin was just telling me about Sirius."

"Yep." Tom's former annoyance flared again in his blue eyes. "No plastic on Sirius. Just trees and crops and all of Nature's bounty."

"And you say there's no art, no literature –'

"Tom exaggerates." Bryon smiled at him. "We have paintings and statues. Wondrous textiles. We have stories, histories, plays. Entertainments similar to yours."

Tom's return smile was unreadable. *"Thus far, with rough and all-unable pen, our bending author hath pursued the story; in little room confining mighty men, mangling by starts the full course of their glory.*

"What we don't have, Wiley, is the same kind of great patchwork of emotions always at play here. Mankind has struggled to become what he is, and that struggle has been accompanied by jealousies and heresies, tragedies and just plain old miseries.

"Adultery? There's no Sirian word for that. We're polygamists, and quite happy with it. There is no starvation, no homelessness, no alcoholism or drug addiction. Because there was never a need to escape from those troubles we've never had, things that alter your consciousness were never invented on the homeworld.

"Like I once told Liz: there are no haves and have nots on Sirius, Wiley. Everyone gets what they need: food, sex, housing, work; rest, relaxation. Everyone is happy and healthy. There is neither murder, nor robbery; no fraud, no scams upon the innocent.

"And our *entertainments* reflect all this wonderfulness. No one writes *The Postman Always Rings Twice* in the Garden of Eden."

"Yet some of you want to visit–"

"Some of us are more monkey than mermaid." Tom's killer smile returned gloriously. "Maybe some of us have a little bit more of the old Berserker genes in us, or the Azteca. We seek a little more spice." His expression became patronizing; he smirked at his cousin. "It's not for everyone."

Wiley clapped the young Sirian on the shoulder. "Byron *comes most carefully upon his hour,* Tom. Give him some time. He just got here. He might warm up to our debauchery after a while."

"And if not, there's always that world-saving to be accomplished."

Wiley eyed Byron hopefully. "Are you in the mood to let us in on more about that now?"

Byron glanced at Tom, and noted that his grandmother's brother returned his gaze evenly, expectantly. He knew that his tale was one that Tom had never heard; it was a legend told only to a select few, and certainly not to those who longed to come to Earth in search of *a good time*. Byron realized that he'd have to convince Tom of its validity as much, if not more, than he would have to convince Wiley.

"All right. I suppose now is as good a time as any." Byron cleared his throat. "As you are aware, there were Sirians here on Earth at the time of the building of the Pyramid of the Feathered Serpent."

"Wait one second, Byron." Wiley offered an apologetic grin. "I know that I just asked you to tell us, but let me see if I can scare up Nate. That way you won't have to tell it twice."

"Nate doesn't believe any of this, Wiley," Tom stated flatly.

"Maybe not. But I'm sure he'd like to hear it, regardless."

Wiley texted his friend: *U need 2 get over here to the bookstore.*

I don't need 2 do anything but die.

And live until u die. U has a hangover?

☹

Tom's gonna make the cure & Byron's gonna tell us about saving the world.

I really don't care about all that bullshit.

What else do u have 2 do 2day?

Sleep?

Sleep when ur dead. I'll have him wait til u get here.

TWENTY-TWO

Vikky and Deneen emerged from *Forever 21,* laden with more purchases, and Janae took the opportunity to suggest lunch. They adjourned to the Food Court and ordered a loaded pizza.

After a few moments, Vikky noticed that an empty paper plate sat before Deneen on the table. "You don't like –?"

"Pizza," Janae supplied. *This chick is so odd,* she thought, not for the first time. *They gotta have pizza in Estonia, yet . . . Maybe she's just dumb. Or innocent, like her brother.*

"Denny's anorexic. She doesn't eat–"

"I am not!"

"Not anymore," Brendee commented, her mouth full.

"May I see your phone, Brendee?" Vikky asked politely. They had all placed them on the table beside their plates; Vikky thought that they were perhaps anticipating important calls, or maybe, as was her case, they anticipated unfamiliar words. She picked up Brendee's phone and typed *anorexic* into the Google search box, as Deneen had instructed her to do, whenever she wanted to know the definition of something.

"I have to do it all the time," she'd said. "Mostly when Wiley's talking."

"An eating disorder characterized by a low weight, fear of gaining weight, a strong desire to be thin, and food restriction. Many people with anorexia see themselves as overweight even though they are underweight–"

"I'm not anorexic, Vikky." Denny glared at Janae. "I'm just not gonna eat that."

"Certainly." Vikky became aware of a sudden tension. She handed Brendee's phone back to her. "You're still nursing. The spices–"

"No. I'm not nursing anymore. I'm just not gonna eat fast food pizza. You have no idea what's in it, Vikky. It's–"

"It's full of poison!" Brendee crammed another bite into her mouth. She chewed, grinned.

"You said not to ask Wiley about what's in our food," Vikky recalled.

"Or Tom, either," Janae advised. "Not unless you want to be there all day."

"There are dangerous chemicals in our food, Vikky. You just have to read the labels to see it, and not eat the ones that contain it. And God only knows what's in that crap." Denny sniffed at her companions. "You just have to be smarter than the sheep."

"You're Wiley's sheep," Janae snapped nastily. "You believe anything he says."

Viktoria wondered at the antagonism now manifest between her companions. Something to do with Wiley . . .

Denny picked up her phone. "It's on the internet, Vikky. What the ingredients really are. Tom and Wiley . . . They know all about it."

She texted Brendee: *Janae wishes SHE was Wiley's sheep.*

Brendee looked at her phone and grinned around another mouthful of pizza.

A chubby guy wearing horn-rimmed glasses passed their table. He made eye contact with Vikky and smiled, offered a little wave. Vikky returned his smile, waved back.

Denny looked over her shoulder. She frowned and the guy scuttled off, embarrassed. "I was just telling Brendee this morning, Vikky. We need to find you a boyfriend. But . . ." Denny made a face. "Do you like fat guys?"

"On my – where I'm from, the men all look pretty much the same. There are different races, of course, just like here, but as far as body type goes, they are alike. We choose our mates based on their personalities, more than their looks, I guess. They're all beautiful." When no one commented, Vikky added, "No one is overweight where I'm from, Denny. Our diet is vegetarian, augmented with fish."

"My mate's a vegetarian," Brendee said absently, scrolling on her phone. "Except when he's not."

Your mate's a lot of things, except when he's not, Janae thought. *He's an outrageous flirt, but when one goes to call him on it . . .* Janae had made an extra-marital suggestion to Wiley once, and she'd believed that he'd agreed to take her up on it. But she'd been mistaken. Wiley had made a fool of her, and Janae would never completely forgive him for that.

"So does that mean you *do* like fat guys?" Denny asked Vikky with a pained expression. "Because you haven't seen too many?"

"There are so many *different* men here." She gestured at the crowded Food Court. "Fat ones, thin ones. Bearded ones, bespectacled ones. And ones that are not. You and Brendee – your men are different from each other, yet each is attractive to you. What does your man look like, Janae?"

Denny barked laughter. "Like Wiley!"

Janae frowned at her comment. "I don't have a man, Vikky. My mate is a woman."

But she still looks like Wiley, Denny texted to Brendee. Brendee nodded, smiled. She would tell Denny about the bombshell later.

Vikky nodded sagely. "I've heard of this phenomenon. It's become more popular recently in my community. Byron–"

"Does Byron have a girlfriend?" Denny asked. "Back in Estonia?" Brendee looked up from her phone, again interested in the conversation.

Vikky noted their expectant expressions and thought that perhaps this monogamous love to which they all claimed to adhere wasn't as ingrained as they wished her to believe. Byron resembled Wiley a great deal, and Denny had said that this other one's homosexual partner also resembled him. Deneen's mate was of a different build and coloring, but perhaps she was also curious. Perhaps Byron could use this apparent attraction they all had to him to his advantage . . .

"Not that I know of," Vikky told them. "He's been immersed in his studies of late, before we came here."

"Byron's an archaeologist," Denny told Janae.

"How interesting," she commented noncommittally. She picked up her phone and texted Brendee: *I've got some bones for him 2 dig.*

Brendee set down her last slice of pizza and replied, *I think bones r paleontology.*

But u get my point.
☺

TWENTY-THREE

A half an hour later, Nate arrived at *Morry's Books*. He was disheveled, and a pulsing headache just behind his right eye was a constant reminder of why he wasn't a drinking man. He'd considered blowing off Wiley's invitation to another one of Byron's interplanetary tall tales, this time about how the self-proclaimed out-worlder intended to save his species. It was all bullshit. Nate agreed with Tom: the world didn't need saving, and he wasn't in the mood for more of this fiction today. Neither Tom nor his cousins were really from another planet.

But Wiley Royce was interested in this ridiculous fantasy, and when Wiley was interested in something, he invariably dragged Nate along with him. It had been that way since high school.

Wiley handed him a glass of Tom Bastion's Miracle Hangover Cure and Nate grimaced. It tasted like grass clippings, but he drank it anyway, because it always worked.

"Byron's been reading *Hamlet,*" Wiley told him.

Nate rolled his eyes, and churlishly asked himself why he hung out with a guy that read Shakespeare and watched ancient movies; all that boring shit that he personally couldn't possibly care less about. A good question for today: *Why do I put up with Wiley?*

Nate sighed and downed another portion of the green wonder medicine. *Because he's my best friend, that's why.*

On the day they'd met, the guy that thought he was smarter than everybody else had made a spectacularly dumb move. He'd insulted the center for their little high school's football team, and while Wiley had been completely unafraid to fight big Neal, he had foolishly misjudged Neal's sense of fair play. Nate came upon the scene just as Neal and two of his teammates were about to hand Wiley's ass to him.

Nate believed Wiley might've had the ass-whipping coming – he'd made an obscene remark about Neal's sister in front of the whole class – but three football players against one skinny dark-haired kid didn't strike Nate as proper odds, so he came to Wiley's aid. He'd once been on the football team himself, and didn't care for any of these guys, anyway.

Once they'd laid the three tough guys out, if only temporarily, Wiley said, "Thanks for saving my life, pal. What's your name again?" He held out his hand. "I'm—"

"I know who you are, Wiley. You're an asshole."

"Better men than you have said so." He grinned, and his teeth were pink with blood.

The two of them went to the cafeteria for lunch, and once seated, Nate watched the smart-mouthed kid take a yellow handkerchief from his backpack and hold it to his bleeding mouth. He noticed that there was already dried blood on it. "Not your first fight, Wiley?"

He looked at the handkerchief. "First this week."

It was then that Nate allowed his curiosity to get the best of him. He'd regret it a few times in the ensuing years. He asked, "What's your deal, anyway? Why did you feel the need to insult Neal's sister? Why would you want to get your ass beat over nothing?"

"I wouldn't have gotten my ass beat, Nate. Neal's big, but he's slow. I'm in a lot better shape than him. It would've been fun. I need the exercise. The occasional fight keeps ya focused, alert, tip-top. Sometimes, ya gotta remind the sheep who the rancher is. I would've held my own, if the odds hadn't suddenly changed."

Wiley grinned again. "You know those people that think they're smarter than everybody else? Those people that consider themselves worldly and wise? The ones that think they're above the petty intrigues of our wondrous high school life?" He gestured at the crowded tables. "Better than the jocks and tramps and dopers? Well, I'm one of those guys."

"But why is that, Wiley? What's so special about you? You haven't got a friend to your name that I can see – you're always by yourself."

Nate would become the friend that Wiley's superiority had never before allowed him to have. And Nate discovered – though he would never admit it, on threat of death – that Wiley Royce was indeed smarter than everyone else.

And since he was Wiley's only friend – until Tom came along – Nate was also the keeper of Wiley's secrets. He knew all about Brendee's undisclosed crush on that old singer, for example; he knew that Wiley had used his resemblance to the guy to make her fall in love with him.

Nate was covertly proud of being his clever friend's confidante, but on the other hand, some of Wiley's secrets – like this whole alien extravaganza – were just plain annoying.

"Okay, Byron!" Wiley clapped his hands together and grinned like a schoolkid. "Nate has arrived. Tell us about saving the world."

TWENTY-FOUR

"Perhaps it *would* be fun to have a boyfriend while I'm here," Viktoria mused aloud to Brendee when they were back at Tom's house. *Why not? It could be a playful diversion, before the real work begins.* "But I'm unsure. Like I say, there are so many types. What's considered attractive here, Brendee? What's . . . *sexy?*"

Brendee smiled. Denny and Dionne and Janae were out in the garden, picking tomatoes or something. It had been Denny who'd suggested the idea of a boyfriend to their odd visitor, but Vikky had chosen to discuss it alone with Brendee. She was flattered that Vikky would ask her opinion.

What's sexy? Wiley was sexy, but Wiley was spoken for, now wasn't he? *Besides my husband, what's sexy?*

Of course. What was the sexiest thing she'd ever seen, besides Wiley? Brendee called up *You Can't Be Shy* on her phone and paused it where Wes looked over his shades at the camera.

This wasn't the video that had ensorcelled her so completely as a teenager, but this was the only other clip from Wes and Rolling Blackout known to exist. Wiley knew that his mother-in-law had liked the old band once upon a time, so he and Tom had scared up this other video from the internet somehow – Brendee never did find out how – and had presented it to Darlene as a birthday present.

But Wiley didn't know that his wife had it on her phone, too, because he didn't know that his wife also appreciated Rolling Blackout. Or at least their singer.

She showed the still to Viktoria. "This is sexy."

Viktoria smiled. "Yes. This is Wiley."

It would seem that Viktoria, with her odd, foreign perceptions, still had perceptions enough to find Wiley sexy. Brendee wasn't sure if that amused or worried her.

"No, this is not Wiley. This is Wes Thomerville."

"He is attractive because he resembles your mate and is evincing a receptive expression in this screen capture."

Brendee looked at her phone. There had to be more to it than that. She abandoned *You Can't Be Shy* and put on *My Disgrace,* her original favorite. "Just watch this, Vikky."

Wes sang, whispered, made eyes at the camera, at Brendee and Viktoria, watching. He alternately manhandled and caressed his guitar. When the song concluded, Brendee sighed. The ancient clip still did it for her. Hot damn, the old guy had been fine! She wondered idly if Wiley was done with Byron's literature lesson for today . . .

She found that Viktoria was looking expectantly at her. "He greatly resembles your mate–"

"And you find my mate attractive."

Viktoria nodded. "But that's because he's kind and friendly to me." *And because he is a keeper of the knowledge. He will be useful.*

Yeah, Wiley's friendliness with the opposite sex is legendary, Brendee thought. There had been that little exchange of flirts with Janae, but Brendee knew that she was the only woman for Wiley, and wasn't jealous. Too much. She hoped once more that newly-single Janae wouldn't start throwing all those incomprehensible quotations at him again, things that Brendee didn't understand, except on a visceral level – she knew that when Janae said them to Wiley, they were come-ons.

Viktoria studied her. "Yet I grasp that you find this individual to be more attractive that Wiley."

"Once upon a time, my friend." She hadn't found Wes more attractive than Wiley since the moment she'd met Wiley, because Wes wasn't real. But Brendee wasn't seeking to make such nuanced distinctions with Viktoria.

"I see very little difference, Brendee."

"Watch it again."

Still Viktoria remained unconvinced, but she truly wanted to fit in, so she catalogued her observances. "This one sings, while looking invitingly at us."

Indeed he does, and ever so invitingly.

"But it's not his words . . ."

"No." *My Disgrace* wasn't a great song. Not at all. Brendee would've long ago forgotten about it, wouldn't have kept this clip for all these years, if it'd been sung by anyone but Wes.

"He and the others accompany themselves on these stringed instruments . . ."

"Yes. Wes plays the guitar, Vikky."

Again Viktoria studied her. "And that makes him sexy?"

"It does indeed."

"We had no guitars in my community. No instruments at all, actually, except drums. Yet I don't find the drummer attractive – do you?"

"I've never been much for drummers." And the drummer for Rolling Blackout was certainly not much to look at.

"What is it about this other instrument that heightens this man's attractiveness to you?"

Now there was a question for the ages. What made guitar players attractive? All of them certainly weren't, not to every woman, but Brendee had no doubt that all of them were attractive to *some* woman.

"I dunno, Vikky. There's absolutely nothing sexier than a good-looking guitar player, so–"

"But why?"

"You *have* been with men, right?" Brendee knew that she had – *I have many friends that are boys* – but somehow, she needed a reaffirmation of it at the moment.

"I have. More than a few, in fact. As I've mentioned, monogamy is not common–"

"And it was enjoyable to you?" Brendee thought of Janae.

Viktoria smiled deviously. "Undoubtedly so. As Deneen said, it would be *fun* to perhaps have a *boyfriend* here. So I seek to know what is considered attractive in your culture, as this place is so much more diverse. Our men are all basically like Byron."

"Built like swimmers," Brendee mused.

Viktoria grinned. "You find that aspect of Byron attractive?"

"I do," Brendee admitted. *But Byron's just as dumb as a post, like you. Maybe even innocent, like Janae thinks.* She wondered suddenly if Byron was at the bookstore right now, not talking about dusty old plays, but instead quizzing Wiley and Tom on American women. *What's sexy?*

"Byron also resembles your mate," Viktoria was saying. "But there are so many other types here. Your men come in all shapes and sizes and there doesn't seem to be one standard of attractiveness." She blinked, and liked everyone else, it struck Brendee as odd. Owlish. "Occupations seem to play a role, such as with this musician."

"I can't really explain it, Vikky. It just has something to do with the instrument . . ."

"A phallic representation perhaps?"

Brendee blushed. "Perhaps." She'd never quite thought of it like that before, didn't believe that was precisely accurate. There had to be more to it than that.

"I can't really explain it," she repeated. "There's just something about a guitar player. You just gotta use your imagination."

"What should I imagine?"

"That he's doing something else besides playing the guitar." Brendee's smile approached a leer. She had it now. "That instead of his guitar . . . he's touching you."

Viktoria's eyebrows went up as she considered that. "Play this again."

TWENTY-FIVE

"As you are aware, there were Sirians on Earth when the Pyramid of the Feathered Serpent was constructed in Teotihuacan. It was at the height of the Dino War, but many knowledgeable and hopeful leaders, many scientists, believed that the end of the conflict was in sight. Some of the Sirians here on Earth also believed that once the threat was eliminated, once no more soldiers were needed, Sirius would forget about this little backwater planet."

"That's what you said did happen," Nate snapped, still feeling churlish.

"Did you eat breakfast, Nate?" Wiley asked brightly. "You sure are in a bitchy mood."

"No, Mom. I was asleep when you called me." He frowned at Byron. "And I'm getting a little tired of all these stories about aliens. If I was into all this garbage, I'd watch Netflix with Dionne. I just can't believe–"

"Hamlet said it best, my son. *There are more things in heaven and earth than are dreamt of in your philosophy.*"

"And therefore as a stranger give it welcome."

Wiley smiled at Byron's seemingly eidetic memory. He might seem a trifle strange; he might be an alien – Wiley was willing to concede that he was, and Tom, too, because there were indeed more things in heaven and earth than were dreamt of in his philosophy. Regardless of where he was from, Byron was definitely intelligent. He learned quickly.

"Just be polite, Nate. Byron's story – you've got to admit, it's not the kind of thing you hear every day."

Wiley closed one eye and squinted at his friend. It was a familiar expression, the one he used to communicate amused doubt, or barely concealed derision. In this case, Nate suddenly got the impression that maybe Wiley wasn't buying all this bullshit as much as he seemed to be. Maybe Wiley also thought that they were nuts – his good buddy Tom and his newfound relative, too. Maybe he was just *being polite.*

Nate had always considered Tom to be his friend, even if he was a little odd, and a know-it-all, just like his other friend. Maybe he was being bitchy. "I'm sorry, Tom."

The old man smiled. "It's okay, Nate. I know it's a lot to take in. As long as you don't call the men in the white coats on me, you can believe whatever you want to believe. Proceed, Byron. I'm kinda curious to hear the world-saving part myself."

"There was a right-handed couple here on Earth, in Mexico." Wiley liked the sound of that, but Byron quickly added, "Whether it was for love or simply for convenience in a foreign place, we don't know.

"The scientist's name was Brice, and his woman, also a scientist – she was called Annett. They had a son named Tyrrel."

Wiley grinned brilliantly at Tom. *"Is thy name Tyrrel?"*

"James Tyrrel, and your most obedient subject," the bookstore owner replied immediately.

"Art thou, indeed?"

"Prove me, my gracious sovereign."

"Another movie?" Byron asked with a touch of annoyance.

Wiley shook his head. "More Shakespeare, my son. Maybe we'll look at that one next. *Richard III.*"

"It's about treachery," Tom explained, and Nate was surprised to see him exchange an unreadable glance with Wiley.

Byron continued.

"Imported Aztec warriors had proved themselves to be fearsome fighters against the Dinos, and Brice and Annett lived here on Earth, among them, overseeing their–"

"Abduction?" Nate suggested.

"Their immigration." Byron smiled, paused. "Towards the end of his life, Brice realized that once the war was over, his people were going to abandon Earth."

"Which they did," Nate repeated. "We've already heard this part. The Dino threat was eliminated, the aliens didn't need us anymore, so they went home. Right, Tom?"

Tom was silent for a heartbeat, then said slowly, "The exact reason that Sirius abandoned Earth . . . The way I heard it, it didn't really have anything to do with the Dinos. We *never came back,* except as tourists, because the Dino threat was overthrown, but that's not why we abandoned this place. But this is Byron's story. I'll let him tell it."

"Brice believed that Sirius would forget all about this backwater rock, *for whatever reason.* He'd grown to love this planet; he'd even grown to admire the fierce and bloody Aztecs, after a fashion. But once all the Sirians left, he was certain that their culture wouldn't endure. But their architecture would.

"So he decided that he'd leave behind a gift for the people of Earth, whose company he had so enjoyed. He left it in the temple, and prophesied to his woman and son that it would be rediscovered at just that point in human history when they needed it the most."

"Like King Arthur's return," Wiley mused.

His phone made a *Ta-Da!* sound, and with an expression of surprised shock, he picked it up off the counter and checked it. This action in turn surprised Nate; Wiley usually ignored his phone when people were speaking to him, and he was the one that was interested in this ridiculous fiction about aliens saving the world in the first place. Wiley frowned at his phone for a second, then gave his attention back to Byron.

"After Brice's death, Annett and Tyrrel returned to Sirius. They spread the word of the gift he'd left behind for our genetic benefactors, and the story was passed down over the centuries to a select few."

Tom laughed. "I've never heard it."

Byron ignored him. "Always, through the generations, those who knew the secret of the gift waited for news from Earth of the discovery of the pool of mercury in Mexico." Byron smiled. "It's not a symbol of the Aztec underworld, as your archaeologists believe. It's a representation of the great lake from which we were all spawned."

"The one on Sirius," Nate said.

"But it said online that the mercury was discovered beneath the temple in 2015," Wiley recalled. "That was twenty-five years ago. What took so long?"

Tom giggled. "Communications between Earth and Sirius are notoriously slow."

Nate got the distinct impression that Tom wasn't buying Byron's story any more than he was, regardless of where he claimed to be from. *I've never heard it.*

"Slow, yes," Byron agreed, "but not that slow. We've known about the discovery for some time. But the way had to be cleared. Volunteers had to be selected to come to Earth." Byron smiled smugly. "Viktoria and I were so honored. When it became known that the treasures from the temple were to be exhibited in this area, we decided to at last pay our *fellow tourist* a visit."

Wiley narrowed his eyes. "So you're not really related to—"

"We are, actually. We're Alba's grandchildren. It's just a coincidence that we were also the ones chosen, I assure you."

"So, this gift from Sirius, that's gonna save the world? It's right over there in San Bernardino? It's part of the exhibit?"

"Don't tell me! Let me guess." Nate consulted his phone. *"There is the famous wooden box and the golden disc it contained, covered with raised markings in a yet undeciphered language.* That's gotta be it, right?"

Byron smiled. "The inscription that they find so mysterious is of course Sirian. It's key to our–"

"Mission?"

Byron's smile widened. "Yes, if that's the term you'd like, Nate. The gold disk is key to our *mission–"*

"Of saving the world," Wiley concluded. His phone made that *Ta-Da!* tone again, and again he looked down at it. Again he frowned, but he kept on talking to Byron: "But you still haven't let us in on the secret. How is this thing gonna save us?"

"What does it say on it?" Nate asked.

"Be just and fear not," Tom suggested.

Again Byron ignored him. "There are . . . I guess you could call them *formulas* . . . When properly deciphered by scholars, they will provide solutions for the phenomenon of global warming. There are treatises, dissertations on détente, as you said, Wiley, which will eliminate political strife. There are essays on germ theory and disease, a cure for–"

"Cancer." Tom frowned.

"The very thing you sought when you tried to return to the homeworld, is it not?"

Tom didn't want to discuss his attempted return to the homeworld with his relative, plus he noted a faraway look in Wiley's eyes. He was buying the Sirian salvation of mankind, the cures for all ills, left behind by a grateful benefactor on a golden disk.

Wiley's apparent belief bothered him, so Tom winked at Nate. "Let me say it before you do, my son: this is bullshit, directly from the bull. If I didn't know better, Byron, I'd think you'd been watching *Ancient Aliens* with Dionne. They harp on the same chord, that the visitors were gods to the primitives in the old times. They came to guide mankind. It's in all the scripture. Viracocha – *he it was, showed men how to bring streams of water to their crops, and taught them how to build terraces upon the mountains where crops would grow.* In the stories, it's told that, eventually, he and his sons walked cross the water until they winked out of sight, but like King Arthur, they're prophesied to return when their people need them.

"But that's not how it was, kiddies. Viracocha and Enlil, Isis and Osiris, Zeus and Prometheus, or even Brice and Annett and Tyrrel. They weren't gods, arrived here to lead the monkeys to enlightenment. They were *scientists*, for lack of a better word, here to take something from you that they needed.

"And just like you said, Byron, after they didn't need anything anymore . . . Sirians were never too concerned with the problems of humanity whilst we mingled amongst you, and surely not after we went home. Surely not your political problems, and not your diseases either. Cancer is unknown on Sirius, so why would–"

"I don't know a whole lot about biology, Tom," Wiley interrupted. "Certainly not anything about this melding of species and whatever you say occurred to make men out of mermaids. But maybe when all that occurred, there was a new possibility that Sirians could get human diseases."

Tom shook his head. "All that happened a long time ago, Wiley, and I'm telling you, there was no cancer on Sirius when I was there."

"You've been gone awhile. Maybe things have changed."

"No." Byron shook his head. "Still no cancer on Sirius."

"Like I've been telling you all along, Wiley, cancer is caused by toxins in your environment. Pollution. Food additives."

"Yet you love it here," Wiley replied with his own tinge of annoyance. "It's all I've got, but you came here especially for the decadence. The cancer-causing ambience."

"You pays your money and you takes your chances, my son."

Tom figured that, like Nate, it was perhaps Wiley's hangover causing this uncharacteristic pique. Wiley rarely became annoyed, and never with him. Or maybe something else was bothering him. As if to underline that idea, the *Ta-Da!* chimed on Wiley's phone a third time and he positively grimaced in annoyance. Tom vaguely recalled hearing this particular notification sound another time, and remembered Wiley had become a little upset then, too . . .

"Excuse me just one minute, gentlemen." Wiley pushed a button and held the phone to his ear. "Hiya, Brend. What'cha doin'?" He stepped into the office for privacy.

Nate was absolutely nonplussed. Speechless. Wiley was not the type to pause a discussion that he had initiated to call his wife and ask her what she was doing. It was unheard of. Nate looked at Tom for an answer; the bookstore owner shrugged. He and Nate and Byron waited for Wiley to return.

After Bo was born, Wiley had become worried about Brendee's new-mother fugue. There was a time when she didn't seem interested in marital activities, which had always been her very favorite pastime before. Wiley had thought that maybe the one fear he had in life had at last come to pass: Brendee had become bored with him.

His gauge to determine this had been that old Wes Thomerville video she'd liked so much before they'd met. Wiley got it into his head that if Brendee started watching Wes again, then maybe it meant that her old fantasy had become more appealing than the reality of their marriage. Nate told him that he'd heard that there was another Rolling Blackout video online, and in the throes of a kind of perverse self-destruction, Wiley decided he'd find that one for Brendee, too. Hell, she could just drown herself in old fantasies.

But despite being an electronics genius, Wiley didn't have enough patience for an in-depth internet search. So he consulted his father, an electronics genius in his own right: "Didn't you tell me that you knew a guy that specializes in finding things online?" Pause. *"Morry's Books?* Ok. Thanks. Bye."

Wiley disconnected the call and told Nate, "The internet search guru owns a bookstore."

"Do they still have bookstores?"

"I've been in there a few times. You want to swing by with me after work? It's only a few blocks from here."

"Sure, Wiley. But why do you want to–"

"Maybe she'll like it," he'd replied.

In the optimistic vein of everything happens for a reason, Wiley's search for a clip of *You Can't Be Shy* had led him to Tom, *the guy who could find stuff on the internet,* and they'd become good friends.

Whilst Tom was looking for the new-old video, Wiley had set up a signal that would alert him – *Ta-Da!* – if Brendee watched the other one, *My Disgrace,* on her computer, if she decided to take any walks down Memory Lane with her old fantasy crush. Tom correctly recalled the electronics genius's pique after he'd heard the notification: Wiley had not taken it at all well when the alarm went off.

At this same time, Janae had been flirting with him; Nate had been amazed and quite disconcerted to watch him flirt back with her.

"What are you doing, Wiley?"

"I'm not doing anything, Nate." But his reply came out uncharacteristically defensive. "It's not like I'm – I'm not gonna . . ."

"What? You're not gonna *what?"*

"I'm just having a little fun. It's not like I'm . . ." Wiley repeated, but he still couldn't say it.

It's not like I'm gonna fuck Janae. Because that's what was on the table for consideration, wasn't it? They flirted with each other shamelessly in front of everyone but Brendee and Denny.

"It's harmless," Wiley insisted. "I'm just keepin' sharp. It's fun to have someone look at *me,* for a change, Nate. To have someone really look at me – because I'm me, not because I look like–"

"I'm not gonna listen to that excuse, Wiley. You're not gonna whine to me that you want to cheat on Brendee because you think that she's been pretending that you're Wes Thomerville all these years."

"I haven't done anything wrong. I've made Janae no promises, told her no lies. It's nice to know that some girl likes me for me–"

"I'm not buying that bullshit, Wiley," Nate repeated.

But it really was just a stroke to Wiley's enormous ego to have a beautiful woman proposition him. He'd never considered taking her up on it, but he'd also never considered that flirting had a purpose, that Janae's propositions weren't just intellectual exercises. Wiley eventually painted himself into a corner, and had pissed her off by jumping out of it.

On the phone now, Brendee blithely answered her husband's question. "I'm showing Viktoria the glories of American music. She says that she's never seen a guitar player before, so I thought it was time she saw a music video."

The same one, three times now. But it was okay. Wiley relaxed. It wasn't like Brendee was watching it all alone.

"Okay, talk to you later." He ended the call and went back to his waiting friends.

Nate and Tom greeted him with silent, *Oh, God, what now?* trepidation. They had both recalled the meaning of that tone on Wiley's device – his wife was entertaining other men, if only in her imagination.

Wiley returned their expectant looks innocently, but Nate wasn't gonna let him off that easily.

"I sense the return of Wes Thomerville."

"Not at all, my son. Not really. Brendee's just familiarizing her new friend with American music. She's showing Wes to Vikky."

96

"And that's okay, right?" Tom had a hard time hiding his smile.

"But of course. She's just showing Vikky what she likes, musician-wise. I don't play the guitar, after all."

Tom had located Wes's lost second clip for Wiley, but when the moment of truth had arrived, when Wiley casually mentioned to Brendee that he'd found the thing – as a gift for her mom, of course – Brendee had ignored Wes and his voice and his guitar in favor of her husband, in the flesh. Their boy was at his grandma's for the afternoon and Brendee wanted to spend time with Wiley, not waste it on a man that didn't really exist.

So all was again right with Wiley's world, and it was still right. There was nothing wrong with Brendee wanting to share an old fantasy with her new friend. Wiley reckoned it was a womanly form of passing the torch, so to speak.

He said to Tom's cousin, "I'm sorry for this interruption. It's one of the Byzantine by-products of all that true love Tom was talking up. Maintenance, if you will. Go on with your story."

Byron concentrated a moment, trying to gather the threads of what he'd been saying. "You mentioned pollution, Tom? And earlier, Wiley, you said something about plastic, choking the planet?"

"It is the devil, my brother. Ubiquitous, in the oceans, destroying the wildlife–"

"Since when do you care about wildlife?" Nate asked in surprise.

"The little fish eat the plastic, the billions of tons of it, floating, sinking. The big fish eat the little fish, then the bigger fish eat them. I eat the bigger fish, except I don't anymore." Wiley flashed a grin. "My alien friend here is not much of a fish eater. Says he got enough fish back home to last for his extended lifetime, so fish isn't often on our menu anymore."

"There are plans on the disc for composting of this plastic–"

"You can't compost plastic, Byron." Tom laughed. "It lasts forever. That's why it's such a problem here."

"Nothing you throw away is ever really gone," Wiley said, mostly to himself, lost in his horrific vision of the oceans, and all that tasty mahi-mahi and bluefin, consuming the plastic-stuffed little fish; and then, thus tainted, winding up on his dinner table.

"Yet there are plans nonetheless," Byron insisted. "Perhaps my idiom – what's properly done with the plastic here?"

"It's recycled."

Nate and Tom grimaced. No one was more adamant about recycling than Wiley.

"Then that's the correct term. There are plans for the recycling of plastics, the removal of them from the environment, the reuse–"

"More bullshit," Tom declared. "When this disk was supposedly left behind, plastic hadn't even been dreamt of. How could wise and grateful Brice have devised a method–"

"There are plans for cleansing this world of man's pollutants," Byron said firmly.

It all seemed so pat to Tom, way too much in line with human mythologies about Sirians as saviors, which he knew to be false. "Who told you about this miracle disk, anyway?"

"As I said, there is a group, descendants and followers of Brice, of Tyrrel–"

"Who want to save this little backwater rock from itself? I'm not buying it, Byron! Nobody on Sirius cares about Earth–"

"You do," Wiley said softly.

"And there you are mistaken, my son," Tom snarled. "Do you think that the Iowans care about the medicine and sanitation, the fucking *recycling,* that the natives in Vegas have to deal with? No! They go to Vegas to gamble, to look at the lights, to eat a big steak–"

"To have a good time," Nate said.

"Exactly. And I'm telling you, Wiley, that's why we come here. To have a good time. I was fortunate–"

"But in the old days, you came here because you needed us. So maybe Brice *was* grateful–"

"Need doesn't necessarily beget gratitude, Wiley. You're not grateful to the hen for your omelet. I think this Brice is a myth; this whole story of golden disks and grateful Sirians is *a myth.*"

There was a heartbeat of silence while Tom's declaration of disbelief died away. Finally, Wiley said, "I guess we'll find out when Byron sees the disc."

"Indeed! After we've had the opportunity to examine it, all Brice's truths will be revealed."

TWENTY-SIX

Brendee and the odd girl from Estonia had just finished watching *My Disgrace* for the third time when Wiley called, just to say a few words. He said them, and hung up; Brendee put the video on again for Vikky, thinking as she did so that it was like she had long ago been infected with insanity – as if a clown had bopped her over the head with . . . with whatever clowns bopped you over the head with, and left her with this incredibly arousing, yet incredibly silly appreciation for a man that wasn't even real. *Ah, Wes, you were so fine!*

It wasn't like Brendee could ever discuss it with Wiley – he would laugh at the idea that she had an impossible-to-requite fantasy that affected her so viscerally, and his insufferable ego would only be bolstered, because Wiley would get it backwards. He would think that his wife was attracted to Wes Thomerville because *Wes looked like him.* The truth would never, ever cross Wiley's mind: Brendee had fallen in love with him because *he looked like Wes.*

The whole thing was just so silly, but since it was her only secret, Brendee enjoyed it.

As *My Disgrace* concluded for the fourth time, Janae came into the living room. As she paused to pick Eric up out of the playpen, Brendee whispered quickly to Viktoria, "Let's just keep this vision of sexiness between ourselves, shall we?"

Viktoria smiled, nodded. She liked secrets.

Janae plopped down with the baby on the couch. "I'm bored. Let's go over to the store and see what the boys are doing. You want to go see your daddy, Eric?"

Eric kicked and giggled. It sounded like a stellar idea to him.

"How do you know that Nate's–"

"He's not with his wife." Janae smiled. "Where else would he be than with Wiley?"

TWENTY-SEVEN

Nate opened his mouth to inquire how Byron intended to copy down all of Brice's complicated wisdom while standing in line at the San Bernardino County Museum's Hall of History with everyone else, but at that moment, the bell over the door jingled and his wife and Brendee breezed into the store, followed by Viktoria, and Janae, of all people.

Without missing a beat, Wiley said, "Speaking of debauchery, have you met Janae, Byron?"

"He has." Janae elaborately ignored Wiley and smiled winningly at Byron, her eyes all a sparkle.

Wiley was surprised to see a return sparkle in Byron's eyes. Maybe he wasn't as serious and on-mission as he seemed. Maybe the kid thought he'd have a moment to indulge in a good time, after all.

"How's Tisha?" Wiley asked.

He caught a warning look from Brendee before Janae replied off-handedly, "Still looking like your sister."

"Just your type." Wiley smiled innocently at Nate, who shook his head.

"Indeed." To Wiley's surprise, Janae continued to ignore him and smiled at Byron again.

"We have shopped," Viktoria announced, and Janae broke eye contact with her brother. "What have you done?"

"I fixed your phone." Wiley ducked into the office, returned with it, handed it to her.

"Thank you. I found that I missed it. It's truly indispensable."

"It was nothing." Wiley considered Tom. "What d'ya know? A grateful Siri, uh, *Estonian.*"

"I learned the story of Hamlet, Prince of Denmark. *A man that couldn't make up his mind.*" Byron shared an unreadable sibling smile with Viktoria. "And we discussed the artifacts from the temple."

"Did you?" Viktoria's eyebrows went up and she looked carefully at each of the men in turn. "Has the way been prepared for our visit?"

"A couple weeks from today." Wiley hugged his wife. "Do you want to come with us, baby?"

"I don't think so, Wiley," Denny answered for her. "Brendee and I – ancient stuff from Mexico's not really our thing."

"Well, I like to try to learn something new every day." He favored Tom and Byron and Nate with his impish smile. "And this ancient stuff from Mexico promises to be something new."

Denny sighed. "The very fact that it's ancient would indicate that it's not new, Wiley."

"Ah! Deneen-logic! Isaac Newton is rolling over in his grave at the symmetry of it!"

Nate grinned in spite of himself, and his wife shot him a dirty look. "Whatever. We've come to see if you guys want to go to the park with us."

"In the middle of the work day?" Wiley feigned outrage.

"It's Saturday, my son. And there hasn't been a whole lot of work going on here, anyway. The park sounds like a plan, Denny."

"Great minds think alike, Tom. Dionne's outside in the car with the boys. We'll meet you there."

The ladies left, and Tom quickly locked up the store. He was glad for an excuse to get away from Byron's odd Sirian mythology. It disturbed him for reasons he couldn't quite pin down, and he wanted to hear Wiley's take on it. So, in the parking lot behind the store, he said to Nate and Bryon, mimicking Deneen, "We'll meet you there. We need to stop back at the Farmer's Market really quick."

Tom watched Nate's car exit the parking lot, then leaned against Wiley's and lit a cigarette. "Byron's playing you, my son."

"So we don't have to go to the Farmer's Market then? What d'ya mean, he's playing me?"

"I can't quite figure out why, but I think he's pegged you for a hippie, so he's telling you everything you want to hear. This great gift to mankind – fixing global warming, ridding the oceans of plastic, everything that you'd like to do."

"Getting my friends to quit smoking."

Tom smiled, puffed. "One of my favorite earthly vices, my brother and only friend."

"I don't want to save the world, Tom. Like Dionne says, let the sheep wallow in the mess they've created, as long as we have our own clean corner–"

"You don't want to save the world, Wiley, unless you think you could. So this story Byron's told you . . . You want to believe it."

"What do I know? You people say you're from another planet, so how do I know that it's not true that some other fucking alien left us all the secrets?"

"It's not true, Wiley. It's mythology. Some hungry tribe dreamt up the horn of plenty, from which the blessed received a never-ending supply of food. The Ghost Dance would drive the invading Europeans from Native American lands. A friendly alien tells Wiley Royce he holds the key to cure all of his planet's self-inflicted wounds. He's just telling you what you want to hear. The question is – why?"

"Maybe he really believes it. Maybe it's not just a myth to him."

Tom shook his head. "I don't know how such a thing could've taken hold on Sirius. We don't have a lot of mythologies, Wiley. No bottomless cauldrons or cornucopias, because we were never hungry. No messianic deliverers, because we were never oppressed. There are stories of the heroes of the Dino Wars, those brave first voyagers here, but Byron's savior shakes out as a hero to mankind, not Sirius. It just doesn't make any sense. Why would he believe such claptrap? Why would he even care enough to believe?"

"I guess we'll see when we go to the exhibit. *All will be revealed.* Let's go to the park."

TWENTY-EIGHT

"I made you a salad, Wiley." Deneen withdrew two brown paper sacks from a cooler sitting on the end of the picnic table, and handed one to him. "Eat it before it gets wilted."

Nonplussed, Wiley looked at the bag, then at his wife.

"I'm not sure how I feel about you feeding my husband, Deneen." Brendee bounced Eric on her knee. "But then your mommy's just as big of a nutcase as your Uncle Wiley, isn't she? So I guess it doesn't matter."

"I was making myself one, so I made him one, too."

"How thoughtful of you, Denny. Thanks."

Wiley considered the bag for another second, then placed it on its side on the table in front of him and tore it down the middle. He started eating lettuce and cucumbers and cherry tomatoes with his fingers.

Brendee again addressed the baby. "I ask you, Eric. Who eats a salad out of a paper bag? Who puts a salad in a paper bag?"

"Here's a fork, Wiley." Deneen handed him a metal utensil and opened up her own salad. "We don't use plastic, your husband and I. What was I supposed to put it in?"

"It's very clever, Denny."

"Thank you, Wiley. I thought so."

"You're both crazy," Brendee reiterated.

It never ceased to amaze her: Wiley annoyed Denny most of the time, with his nonsensical movie and literary quotations, his singing of ancient songs, his interest in museums and art galleries. Most of the time, Brendee knew, her husband made Denny feel stupid.

And most of the time Wiley thought Denny *was* stupid, and he occasionally took a potshot at what he perceived as her lack of intellect, such as his remark earlier about *Deneen-logic.*

But when it came to food and those modern, evil, chemical-leaching conveniences in which food was packaged and cooked, they were simpatico. Copacetic. No multi-syllabic additives, no plastic bags, cups, or utensils; no non-stick cookware. It was all laced with poison, according to Denny and Wiley. They believed it because the internet, and more importantly, Tom Bastion, had told them so.

"What did you have for lunch, my wife?" Wiley asked.

"Pizza," Denny sneered. "From the Food Court at the mall."

Wiley shook his head.

"I know. You guys'll dance on my grave." Brendee smiled at Denny, and kissed her husband on the cheek, because she loved them both, despite their chemical paranoia.

She nodded at the rest of the Tribes, tossing a Frisbee back and forth a little distance away. "I think our Estonian friend may be in danger. Janae told me she broke up with Tisha."

"No way!" Wiley glanced over his shoulder in astonishment.

"Don't stare at her, Wiley. I think she wants to keep it on the down low for the time being."

"If she told you guys, then it's probably not a secret."

Denny also looked over at Janae. "She didn't tell me."

Wiley squinted at his wife. *"If you haven't got anything nice to say about anybody, come sit next to me."*

"Well, maybe it's not a secret, then," Brendee said quickly, flustered at being a gossip.

"So which Estonian do you think's in danger?" Denny smiled guilelessly at Brendee, as if she didn't know.

Wiley knew. He'd observed their shared smiles at the bookstore. "Byron."

"Why do ya think that, Wiley? Because he looks like you?" Denny asked sweetly.

"I hadn't thought of that, but now that you bring it up . . ."

Wiley turned and looked at the rest of the group again. In three pairs of two, they formed a rough triangle, teams for Frisbee throwing: Tom and Nate, Dionne and Viktoria, Janae and Byron. This last pair had an extra teammate: Janae was kneeling beside Bo, showing him how to hold onto the Frisbee. He made a game attempt at a toss and Janae clapped her hands and gave him a hug. Then she smiled up at Byron, standing beside her. He smiled back.

"Look at them. They look like a little family already." Wiley turned back to his wife. "Although I don't think Byron's the marrying kind."

"We heard," Denny said. "Vikky told us, *among my people, monogamous pairing is sometimes achieved, but it doesn't often last.*"

"Really?"

Brendee eyed Wiley suspiciously. She was aware that men talked, *gossiped,* just like women. "Byron didn't tell you that?"

"Maybe something in passing."

"It's not like Janae's that big on monogamy, either," Denny said to neither of them in particular.

"Maybe it'll work out then," Wiley opined.

TWENTY-NINE

After dinner that night, Byron and Viktoria took a walk around the block.

"What have you learned today?" Byron asked.

"The dark hair and blue-eyes of the Sirian male appeal to the women of this group." Vikky pinched him playfully on the arm. "If you were so inclined, I believe that with but a little coaxing, you could have your choice."

"They are paired, right-handed. You flatter me." Bryon grinned back at her. "Except perhaps for the one who calls herself kin to Tom. Janae."

"Her mate is a woman."

Byron shook his head. "She tells me that that pairing has been dissolved. She seems to show me interest, then she backs away. She smiles invitingly at me one moment, then seems to ignore me the next."

"The women here play games."

"Yet her motives are clear."

"Maybe she just hasn't made up her mind yet," Viktoria teased, with a false-innocent smile.

"Janae's mind is made up. She just doesn't want me to perceive that such is the case." Bryon returned his sister's smile. "Maybe you should learn these games. I find them quite amusing, as I think their men do. Perhaps you might choose to inveigle a monkey, sometime, by pretending that you haven't yet made up your mind. It could prove useful."

"I will continue to observe how it works." Viktoria giggled. "Wiley–"

"Ah, yes. *Wiley.* He's different. Perhaps unique."

"He is a keeper of the knowledge. He knows how things work."

"That explains why he considers himself to be above the other members of the – what did they call themselves?"

"The Tribes."

"Wiley is fond of them all, but he has little . . . *respect* for their opinions, I think. Except for Tom. He listens keenly whenever Tom speaks."

"Do you think Tom will be amenable to our–"

"Our *mission?*" Byron smiled again, then his face clouded. "It seems doubtful at this point."

"I could have told you as much."

"Wiley, however . . ."

"Ah, yes. *Wiley.*"

THIRTY

The following Thursday morning, Wiley emerged from the office behind the counter and frowned at Tom. "I don't think your cousin is assimilating very well, my son."

Tom was sitting beneath the window on a folding chair, with his legs propped up on another. He looked up from his laptop. There had been no book-buying customers all week, but as usual, Wiley had been doing a land-office business. The printed word was a part of the past, but repairing electronics was most certainly the future. There were no customers in the bookstore now – they'd all dropped off their devices and went happily on their ways, secure in Wiley's knowledge and impressed with his incredibly reasonable prices.

"How so?"

"He keeps sending me weird texts."

"Such as?"

"On Monday night, he says: *I'm at Mickey's. The music's amazing. Why aren't you here?*"

"I sent him over there. The music's all right. What's wrong with–"

"Or this one: *I just had the most incredible hamburger. It was almost sexual.*"

Tom shrugged. "No hamburgers on Sirius, Wiley. I'm telling you, that's the kind of stuff we come here to experience–"

"But why is he telling *me*? And this last one – *It's a good thing that you're Tom's friend, lest you and I would be trouble for each other.*" Wiley looked up from his phone and frowned again. "What is that supposed to mean?"

Tom grinned. "I think I'm sensing a pattern here. Maybe that's why he's telling you all these hippie fairytales about saving the world. I thought it was a little odd that he would . . . But it would certainly explain . . ." Tom nodded at a small, pink cardboard box on the counter, like the kind donut shops use. "Byron made that for you."

Wiley set down his phone and opened the box, sniffed the contents. "What is it? It smells delicious."

"It's called an Asparagus Gruyere Tart." Tom pretended to look at his laptop again. "But I wouldn't eat it if I were you, my son."

Wiley was immediately suspicious. "Why not?"

"In the mood it will put you," Tom replied, Yoda-stylie. He giggled.

Confused, Wiley said nothing.

"For a smart guy, sometimes you is dumb, Wiley. That little pastry is an amatory appetizer, my son, the Sirian equivalent of Spanish Fly, an aphrodisiac, if you will . . ."

Wiley quickly set the box back down on the counter. "Why would Byron give me an aphrodisiac?"

"Why would he send you weird texts? Apparently, things *have* changed on the homeworld. We used to be a mostly heterosexual race, but perhaps nowadays . . ."

"Surely Byron doesn't think that I'm gay?" Wiley blinked rapidly in disbelief. "I got the impression that his sister might be more inclined to . . .

"Who knows? Maybe he brought it on her behalf. Maybe he's testing to see which way you . . ." Tom mimicked Byron. *"What is the idiom?* Which way you *swing."*

"Your goddamned relatives, Tom. First Janae, now them." Wiley paraphrased an ancient movie, quite sure it would be one Tom hadn't seen. *"I knew I was in with a bad crowd, but it was worse than I imagined . . . Aliens!"*

"What can I say? You're a fine specimen of Earthling *Homo sapiens,* Wiley. You carry *the Charles Atlas seal of approval."* Tom was familiar with the reference.

Wiley wasn't offended. He believed that he was smarter than everyone else, and even though attention from another man was a new occurrence for him, he figured that any kind of collateral admiration, well, that was probably just par for the oft-mentioned course. How did the old saying go? Women wanted him, men wanted to be him. Now there was apparently a man that wanted him, too.

"How does *Rocky Horror* play on the homeworld, anyway? With all ya'll being heterosexual?"

"There's not a two way street between your culture and Sirius, Wiley. We come here, we enjoy. We seldom return. Those that do return, it's usually because they *didn't* enjoy it. They don't take anything back. Your culture has no more of an effect on ours than ours has on yours. We assimilate or we go back."

"Well, I'm just going to have to tell Byron . . ."

"I'd like to be a fly on the wall for that one. What exactly are you gonna say? He hasn't quite propositioned you yet. Maybe he's just being friendly."

"I'll tell him that it's . . . inappropriate."

"Really. When have you ever been appropriate?"

"Regardless, I'm not–"

Tom giggled. "What did he say? *We're practically brothers!* Maybe he's just being *brotherly."*

Wiley discovered that he was discomfited about how to approach this. It was a situation he'd never encountered before. "I'll tell him that I'm married. *Monogamous.* Or even better . . . You can fucking tell him for me, my son. He's your relative."

"I don't see how it would come up in conversation, but I guess I could–"

"You could *bring* it up."

"I think you're overreacting, you sexy thing, you." Tom batted his eyelashes and Wiley laughed. "If he puts his hand on your knee, let me know, and I'll say something to him."

Wiley sang, *"Don't hand me no lines and keep your hands to yourself."* When Tom looked puzzled, he said, "You don't know that one? It's a real oldie."

Tom repeated Nate's words. "You can't expect me to know every ancient thing that was ever broadcast."

Wiley scrolled on his phone for a while, then at last brought up a YouTube video of The Georgia Satellites. "That's why I'm here, my son. To play every Jurassic one-hit wonder tune I've ever heard for ya. To help you *assimilate."*

THIRTY-ONE

Janae and Tisha had seemed so devoted to each other, so Wiley was surprised by the news of their breakup. It was sad, but he knew that people changed. Affections faded; life intervened. He'd had a lover once, before Brendee . . . Wiley sighed at her memory. Their thing, idyllic though it had been, hadn't lasted. Life goes on.

Wiley had also been surprised by Byron's maybe come-ons, his weird texts and gifts of Sirian aphrodisiacs. But Tom was right; it wasn't as if Byron had made any kind of out an out pass at him. Wiley had seen the shared smiles between Byron and Janae at the park; he supposed that maybe the young Sirian was bisexual, just like she was.

And that gave him an idea.

He invited Byron and Nate for a beer at *Mickey's* after work that evening. Believing that Janae's newly single status would offer him the unique opportunity to observe the heterosexual side of bisexual alien-human interaction first hand, Wiley got directly to the point.

"I think you should ask Janae out on a date."

"A –?"

Nate shook his head. This guy just wasn't for real. "Call it . . . a precursor to sexual relations."

Wiley smiled in surprise at what were, for Nate, some pretty big words.

Byron put on an expression of amused, flattered surprise. "Why do you think she'd want to – I understand her last mate was a woman."

Nate grinned. "Janae plays for both teams."

"Why not?" Wiley asked. "She's cute, and I think maybe she's of a mind to . . . switch back. I saw how she looks at you."

"Wiley thinks he knows what women want, Byron."

"Does he indeed?" Byron sipped his beer. "What does Janae want from you, Wiley?"

"Ah, does it still show?" Wiley offered his inimitable shark's grin, showing all his teeth.

"I saw how she looks at *you.*"

"We must not promise what we ought not, lest we be called on to perform what we cannot."

At Byron's blank expression, Nate explained. "Wiley's the dictionary definition of a happily married man. He'd never cheat on Brendee, regardless of the temptation. That being said, it's also a well-known fact that if a woman flirts with him, he'll flirt back."

Wiley defended himself. "It's not like it happens all the time."

"The one time it did happen . . . What exactly did she say?"

"There had been some mention of cleaning the store room above the bookstore. I told Janae, *anon,* as in, some undefined, future timeframe. She thought I meant *later,* like that same night. When I didn't show up, she called me, and it became immediately apparent from her tone that cleaning the store room had not been her intention at all." That shark's grin again. "When I told her that I wasn't interested, she got pissed and hung up on me."

"He led her on," Nate stated.

Byron continued to hold Wiley's gaze. "Did you?"

Wiley broke eye contact, shrugged, looked over his shoulder for the waitress. "Maybe." He signaled for another round, then looked back at his friends. "It was just harmless flirting. It was fun. I never intended for it to go anywhere. Janae's a big girl. She should've known better."

"I'll say it for you, Byron, so you don't have to. You're a son of a bitch, Wiley."

"Ah, don't blame my mom, Nate. She's a grand ol' gal."

The waitress returned with their beers. She ignored Wiley and Byron, because, like Deneen, skinny, black-haired, blue-eyed guys were not her type. She reserved her winningest smile for big, blonde Nate.

"So what d'ya think, Byron?" Wiley asked after her departure. He hadn't noticed that he'd been snubbed. "Janae's single again, and I am still, unfortunately, unavailable."

"Where would I take her?"

He is an odd one, Nate thought. *I don't believe he's from Sirius, but he's certainly not from around here.* "Take her to a movie."

"You do have dates on Sirius, right?" Wiley asked.

Byron grinned smugly. "Yes, sex has its precursors, just like here."

"But how do you . . ."

Nate's eyebrows went up at Wiley's uncharacteristic loss for words. He began again. "From what you've said, I'm assuming that your women . . . They don't have to pretend that they don't know what it is that you want. They don't have to pretend that they're shy and virginal."

Byron considered, still smiling with amusement. "That's a fair assessment."

"Then, if you know it's gonna happen, what's a first date like?"

"You don't always know it's gonna happen, Wiley. You smile and converse with her, just as you do here, I imagine."

"You get to know one another," Nate suggested.

Byron nodded.

"Right. But if it *is* gonna happen, if you hit it off, so to speak, she's not going to pretend like–"

"She hasn't yet made up her mind?" Byron smiled. "Women are women, Wiley. Sirian women don't necessarily immediately like us and decide to sleep with us–"

"On the very first date." Nate giggled, and smiled at the waitress as she passed their table. "What kind of tramps do you take Sirian women for, Wiley?"

"But if they are interested, even on the very first date – what I'm asking – they don't pretend they're *not* interested, right?"

Byron's eyes twinkled merrily. "No, not generally."

"Hell, Wiley, all your years of study would be for nothing on Sirius. Imagine a place where women let you know what they want right away."

Wiley imagined it for a moment, then told Byron, "It's definitely not like that here."

"I'm grasping that already." Byron sipped his beer with an air of contemplation. "Yet the signals are the same, I think. On Sirius, there is an interest, or there is not. The interest is apparent, and may lead to more, or it may not. It usually does, however. Here, I note that there is a receptiveness, then an indifference, a pulling back, then more indication of interest . . ."

"You just gotta strike when the iron's hot, as they say," Nate advised. "Make your move during one of those receptive times."

"No." Wiley shook his head firmly. "If you make a move when she's signaling you to, then she thinks she's the one pulling all the strings. You gotta make her wait, my son. Be receptive, show interest, of course. But make her wait. They expect us to be eager; it's how they're brought up. So be anything *but* eager. Trust your big brother Wiley on this one, Byron. I know wherein I speak. Make her wait."

All trace of that innocence Janae thought she saw in Byron was absent when he said, "I believe I've got this one, big brother. It's not my first – what is the idiom?"

"Not your first rodeo."

"Right. Not at all. I know what to do. I just needed to know where I was to take her to commence."

THIRTY-TWO

When she and Tisha called it quits, Janae had again moved back in with her parents. When Byron rang the bell on Saturday evening, her father answered the door, and she made introductions.

"This is Byron, Dad. He's Tommy's grandnephew. He and his sister are visiting from Estonia. We're going to the movies."

Janae felt ridiculous, as if she was a kid again, introducing Daddy to her latest beau. It was worse than being a kid – she'd never brought her beaux (or belles for that matter) home for her parents' inspection. Their opinions didn't matter to her, and her relationships were mostly transitory, anyway. The partners of which she'd been fondest, the ones that had intrigued her, if only momentarily – these she'd introduced to Tommy.

But Tommy already knew Byron; Byron was his relative, was living at his house. So it was only fitting that, being a polite suitor, Byron would want to pick Janae up at her house.

Sam Rossmore tried to hide his pained expression as he shook the young man's hand. He knew he could never remove crazy Tom's influence from Janae's life, and, sizing up this young man that looked so much like Tom, he was also pretty damn sure he wasn't pleased with another one of the oddball Bastion clan squiring her around, either. He surprised himself by thinking that his daughter might've been better off if she'd stuck with girls.

Conversation was expected of him, so Sam said the first thing that came to his mind. "Is that where Tom's from? Estonia?"

"No . . ." Byron wondered what *backstory* Tom had told these people. He thought quickly, making things up as he went along. "To tell you the truth, I'm not exactly sure where Tom's from. He's rather a distant relative. My sister and I were coming to the U.S., so our mother suggested we look her uncle up. She doesn't really know him either, though, except from stories Grandma told."

"Yeah, nobody's really sure where Tom's from." Sam smiled, but it didn't reach his eyes. He wondered distantly if insanity ran in their family. "In fact, years ago, he told my wife he was from another planet."

Byron appeared to be only mildly surprised. "This was about the time of his wife's passing, I would imagine?"

Sam nodded sadly. "I figured the tragedy of her illness just made him snap."

"Stop, Dad," Janae said angrily. "I won't listen to you talk about Tommy like that. Especially not in front of—"

"It's okay, Janae. Viktoria and I are not unaware – you might say it's something of a *family secret.* That our cousin is—"

"Delusional?"

"Tommy is not delusional, Dad! He's never once mentioned anything to me about being from another planet! And I think I know him a lot better than you do!"

Byron laid his hand on Janae's shoulder, again told her that it was okay. "He's never mentioned it to me, either. Perhaps he doesn't ascribe to it anymore. And if he does . . . Well, it's a harmless enough delusion, don't you think?"

"Tommy's not delusional, Byron."

Byron shrugged, shared a glance of understanding with Sam. "It doesn't seem to adversely affect him. He runs a business, he has a wife—"

"He's not married to Dionne," Janae said sourly.

"He has friends. Wiley—"

"Yeah. With friends like Wiley . . ." Janae frowned. "Once upon a time, Tommy told Wiley about the additives in our food, Byron. About how we're all being poisoned. Wiley took all that nonsense to heart, went on a big campaign . . . Since then, Wiley believes anything Tommy tells him. If he really was from another planet, I'm sure Wiley would believe that, too." She glared at her father again. "But I really don't appreciate you talking about my grandfather like he's some kind of a—"

"He's not your grandfather, Janae," Sam said wearily.

"I'm glad he's not," Byron patted her on the shoulder again, then looked at his phone. "The cab's waiting, and we should go if we're going to make it on time. It was nice meeting you, Mr. Rossmore."

"You, too, Byron."

Janae picked up her purse and walked out the door without saying goodbye to her dad.

THIRTY-THREE

Byron discovered that movie theaters were quite dark, and he wondered if they'd been constructed solely for first date activity. He knew these colorful fictions could be watched at home; Tom had not one but two large screens for just that purpose. But the tentative steps he and Janae took whilst watching the movie – holding hands, snuggling close to each other – could not be achieved at their respective abodes. Byron was familiar enough about Earth customs to know that these things would not be socially acceptable in front of Janae's parents and certainly not her "grandfather," as he had so obviously gone native, with his meaningless talk of true love.

So Byron was delighted with the theater experience. He smiled to himself when Janae casually laid her hand on his knee, but he took Wiley's advice and didn't make any propositions to her. It was not so much because he wanted to make her wait – he was confident that she would've acquiesced to anything he asked – but they didn't have anywhere to go, and it amused him to think, also as Wiley had suggested, that Janae believed she was in control of the situation.

When and if he thought the time was right, Byron was sure that Janae knew of places for these things, where parents and grandparents weren't watching.

THIRTY-FOUR

The next morning, Tom was again lounging across two folding chairs, surfing the internet. Wiley explained patiently to a customer, "Okay, this is called a shockproof external hard drive, Mrs. Lucas. But I don't want you to test their claims."

"I'm sorry, Wiley. I'm just so clumsy. I only had the other one home for a minute and then I knocked it off the arm of the chair. And then . . . Well, you know. It wouldn't let me see my grandchildren's photos anymore."

"I know." Wiley glanced over his shoulder at Tom. *"It approaches, collision, damage, blackness. I am Nomad."*

"You are in error," Tom returned mildly, not looking up from his laptop. *"You did not discover your mistake; you have made two errors. You are flawed and imperfect, and you have not corrected by sterilization; you've made three errors."*

Wiley turned back to Mrs. Lucas. *"Error?"*

"You're so silly, Wiley! How do you know *Star Trek?* My grandmother had the boxed set. She used to play it for us when we were kids. It was one of my favorites."

"He's seen all the old stuff, Mrs. Lucas. He's rather a connoisseur."

"Maybe that's why you're so good with these gadgets, Wiley. They had 'em all on *Star Trek.* I remember – way before your time – when they first came out with cellphones. They flipped up, just like a Star Fleet communicator."

"I've seen pictures," Wiley told her. "All your grandchildren's photos are on this new hard drive, but–"

"I'll try not to drop this one." She asked him how much she owed him, and Wiley rang her up. She paid gratefully and gave him a maternal smile.

As Mrs. Lucas left the store, Janae entered.

"How did Byron like the movie?" Wiley asked.

She shook her head from side to side: *comme ci comme ça.* "I'm not sure. He seemed to have trouble with the idea that the woman was torn between two men, that she loved them both."

"I'll bet," Wiley said.

Tom laughed. "What did you show him? *Casablanca?"*

"No, Tommy. We went out to the movies. It was the new one. *Servants of the Storm.* It's by the same guy that directed *Eileen's Mother.* That won an Oscar, so I figured–"

"Wait a minute." Tom suddenly snapped his laptop closed, stood and set it on the counter. "You went *out* with Byron? Like on a date?"

Janae waited for a punchline, because surely this had to be some kind of a joke, Tom's pretending that he was upset that she'd gone to the movies with his cousin . . .

"Answer me, Janae!"

She jumped at his harshness, laughed nervously. "Yes, Tommy. Byron and I went on a date. What's wrong with–"

Now Tom turned on Wiley. "I suppose you had something to do with this?"

Wiley's mouth fell open in utter surprise at Tom's unprecedented anger. "This seems like something you'd like to discuss privately with Janae. If you'll excuse me . . ." He ducked from behind the counter and quickly stepped out the door.

"What the hell's wrong with you? Why do you care if Byron and I–"

"I don't want you dating him."

"What?" Janae was amazed. Never in her life had Tommy said such a thing to her. "Why not? What's wrong with–"

"He's not like the men you're used to. He wasn't raised like Wiley or Nate. Or you, for that matter. The customs are different where we're from–"

"Where exactly are you from, Tommy? Certainly not from Estonia." A clammy fear laid a damp finger on Janae's heart, and her father's words echoed in her mind: *Years ago, he told my wife he was from another planet.*

"No, I'm not from Estonia. And my sister, and Byron and *his* sister . . ." Tom looked away, out the window. "It's not so much where we're from, it's how we were brought up. The way that people . . . *relate* to one another is different than here."

Now Janae heard Byron's voice. *Viktoria and I are not unaware – you might say it's something of a family secret. That our cousin is–*

Delusional.

Janae would not believe it. There was absolutely nothing wrong with Tommy. She'd always loved him; he was the most easy-going, most charming, most brilliant person she'd ever known. Janae refused to believe it, but this sudden, completely irrational attack on his cousin prompted her to *say* it. "You're crazy, Tommy. There's nothing wrong with Byron."

"Not wrong. Just different. Like you said, he couldn't understand how a woman would be so upset about having to choose between two men–"

"It was just a movie, Tommy!"

"He didn't get it because where we come from, women don't have to choose–"

"And where is that again?" Outrage at the ridiculousness of Tom's telling her what to do surpassed Janae's now undeniable fear for his mental health. "Are you trying to tell me that Byron is from another planet, like you are?"

Tom narrowed his eyes. "You've been listening to Sam."

"No, Tommy. I've never listened to him. I've heard it all my life, since I was a little kid. Since Liz died. *Tom's nuts.* When he thought I couldn't hear him, or I was too young to understand; and then when he was sure I could. *Tom's crazy. He's delusional. He thinks he's from another planet.*"

"Janae–"

"No! I'm not gonna listen to any of this! There's nothing different about Byron, and neither he nor you are extraterrestrial!" Janae almost sobbed. "I won't hear any of this crazy shit!"

When Tom opened his mouth to speak again, Janae turned and ran from the store.

Through tears, she fumbled to unlock her car. Wiley materialized beside her, seemingly out of the thin air, and while he knew better than to touch her, even in an attempt at comfort, he asked with concern, "Are you all right?"

"Do I look all right?" She swiped at the streaming tears. "What's wrong with him? Why is he acting like a lunatic all of a sudden? He's never yelled at me in my life, and now he starts babbling about how Byron's different . . . It's freaking me out, Wiley! My dad's always said he was crazy and now, out of the blue, he's acting like it!"

"Tom's not crazy, Janae." *He just tells a great story.* Wiley smiled. "Calm down. Maybe he's just trying to look out for you."

"Byron's a nice guy, and even if he was some criminal drug dealer, I'm twenty-six years old, for Christ's sake! Now, all of a sudden, Tommy decides he's gonna start telling me who I should . . ." Janae stopped abruptly.

Of all the people in the world to whom she knew better then to pour out her heart, Wiley Royce was at the very top of the list. Compassion, understanding – these were not his long suits. The emotions of others were merely fodder for his derision. Whatever her interest in Byron, and whatever she thought about Tommy's sudden display of what could only be termed mental illness, were none of Wiley's business.

"I gotta go."

"Are you sure you're okay?"

Janae could've told Wiley that she'd heard her father's veiled and blatant insinuations about Tommy's insanity all her life, and, because it was inescapable that he *was* a little odd, she'd always feared that it could be true. Wiley was Tom's best friend – his only friend, really – and he would undoubtedly assure her once more that Tom was all right. But then Wiley, being the superior son of a bitch that he was, would go back into the bookstore and make fun of her and her fears. He and Tommy would have a big laugh at her expense.

Wiley had laughed at her enough. Janae wasn't going to provide him with another opportunity.

"I'm okay. Just tell him to stop acting like a lunatic. I'm a big girl. I don't need his dating advice."

THIRTY-FIVE

Wiley watched Janae drive jerkily out of the parking lot, but he didn't go back inside right away. It was Sunday, and Nate spent most Sundays hanging out at the bookstore with his friends. He was due any minute, so Wiley decided to wait outside for him. It would give Tom a minute to cool down from his bizarre fit of anger.

Wiley didn't have to wait long. When Nate got out of the car, he said, "Prepare thyself, my son. Tom's pissed."

Nate's eyebrows went up in blank surprise. In all the time he'd known Tom, he couldn't remember a single time that he'd shown anger. He was a very laid-back kind of dude. "About what?"

Wiley, ever mysterious, said, "You'll see. Come on."

They entered *Morry's Books,* and before the tinkling of the bell had died away completely, Wiley said, "What the fuck, Tom?"

"Did you fix them up?"

Wiley's glance at Nate said, *See? He's furious.*

"Yeah. I did. I suggested that Byron ask her out–"

"Why would you do that, when you know he's–"

"What? When I know he's from another planet?"

Tom shook his head. "When you know he has no idea what love means–"

Nate spoke up. "Maybe Janae'll teach him. Liz taught you."

"I was twenty years older than him, Nate, and I had some good advice from someone who had experienced a lifetime with a good woman–"

"Are you saying that Janae's not a good woman?" Wiley smirked.

"I'm saying that Janae isn't expecting someone who's not looking for–"

"Listen to yourself, Tom. You sound ridiculous. Just like Janae said, she's a big girl. In earthly parlance, Byron's simply a player. There are plenty of men here who're not looking for love, who are just out to see what they can get. I'm sure Janae's met her share–"

"So why expose her to another one?" Tom shook his head. "You guys just don't understand. Janae's not prepared for the way that we . . ." Tom looked down at the counter and said no more.

Nate rolled his eyes. "Is this another Sirian thing? You guys have two dicks or something?"

Wiley, who reveled in the occasional profanity, still couldn't help his shocked expression at Nate's words.

Tom considered them silently for a good half a minute. "You won't believe me."

"Oh, hell, why would you think that, Tom?" Nate leaned against the counter in an attitude of rapt attention. "You've never told us anything unbelievable."

"All right," Tom replied with a tone of minor offense. "What do I care if you believe me or not? You know how Wiley is a student of women? How he thinks he's unraveled their mysteries?"

"Yeah. So? I tend to think Wiley's a legend in his own mind on that score. What does that have to do with Janae and Byron?"

"Remind us how you came to believe you know what women want, my son."

Wiley said evenly, "One of them told me."

Nate sighed. He knew to whom Wiley referred. He'd been involved in some kind of farm accident when he was a teenager, had broken his leg in three places. The local veterinarian's daughter was studying physical therapy at college and had offered to help with his healing process.

Her name was Kitana. She was twenty to Wiley's just-turned-seventeen, and helping regain his range of motion was not her only contribution to his life.

"My parents suspected nothing," Wiley had told him. "Surely this gorgeous *woman* and their skinny, half-crippled boy weren't doing anything they shouldn't be doing, up there in the attic? Mom just considered her to be a kind and compassionate health care professional, who felt it was her calling to keep a lonely boy company, and to help him mend, straight and true.

"But Kitana put the *passion* in *compassionate*, Nate, my son. She used me as her completely willing sex toy, all in the name of physical therapy. I could have this if I'd just *reach* for it. I could have that if I'd just stretch out my wounded leg and *bend* for it.

"All through that summer, Kitana was there. Sometimes she'd leave after supper, then sneak back in and spend the night with me, after my parents had gone to sleep. 'You're mending like a tough old plow horse,' she'd tell me. Then she'd climb on top of me and ride me like one." Wiley positively leered. "Kitana taught me to *do things to her,* my son, and *praise Jesus!* the things she did to me . . .

123

"But she also talked to me, for hours on end. Kitana collaborated with the other side in the battle of the sexes, Nate. She told me all their secrets. She told me what girls like, what they want, how they think. Girls have been my favorite subject ever since. I like to study them, to *watch them.*"

Now Wiley opened his mouth to reiterate what he'd been taught, but Nate cut him off. He summarized. "I know. The physical therapist. She's the one that told you to make 'em wait."

"I've also heard about all the things this limber young woman taught him. In detail."

"It's one of my favorite stories." Wiley was inutterably smug.

"So? Wiley got lucky once. What does that have to do with Janae and Byron?"

"Wiley was fortunate–"

"Exceedingly fortunate."

"Yes, my son. You were exceedingly fortunate to meet a young woman who told you the ins and outs, shall we say, of the complicated and sometimes inconsistent female mind. Without the things she told you, you would've had to stumble along, guessing, taking hit or miss actions, just like Nate and all the rest of the men here. You were gifted with a guidebook – what good girls do, what bad girls do."

"What bad girls do that good girls want to do." Wiley leered.

"Exactly. You were given a glimpse into the effects of a thousand years of moral strictures upon the female mind. They think they know what they want, but do they really want that? If they do, why do they feel guilty about wanting it? What would Daddy say? They fear those words – *tramp, whore, adulteress.* They are, in a word, *confused.* It is a rare young woman indeed, who can ask for what she wants, even behind closed doors, nonetheless in public. Would you not agree, Nate?"

Nate nodded reluctantly.

"I'm not gonna get into the whole history of the suppression of the female psyche here, how men have always considered them and their bodies as our property–"

"Please don't," Nate requested.

"Yet all those ugly words spring from that very concept. A tramp shares her body with whomever she chooses. A whore does the same, for payment. An adulteress – she's perhaps the worst of all. She has pledged herself, before God and man, to her husband, yet she goes right on ahead and changes her mind–"

"I know what those words mean, Tom. Do you have a point?"

"Here's my point, Nate. On Sirius, we have no such words, so detrimental to a young woman's self-esteem. We're polygamists. Our women are free to share themselves with whomsoever–"

"I know what polygamy means, too."

"You do go on, sometimes, my son," Wiley observed.

"Like any of us have anything else to do today. But here's what I'm trying to tell you. On Sirius, the women don't have to pretend–"

"I asked Byron about that."

"And what did he say?"

Wiley shrugged. "Not much. He's not as fond of windy explanations as you are. He said that Sirian women generally don't pretend they're not interested if they are."

"And I'm here to tell you that it's because they don't have to. They don't have to pretend ignorance of the act, nor that they're not down to participate in it. They don't have to act like–"

"What does this have to do with Byron?"

Tom smiled. "Our women are completely forthcoming with what they want, Nate. So, the result of this is that, our men . . . *know*. We have no textbooks with diagrams of the female anatomy . . ." He gestured out into the bookstore. "No *Art of Touching a Woman*. We need no written instruction, gentlemen, and we don't have to guess, *because they tell us.*"

"And your point is?"

Wiley slapped him on the back. "Tom's humbly telling us that Sirian men are good in bed, my brother. Much better than us, or anything that Janae's had, so–"

"Hence my apprehension," Tom concluded.

"He's afraid Janae's gonna think she's in love–"

"Oh, for Christ's sake, Tom! I think Janae knows the difference between love and a good lay!"

"Maybe. Maybe not." Tom displayed the ghost of a leer. "I've been awarded such superlatives as–"

"Spare us," Wiley requested. "Regardless, it's too late for you to start warning her about who she decides to date. You've never done it before. She thinks you've lost your fucking mind."

Tom sighed. "And we can't be havin' that. She's already heard that enough from her daddy."

"If you're so concerned about it, say something to Byron. Tell him . . . Christ, I dunno, Tom!" Nate shook his head. "Tell him that

125

Janae's expecting monogamy, so if he's gonna be seeing her, he'd best toe that line."

Wiley remembered the lecherous light in the young Sirian's eyes when he said, *I've got this,* and didn't think anything Tom could say would make any difference. Byron wasn't looking for love.

"Tell him, *when in Rome, do as the Romans do.* "

"Tell him if he hurts her, you and me and Wiley'll kick his ass."

"That might just work. He *likes* Wiley." That little leer again.

"What?"

Wiley explained. "We think that, in addition to the legendary Sirian way with women, Byron might amaze the occasional fella, also."

"And he likes Wiley."

"You don't say." Nate considered them curiously for a moment. This was a new one. "At least somebody likes him." Nate paused again. "Christ, Tom! If that's the case, then maybe he's not after Janae the way you think. Maybe he's just being polite."

"Maybe you're right, my son." Tom's smile returned, and he elbowed Wiley. "You're the one that suggested he take her out. Maybe he just did it to please you. Maybe he's after *you.* "

THIRTY-SIX

Janae had been a little late in discovering the most enjoyable game between men and women, not succumbing until she was a freshman in college, to a brooding, black-eyed Russian exchange student, stereotypically named Boris. It wasn't any illusion of love that had prompted her to agree to his proposal; she was just curious about his dark foreignness, at last curious enough about the whole sex thing in general.

Tommy had liked Boris, had found him to be serious and intelligent. While Janae had also liked his intelligence, his seriousness was a drag, and she'd quickly become bored. Not long after she ended her first brief relationship with a man, Janae met a girl named Jaycee. By the following morning, Jaycee and her soft mouth and hard, toned body were one less thing Janae was curious about.

Unlike bright and studious Boris, Jaycee was unimpressed with Tommy, so she'd swiftly made excuses and decamped from his house. She had places to go, people to see. After she'd gone home, or wherever, Tommy had tilted his head curiously at Janae – it was his trademark gesture. "You know, where I come from . . ."

Janae had blinked in alarm, even then. Because of her father's cruel remarks about Tommy's mental health, just where he was from had been a subject that she'd always studiously avoided. She'd scared up the courage to ask her mother once, but Maxine would only say, "I'm sure he'll tell you when he's ready," and Sam had added, "Whatever he tells you, don't believe any of it."

So Janae had never pursued the topic. What difference did it make where Tommy was from, or even where he *thought* he was from? Janae loved him. That was all that mattered.

"Where I come from, bisexuality is virtually unknown," he'd said, nodding after Jaycee.

"Is that a fact? You've got fifty percent more of a chance of getting a date on a Saturday night."

"You'll have to tell me about it sometime."

It had been nice to be acknowledged without judgment. Janae would always believe that, while they seemed to accept it, her parents would always be uncomfortable with her sometime choice of women as companions. They'd always seem infinitely relieved when she was dating a man. But it never mattered to Tommy, either way; he was always just happy to see that Janae was happy, regardless of the gender of her current partner.

And that was why she couldn't understand his utterly uncharacteristic condemnation of her seeing his cousin. Janae had never worked a day in her life, because Tommy had always generously volunteered to pay for her to attend college; her parents had always been begrudgingly tolerant of her ways, so she'd never before felt any desire to dye her hair blue and rebel. But this disapproval of Tommy's struck a note of latent mutiny in her now: just who the hell was he to start telling her what to do?

She realized that she might not have slept with Byron had it not been for Tommy's ridiculous warnings.

Janae smiled to herself. She probably would've, though. He was cute. She stubbornly refused to acknowledge the obvious family resemblance between Byron and her adoptive grandfather: that would've been too weird. She told herself that she'd always preferred dark-haired men, and women, as well. There'd been black-haired, Slavic Boris, and of course Wiley, with his inviting blue eyes. And there had been Tisha.

What Janae had shared with Tisha . . . If she was honest with herself, she had to admit that it had been the closest thing she'd ever felt to love, as it had been expressed by the poets of which she was so fond. All her other conquests – Janae had simply *wanted* them, for the night, for the weekend, for however long it would last. But Janae had also enjoyed Tisha for her bubbly personality, her irrepressible friendliness.

From a lifetime of privilege and an incomparable education – like Wiley, Janae tended to think of herself as smarter than everyone else – she'd become aloof and easily annoyed with persons or ideas that struck her as ridiculous. Thus she had no patience for Deneen and Wiley and even Tommy's food-chemical phobias; or Dionne, whom she loathed, anyway, and her convictions that the end of civilization was at hand.

But Tisha had listened attentively to them, simply because she knew that it would please them if she did so. Tisha was a good soul, generous to others with her time and affection, qualities which Janae didn't possess. They had eventually discovered that these differences made them incompatible as a couple. It was as Janae had told

Brendee: she and Tisha would always love each other, but they were no longer in love.

Janae would also not allow herself to speculate on the possibility that she had glommed onto Byron so quickly because it was true that she was feeling exceptionally lonely after this breakup, that she might be a little vulnerable, that she was indeed on the rebound. No, that wasn't it at all. She wasn't feeling at all heartbroken; she was once again her cavalier self. It wasn't because she was feeling an unfamiliar emptiness and was (desperately) seeking to fill it again, from the next available source.

Janae refused to call what she felt for Byron *love,* anyway. She was too old for such fairytales; it was entirely too soon to entertain such possibilities. Love him? She'd just met him. It was too childish to even contemplate such a thing already.

But she would admit that she was fond of him, and that she did love talking to him. He said nothing of his life in Estonia, but was very curious about American culture. This allowed Janae to hold forth on any and all aspects of history and current events, and again, not unlike Wiley, one of Janae's greatest joys in life was listening to herself talk. Having an interested audience that asked intelligent questions but didn't offer any dissenting opinions warmed her. She'd been attracted to Wiley for his intellect as well as his looks, but unlike *Brendee's husband,* Byron didn't infuriate Janae with relentless logic or caustic derision if he disagreed with her thoughts. Byron didn't disagree at all. He just listened, and that was incredibly flattering.

And Janae was indeed *quite* fond of other aspects of Byron, ones that she'd never had the chance to experience with Wiley.

She'd sampled the charms of many lovers, and had been impressed on many occasions. She'd known women that had caressed her body as if it was merely an extension of their own, awakening the most exquisite pleasures at precisely the moments they were called for, as effortlessly as a sigh. She had known men that, whether from an honest desire to please or from an overabundance of ego, had amazed her with their prowess.

But the young man from Estonia had surpassed them all. Janae had arranged to borrow the apartment of a girl from school, and while the not-so-subtle concept of *Netflix and chill* had been lost on Byron, once he understood that the absent apartment owner would not be returning that night, he'd shown himself to be, to Janae's delight, neither shy nor innocent, had proceeded with no hesitance whatsoever. It was as if, once he had gained Janae's assent, he didn't pause to wonder what avenues of lovemaking might be better explored later, after their relationship had further progressed. He seemed to know instinctively that Janae was not shy either, and she was amazed at his perfect intuition, his complete confidence.

She'd once imagined that Wiley would be thus; his superior smile and own insufferable confidence whispered to Janae, assured her that what he always maintained was fact: Wiley Royce knew what women wanted.

Be what thou wouldst seem to be, Wiley, Janae had feverishly thought. She'd never felt anything akin to love for him, though; hell, she didn't even like him very much. Instead, Janae's fantasies of Wiley had always been shot through with a yen for triumph. He was always in control, and Janae had longed to see him lose it. She'd wanted to cause a helpless desire in him, one that would compel him to act on all the filthy little things that he said. In the throes of lust, Janae had wanted to see him lose his brilliant mind.

But it had been Janae who'd lost control. Wiley's clever flirtations had caused her to tip her hand, to call his intricate and intriguing bluff, to let him see that she was down to be toss loyalty and friendship aside for a good time. His turndown had enraged her, so purely out of revenge, Janae had made a pass at Wiley's bride.

To this day, Janae was confident that Brendee would've gone for it, had not Wiley himself interrupted them. They had been in the midst of a kiss – Janae had felt Brendee begin to respond, then the front door to her apartment had slammed, and Brendee's somewhat commonplace sense of morality had then had the time to reassert itself. While she may've considered that what she had been about to do with Janae could've been written off as just a little harmless fun between girlfriends, Wiley's appearance in the doorway, his curious, not-jealous-at-all glance, had made her realize that her concepts of *infidelity,* of *adultery,* indeed stretched to include both genders. She had enjoyed kissing Janae, and might've enjoyed anything else they'd been about to undertake, but Brendee *loved* Wiley, and she decided in a single heartbeat that *forsaking all others* meant women as well as men.

After these twin failures at seduction, Janae had believed that she could've worn her scarlet badge of attempted homewrecker proudly. *And therefore, since I cannot prove a lover, I am determined to prove a villain.* She would've gladly eschewed the friendship of Brendee and Deneen and Nate, would've withstood

Tommy's reproachful embarrassment at her party-foul. She thought Denny was a ninny, anyway, and Nate was just a whupped sheep, a spineless puppet that danced to his wife's tune, when he wasn't dancing to Wiley's. Brendee was just a pretty face, and Wiley . . . the hell with Wiley and his little, happy domestic life. The hell with all of them, including Tommy. Wiley Royce had made a fool of her in front of all the Tribes, and it gouged at Janae.

Shame and eternal shame, nothing but shame! Let life be short; else shame will be too long. She wasn't ashamed that she'd a made a play for a married man and subsequently his wife; Janae was only ashamed that everybody, even Tommy, was laughing at her failure at it. In one bout of drunken melodrama, Janae had even thought of embracing her ostracism in Miltonian terms: she might be lonely, friendless, but *here at least we shall be free;* free from everybody's sly glances and half-hidden smiles at her foolishness. As an unrepentant bad girl, Janae would *reign secure.* And even if she was thereby without company, she thought it *better to reign in Hell, than serve in Heaven.*

Wiley was a coward; if she refused to associate with him anymore, Janae would retain her own sense of superiority, and it would lend her a modicum of triumph in the situation. The hell with all of them. They weren't gonna laugh at her anymore.

But Wiley had not allowed this little bump in the road of his marriage to dissolve his and Brendee's friendship with Janae. He'd pontificated – that was really the only fitting word – to the Tribes at another family barbeque: he told them all that while he was forever loyal to Brendee, all women (including her) should take note: if a girl flirted with him, he would flirt back. The girls in question should thenceforth be aware that they did so at their own risk, however. While he enjoyed the banter, no temptation would ever cause him to stray.

After this pronouncement, Janae had still considered avoiding all of them, but then she had met Tisha. Her embarrassment at having been rebuffed in her adulterous suggestions faded to nothingness. Everyone loved Tisha and no one ever reminded Janae of her attempted treachery again.

But now, Tisha was gone, and Tommy was acting like a crazy person because she was dating Byron. That sense of *the hell with all of them* flared in Janae again. Byron was great; she was quite fond of him. She thought a little hysterically that if she was forced to make some choice in the future, between perhaps-insane Tommy and the

Tribes, and this unique and intriguing young man she had so fortunately discovered . . . Janae knew where she would place her loyalty.

THIRTY-SEVEN

To Wiley, the line of people waiting to get in to see *River of Mercury – Artifacts from Teotihuacan's Temple of the Feathered Serpent* appeared to stretch out infinitely. It seemed to him that they were at least two blocks away from the entrance to the museum.

Tom and Wiley, Viktoria, Byron, and a somewhat reluctant Nate took a few steps forward as the line inched toward the door. Janae again had some school activity and had sent her regrets that she couldn't join them. Wiley was sure that Tom's displeasure at her dating Byron also had something to do with her absence.

"Who would've thought that there'd be so many people interested in an Aztec exhibit?"

"They had human sacrifice, Tom," Nate replied. "That interests people."

Wiley frowned at the crowd. "Maybe they had the right idea."

"You don't like mingling with your fellow man, my son? All these masses that Byron wants to save?"

"Baaa," Wiley bleated. The line shifted again, but he still frowned. "I dunno, kiddies. Maybe we should come back during the week. After it's been open for a while. All these people . . . We're not gonna be able to see anything."

"No," Viktoria objected immediately. "We must go now. We must touch the artifact."

Tom narrowed his eyes. "Why do you have to–"

"Touch it?" Nate thought, *She is so bizarre.* "Hell, Vikky, like Wiley says, with this crowd, you're not even gonna be able to see it."

"Why do you have to . . ." Tom trailed off.

"You're not gonna be able to touch it, Vikky." Wiley looked at Tom with a completely false air of seriousness, his earlier annoyance forgotten. *"Neo, this is loco. They've got Morpheus in a military controlled building. Even if you somehow got inside, those are agents holding him. Three of them. I want Morpheus back too, but what you're talking about is suicide."*

Byron peered at the entrance to the building. "I see no uniforms–"

"Wiley's kidding, my son. It's from a movie. But he's right. You're not gonna be able to touch it. That's not the way things work

here. They don't just let anyone handle the priceless treasures."
Again Tom considered his cousin closely, then his eyebrows rose.
"Surely you don't think–"

"Yes. The artifact is imbued."

Tom barked laughter and a portly lady in front of them turned
around. He didn't notice her looking at him. "Not after all these
centuries, Vikky. Maybe if it was still on Sirius–"

"Did you say Sirius?" the portly lady asked.

Her companion, equally stout, also turned. "That's where the
aliens are from." Tom's mouth dropped open and the fat lady smiled.
"That's what they say, anyway. And some of the stuff in this exhibit
– they say it's from another planet, too."

"The Aztecs knew too much about the stars to have figured it
out all on their own," the first woman stated wisely. "Those funny
pyrite balls. They have to be from someplace other than Earth."

"The balls symbolized constellations," Viktoria informed her.
"They were laid out in specific patterns in the chamber, but degraded
and shifted over the eons." She smiled smugly. "Therefore, by the
time they were discovered, your scientists were unable to grasp their
meaning. They are strictly terrestrial in origin, I assure you. It's only
the disc that's from–"

"Baaa," Wiley sneered at the ladies. "Don't talk to the sheep,
Vikky. Like Mary's lamb, they're liable to follow us to school one
day."

"And that's against the rules," Nate added. He might not know
any lines from old movies, but he had a little boy. He was up on his
nursery rhymes.

The ladies turned away in shocked affront.

Byron now surveyed the crowd and also frowned. "There *are* a
lot of people. You really don't think that we'll be able to–"

"Or even see it," Wiley said. "Let's come back after it's been
open for a while."

Byron sighed. "All right. We've waited this long, I guess we
can wait a little longer."

THIRTY-EIGHT

They returned to the parking lot. The three Sirians crammed together into the backseat; Nate rode shotgun. It took Wiley several minutes to maneuver his way out onto the street – still more patrons were arriving to see the exhibit, looking for a place to park. When he finally achieved the freeway, he glanced in the rearview and asked the same question that Tom had asked.

"Why do you have to touch this thing?"

"It's imbued," Viktoria repeated.

Nate turned in his seat. "You said that before. What does it mean?"

Before she could answer, Tom said, "It has to do with our methods of learning on Sirius. Wiley quoted *The Matrix* earlier. Did you happen to see that one?"

Nate grimaced. "Yeah. It's one of his favorites. The one where the computers have taken over, and we're all hooked into–"

"A neural-interactive simulation."

Nate frowned at his friend. "I thought it was stupid. All that bullshit about AI. Computers are never gonna get smarter than us."

"You're living in a dream world, Neo. Computers are already smarter than you, which isn't really difficult. The phone in your pocket–"

"Remember the part where they plugged the thing into their heads in order to learn?" Tom didn't want to get into a discussion of AI with Wiley. They'd be there all day.

Wiley glanced at him in the rearview mirror. *"I know kung-fu."*

"Show me." Tom smiled. "The way we learn on Sirius – it's kind of like that. But without any holes. Without any computers or machinery. The elders, the teachers . . . They're able to imbue things, such as this gold disc, with information."

"Like writing to a hard-drive," Wiley said. "But how? Without any machinery?"

"Simply by holding it in their hands, and willing it to be so," Vikky retorted haughtily. "And the student can receive the knowledge the same way, by holding the–"

"This is insane. Just fucking nuts." Nate wondered again why he had even come along on this adventure. "You're saying that Sirians possess some kind of telepathy, that they can pass on their knowledge through inanimate objects? All ya gotta do is hold 'em? How stupid do you think we are?"

Vikky opened her mouth to tell him just how stupid she thought he was, but Tom shook his head, cutting her off. "I guess you could call it telepathy, after a fashion. It's an innate Sirian ability."

"They say the Dinos had it, too," Byron said quietly.

Wiley glanced in the mirror to witness Tom's reaction to this comment. Whenever any aspect of Sirian culture or history came up, the younger out-worlder always had to throw in something about the lizards, and Wiley kenned that Tom didn't appreciate Byron's constant mention of their ancient enemy.

Tom caught Wiley's eye. *"The better to eat you with,"* he murmured. Wiley paled, as had been Tom's intention, and he smiled. "Telepathy was always a Sirian trait; it's sometimes difficult for an amphibious race to communicate verbally while underwater. It faded a great deal once we became terrestrial, so it's not like we go around reading each other's minds. And since our genes were mingled with yours, it sometimes appears in the population here, also, with people who can handle objects and read things from them. They call it–"

"They call it bullshit," Nate suggested.

"They call it . . ." Viktoria paused, then read from her phone. *"Psychometry. Also known as token-object reading, or psychoscopy, it is a form of extra-sensory perception characterized by the claimed ability to make relevant associations from an object of unknown history by making physical contact with that object. Supporters assert that an object may have an energy field that transfers knowledge regarding that object's history."*

"So the elders use this energy to imbue the object with whatever knowledge they want to pass on?" Wiley asked.

"I don't see how it could be imbued anymore. It's been under that temple for centuries. The knowledge – the energy – has to have dissipated, if it was ever there in the first place, which I doubt. I don't think that our ancestors left too many things like that lying around here. Who would've been able to read them?"

"It was left here for a purpose," Byron said firmly. "And we're sure it's still imbued."

"Is there any way that we could somehow arrange to sleep at this facility?" his sister asked suddenly.

Tom laughed. "That wouldn't work, Vikky. Surely not after all these years."

"What now?" Nate asked.

"About that Sirian capacity for telepathy. Sometimes, when we sleep together–"

Nate frowned suspiciously at whatever this was going to be.

"No, Nate. I don't mean sex. I mean sleep. Together in the same bed or even in the same dwelling. Sometimes we can share our dreams."

"Oh, for Christ's sake!" Nate shook his head. "You people are crazy."

"The very young are capable of learning in this way," Vikky told him. "When they're asleep, the teacher can also sleep and pass on simple–"

"That's a helluva naptime." Wiley nudged Nate.

"The ability lasts into adulthood. When we sleep, we can oft times see each other's dreams."

"I slept through a few study groups in college, Vikky." Wiley nudged Nate again. "But I didn't learn a damn thing."

"Sometimes, people here have the ability to see our dreams," Tom said, mostly to himself. "One time, Liz–"

"Now you're saying that you *can* read my mind, Tom?" Nate demanded. "What am I thinking right now?"

Wiley made an obscene gesture. "And I'm not even from Sirius."

Tom ignored Wiley's attempt at humor. "I can't read your mind, Nate. I can't even read your dreams. It doesn't quite work that way. Sirians can share their dreams with each other, but here . . . Sometimes, if we're close with a person that's not from Sirius, and we're asleep at the same time, they can get a glimpse of what we're dreaming. But it doesn't work the other way around. You can sometimes see our dreams, but we can't see yours."

"Or you could've invaded centuries ago," Wiley proposed. "Just landed and taken over our dreams, made us all dance to your all-natural tune. Telepathically controlled our minds. Commanded every man, woman and child to recycle their plastic. *All shall obey the Hypnotoad.*"

Nate shook his head again. "I don't even wanna know."

"Why do you always talk of us as invaders, Wiley?" Viktoria asked in exasperation. "We have no desire to take over your planet. We simply wish to–"

"Assimilate." Tom considered her narrowly for a moment, then shook his head, as if his thoughts were again bothersome to him.

"And you want to save us." Wiley eyed Byron in the rearview. "And you're sure the formula for that is on this disc at the museum?"

"Yes."

"So you plan on stealing this thing?" Nate fairly screeched in disbelief.

"No. We don't need to steal it, we just need to handle it. The knowledge will be absorbed, then it can be dictated onto one of your computers."

"Then disseminated to the masses," Tom said skeptically.

"So you don't need to steal it . . ." Wiley ruminated. "You just need to borrow it for a little while." He made eye contact with Byron in the rearview again. "For how long?"

"A few hours."

"They're not going to let 'em *borrow it,* Wiley," Nate spat derisively. "Like Tom said, they don't let the sheep handle the priceless treasures."

"But Byron's not your run-of-the-mill sheep. He's an archaeologist."

Tom giggled. "I told Liz I was an anthropologist. A student of mankind. She asked if I worked at the university. I had to do a little backpedaling on that one before she got the chance to decide that she wanted to see my credentials. I told her that I wasn't actually a practicing anthropologist–"

"Credentials can be faked," Wiley stated. "As can priceless treasures. Especially if it's just temporarily." He squinted craftily at them. "Let me do a little research."

THIRTY-NINE

Three weeks passed. Byron continued to go out with Janae. They went to more movies, traveled out of town and stayed in hotels to facilitate that alone-time that Janae had begun to positively crave. The excuse for these road trips were visits to the San Diego Museum of Man, the J. Paul Getty Museum, the LA County Museums of Art and Natural History; the Petersen Automotive Museum; the California Science Center. They even took a trip to the Hollywood Wax Museum. Wiley listened to Byron's enthusiastic descriptions of these places, and when Byron wasn't on hand, he listened to Tom bitch about the attention his cousin was paying to Janae.

"Christ, Tom! They're going to museums. It's not like they're going to Vegas for the weekend. He's assimilating!"

"He can assimilate with his sister."

"I'm sure Janae is a much better guide. They *like* each other! What's wrong with that?"

"He said he wasn't here for fun, Wiley. He's here for a purpose. I just haven't quite figured out what it is yet."

"To save the world."

"Right. I'm not buying that. It's not . . . it's not *Sirian.* He's here for something else, and I don't want Janae–"

"I said it before, Tom. *She* said it. She's a big girl." Bo was sleeping in his playpen, and Wiley crossed the room and adjusted his blanket, so he wasn't looking at Tom when he said, "I haven't noticed her floating around all smiles. Do you think they've . . ."

"How the hell would I know?"

Wiley smiled innocently. "All you Sirian Casanovas don't kiss and tell?"

"It's not something he's likely to discuss with–"

"Her foxy grandpa? But you could ask him."

"It's not really any of my business."

"Still . . . You could just bring it up."

"I don't see how it would come up in conversation." Tom recalled their discussion about Byron's apparent interest in Wiley, his weird texts and aphrodisiacs. "You could fucking ask him for me, my son. He's your peer. Your buddy."

"All right. I will."

But the opportunity to ask Byron about the extent of his relationship with Janae didn't present itself. It seemed that whenever Wiley saw him, there were too many people around. There was no time for a private word.

So he asked his wife what she'd heard. "Have they done the deed?" Wiley liked that expression. It smacked of a kind of raunchy poetry to him.

Brendee considered him across the dinner table. "Janae doesn't call me and tell me about her love life, Wiley. We're not that good of friends."

You were almost exceptionally good friends, Wiley thought with nothing but amusement. He knew his wife was what could only be called *addicted* to him. He wasn't Sirian, of course, but he had been taught, nonetheless. Brendee's almost-misstep with Janae had been just that; he didn't worry that she would every reconsider it.

Brendee wasn't thinking about the time she'd kissed Janae. She was remembering how innocent she'd said Byron had seemed to her. Now that Wiley had brought it up, Brendee wondered if Janae had indeed taken the opportunity to instruct him; she wondered if he'd been as surprised as she'd speculated he might be. Brendee considered calling and asking her. Not for Wiley's benefit, but because she'd enjoy hearing about Byron's performance, whether or not this perceived innocence was a sham, like her husband's had been. Janae would tell her if she asked. They *were* that good of friends.

"Why do you care?"

Wiley shrugged elaborately. "Just curious. *The problems of two little people don't amount to a hill of beans in this crazy world,* really. I'm just making conversation, baby."

FORTY

In addition to taking the Southern California museum tour with Byron, Janae also accompanied him and Tom and Vikky to the *Rivers of Mercury* Exhibit on their second visit. Wiley stayed in Riverside. He claimed it was no longer necessary for him to see the golden disk, although he did request a description of how the artifact was being presented to the public.

"It's in a typical museum display case in the middle of the room, so you can walk around it, see it from all angles," Tom told him. "The case is made of some kind of molded acrylic, I'd say, hinged on one side. Locked, of course. The disk's sitting atop the wooden box they found it in, propped up on a Lucite stand, like a plate holder. They've got a couple of baby spots trained on it from the ceiling. The case is cordoned off, of course, but you could probably reach over and touch it if you wanted to . . . I notice you're not writing any of this down, Wiley."

"What?" Wiley looked up from his phone. He hadn't really been paying attention to Tom's detailed description. "I'm sorry. It sounds very secure. Did you notice any cameras?" He looked at his phone again.

"The standard black half-dome cameras in the ceiling, like in grocery stores. I don't think they were installed specifically for the exhibit; I think they're just in the gallery . . ."

Wiley giggled and typed something.

"I think I'm insulted, my son. Aren't you the one that always says it's rude to be on your phone when someone's talking to you?"

"It is indeed, and I apologize." Wiley set his phone down on the counter. "I had to return that text. You now have my undivided attention."

"Why didn't you want to go to the museum with us? I thought you were interested in this thing."

"It's gonna save the world, after all. But I don't need to wallow in the chute with the sheep anymore. I figure I'll be seeing it soon enough."

Tom studied him suspiciously. "What exactly is the plan for that?"

"Be innocent of the knowledge, dearest chuck, till thou applaud the deed. You won't have to wait much longer to hear about it." Wiley picked up his phone, pushed a button, held it to his ear. "Can you come over to the store after work, Nate? I do believe I've solved the dilemma of our Sirian friends' need to handle the artifact."

Nate sighed. "Is this plan gonna piss me off, Wiley?"

"It depends on how larcenous you're feeling, I guess."

"You're not gonna steal it, are you?"

"No. I told you. We're just going to borrow it." Wiley winked at Tom. "Come on, Nate. I made a PowerPoint and everything."

"I'll be there."

FORTY-ONE

Wiley had the store's four folding chairs lined up in a semi-circle around his desk in the office. On the wall behind it was the large monitor from which he oversaw the shop's security cameras, ran diagnostics on his customers' devices, debugged code, and any other electronic/computer/internet related activity that he felt like pursuing, more than a few of which could not be termed strictly legal.

On the other desk across the room Wiley had placed a large, black metal box with three glass windows in it. It had a dial and a keypad on the front, and a scratched, half-peeled off label: all Nate could make out was *MakerBo* and *plicator.* The interior of the machine was dark.

"Pay no attention to that man behind the curtain, Nate." Wiley directed his friend's attention away from the black box. "Have a seat, my son. All will soon be revealed."

On the monitor, a stylized, artistic rendering of the golden disc from the Temple of the Feathered Serpent spun lazily, glinting mellowly against the black background.

"I didn't figure you for a graphic artist, Wiley." Tom took a chair.

"I'm not. There's a million pictures of that thing on the internet. I just borrowed that one." He directed Vikky and Byron to the remaining chairs. "As you know, I'm a jack of all trades and master of most, at least anything of an electronic nature. And there are few things these days that aren't electronic. If not in essence, then in discovery."

His audience now seated and attentive, with his trademark sly, self-satisfied grin, Wiley Royce began his presentation.

"On the screen, you see the object we seek. Designated Artifact AQ175, it has been exhaustively studied by archaeologists, metallurgists, linguists, code-breakers. No psychics, however. It has been determined that it's made of solid gold, so many millimeters thick, so many wide."

"That's not very precise, Wiley."

"You know how I am with the math, Tom. Not to mention that I'm an American. So, I converted. Fuck the metric system. You want precision? The disc is exactly 1.275 inches thick, and 7.138 inches in diameter.

"Because it's been studied so thoroughly, by so many different disciplines, there are, as I said, any number of depictions of it online." Wiley pushed a button on a tiny remote control, and other representations of the disc flashed on the screen. "Exacting specs; 3D maps. How this unspeakable wealth of information will be useful to us – I'll get to that in a second.

"Allow me to digress momentarily and describe the human element of our quest. We are, as you will soon see, exceptionally fortunate." Wiley pushed the button again, and a picture of a bespectacled, scholarly-looking man appeared.

"This is Dr. Douglas Michael Cooper, age thirty-six. He holds an M.A. in Prehistory and Archaeology from UCLA; and he is an RPA, scholastic jargon for a Registered Professional Archaeologist. He's the Curator of Anthropology at the museum, and is in charge, therefore, of the *Rivers of Mercury* Exhibit.

"But don't be put off by the good doctor's educational achievements and scholarly mien. He's just Dougie to his friends."

The next photo showed Dr. Cooper, shirtless, wearing pink lipstick and green eyeshadow. He had a pair of translucent fairy wings strapped across his shoulders; he carried a glitter and ribbon bespangled wand with a silver star at the top. He was blowing a drunken kiss to the viewer.

Wiley clicked the remote. The next photo showed Dr. Cooper bussing the cheek of a somewhat surly, dark-haired young man, who glared smokily at the camera. The picture was arty, in black and white.

"The attractive young thing on the left is Francois Johnson, age twenty-six. Occupation, photographer. He and Dr. Cooper met when Dr. Cooper was on a Caddoan Mississippian culture dig in Arkansas. They hit it off immediately . . ." Wiley clicked through several more photos of the men. Dr. Cooper was always smiling happily; Francois looked alternately bored or bemused.

"They hit it off so well, as a matter of fact, that when the dig was over, Dr. Cooper brought his new friend back to sunny Southern California with him. They lived together in Dr. Cooper's not unimpressive house in Redlands for about eighteen months . . ." Wiley showed a picture of it. "But sadly, Dougie and Frankie's friendship has not endured. Seeking greener pastures and an outlet for his art, Mr. Johnson has recently relocated to a small apartment in North Hollywood."

"How do you know all of this, Wiley?" Byron asked.

"I am simply – but ever so thoroughly, my son – Wiley Royce. *Hacker.* At your service."

"That means–"

"That means that there are very few secrets I cannot uncover, Vikky, my sweet. About damn near anybody. No one can hide online from Wiley Royce. Of course, some people's internet footprints are bigger than others'. *Sásq'ets*, if you will."

Tom smiled. Of course the smart monkey had looked up a term unfamiliar to him. Now he knew: *Sásq'ets* was another name for Bigfoot.

Wiley continued. "For the past two weeks or so, Dr. Cooper has been receiving emails from an earnest young grad student. He has flattered the somewhat vain doctor with knowledge and praise of his various theories on anthropology in general and Mesoamerican cultures in particular. All of which, one can of course find online in various scholarly compilations. This grad student has humbly asked Dougie if he might have the honor of meeting him, if he might be so bold as to request a personal tour of the *Rivers of Mercury* exhibit, with the esteemed archaeologist as a guide. After hours, perhaps. He has expressed a particular interest in AQ175.

"Dr. Cooper has responded eagerly. The two have chatted via text, become friends on Facebook."

"And this grad student is . . ." Tom was sure he already knew. Despite the annoying, totally unfathomable attention that Byron was paying to Janae, Tom suspected his young cousin had, as Earthling parlance might term it, a gay streak a mile wide. And he was pretty sure that Wiley thought so, too.

When Wiley clicked a Facebook page onto the screen, Tom's suspicion about the mysterious grad student was confirmed: Byron smiled serenely in the profile picture. His cover photo was the Temple of the Feathered Serpent.

"That's from Wikipedia," Wiley told his audience. He scrolled through the Facebook page that he'd manufactured. Byron's relationship status was single; he'd graduated from Texas A&M–

"Texas? I've never been to Texas."

"You've never been to Estonia, either, and I couldn't find an archaeology school there." Wiley displayed Byron's favorite books and movies, and when the young man looked askance at the utterly unfamiliar entries, he explained, "Your tastes are similar to Dougie's. That's the basic premise here."

"Why–"

"The good doctor has invited you to that after hours viewing of the *Rivers* Exhibit which you requested. He's even said that he might be able to show you the golden disk – allow you to *touch it,* if you so desire – because apparently they've been having a lighting problem in the Hall of History, and the artifact and its box are going to be in his office when the museum is closed on Monday. While they repair the faulty lights."

"Did you have something to do with that, Wiley?" Tom asked.

"Strictly a provident coincidence, I assure you."

"Christ, Wiley! You are a piece of work! What do ya think Dr. Cooper's gonna want in exchange for showing the goods to Byron, all up close and personal?"

"You malign the doctor, Nate. Just because a young, good-looking grad student shows an interest in the man's work, is a little friendly toward him–"

"How friendly?" Vikky at last spoke up.

"Just a little. Besides praising his archaeological theories, Byron complimented the shirt he was wearing in one of his pics. From the Palm Springs Gay Pride Parade."

"Christ, Wiley!"

"You act like I would so cavalierly throw Byron to an unknown fate, Nate. That's not the case. Byron's not going into the lion's den alone. He's bringing his entourage with him."

"Does Dr. Cooper know this?" Byron asked with an amused smile. Wiley's offering him up as bait bothered him not at all. This archaeologist wasn't at all unattractive, and it just might work.

"Of course! The man is an academic, my son! He doesn't think this is some kind of . . . assignation."

"At least not the first time," Tom murmured.

"And there need not be a second time." Wiley triumphantly pointed the remote at the big metal box on the other desk, and theatrically, the light came on inside it. "Here's your cue, Nate."

Nate sighed. "Okay, Wiley, I'll bite. What is that?"

Wiley smiled at his friend's cooperation, and crossed the room. "This, kiddies, is a *MakerBot Replicator.* I love that name. Sounds all science-fictiony, doesn't it?"

"What is it?" Nate repeated.

"It's a 3D printer, my son." Wiley opened the door. "And this is a 3D copy of Artifact AQ175. All those pics and specs? I just uploaded them, ran a little compile app, and voila! All hail, the internet. Catch, Lefty." He tossed the disc to Tom.

"But it's not gold," Vikky observed. The disc looked exactly like yet another photo that revolved on Wiley's computer monitor, except that it was dark gray in color.

"Not yet. But like the Maltese Falcon, all we gotta do is put a coat of paint on it, antique it up a little bit . . ."

"The Maltese –?"

"A movie," Tom told her absently, turning the disc over in his hands.

"It's made of a polymer resin. It weighs exactly the same as the original. Whilst Dr. Cooper is holding forth on Aztec history and gazing into Byron's big blue eyes, one of us'll just replace the real one with this one, and then–"

"I thought you said you weren't gonna steal it."

"We're not gonna *steal it,* Nate! We're just gonna borrow it for a few hours. When Byron and Vikky are done reading what's on it . . . Hell, we'll mail it back to them."

"They'll know who took it."

Wiley shook his head. "They'll never even know it was gone. Anybody could've made the switch any time during its long journey from Mexico. And when they get it back . . . Why and to whom would they even mention such a security breach?"

Nate shook his head. "Your entourage-ing this one on your own. I'm out."

"God hates a coward, my son."

"I dunno, Wiley." Tom handed the fake disc to Byron. "Maybe Nate's right. This is grand theft you're talking about–"

"Oh, for Christ's sake! It's grand *borrowing!* They won't even miss it! What happened to having a good time?" Wiley looked at the Sirian siblings. "What about you guys?"

Viktoria grinned in unabashed admiration. "You're brilliant, Wiley! We're in!"

FORTY-TWO

"It's so nice to finally meet you in the flesh, Byron!" Dr. Cooper enthusiastically shook the young man's hand.

"And you as well, Doctor."

"Please, call me Doug. I feel as if we're friends already."

I'll bet you do. Wiley exchanged a glance with Tom. Through wheedling and cajoling and derision, Wiley had persuaded the bookstore owner and longtime tourist from Sirius to accompany them on this caper, after all.

"My family is looking forward to viewing the disk as much as I am. We're all quite honored . . . Doug."

"It's really nothing. The exhibit's been open for a month now, and after the initial crowds . . ." Dr. Cooper sighed. "I haven't heard from a single person, not even any students. No one besides yourself has contacted me expressing an interest."

Tom wondered if Wiley had anything to do with that, if he'd excised any email queries from the archaeologist's inbox, freeing up his schedule for this meeting.

Byron introduced his family – Wiley was amused that Byron would include him under that heading – and Dr. Cooper shook hands with them, offered each a friendly and welcoming smile, said it was nice to meet them. But as they proceeded into the silent, dark and empty museum, Byron's *family* noted that the academic spoke exclusively to the young Sirian, asking him questions about his studies, his interest in Mesoamerican culture and the Temple of the Feathered Serpent.

Wiley smiled smugly at his companions. His plan was working.

Dr. Cooper led them past a sign that said *No Admittance,* and then up a staircase and into the behind the scenes portion of the museum. He opened the first door on a long hallway, marked simply *Workroom B.* He told them that the disk was not in his office as he'd previously thought it would be.

"This is Natural History's bone room," the doctor explained, somewhat unnecessarily: three large tables were covered with animal skulls and leg bones and ribs and other osseous remains. Wiley thought he recognized some species of cow, by the horns, and thought that maybe that one was a lion or a tiger or a bear, based on its teeth.

"These appear to be modern bones," Viktoria observed.

"Yes. No mastodons or saber-toothed tigers in this room. They decided to store the artifact in here because it's the closest to the service elevator that leads downstairs to the exhibit."

"Have they fixed the lighting yet?" Byron inquired politely.

"They're working on it. The spots kept flickering. All we needed was a disco ball and we could've had a party." When Byron only smiled blankly, the doctor gestured across the room. "The disc is over here."

Beside the skull of a giraffe – Wiley knew it was a giraffe because it was labeled as such – the golden disc that was supposed to save his planet shone atop its box, propped up on a Lucite plate holder, just as Tom had described.

Dr. Cooper indicated the box, carved on all sides with hieroglyphics.

"The glyphs describe a serpent of some kind, but they don't specifically reference Quetzalcoatl, the *feathered serpent*. We figure that they're talking about him, however, because the glyphs mention his common symbols, the wind, dawn, that he's associated with a planet–"

"Sirius?" Wiley asked, and those from that world turned to look at him.

Dr. Cooper smiled, a trifle patronizingly, Wiley noted. "Quetzalcoatl was associated with the planet Venus, actually. The morning star."

Wiley returned his smile. Masquerading as Byron, he'd led Dr. Cooper down the garden path with lightly disguised, flirtatious innuendo, and lonely Dougie had keenly responded: Nate had hit the nail squarely on the oft-mentioned head when he'd speculated that the good doctor was interested in giving Byron more than just a tour of the treasures. Wiley didn't like to be patronized, and especially not by someone so easily manipulated, so he pressed, "But does it say Venus? On the box? Or does it say some place else?"

"The glyphs tell of a serpent–"

"That's another word for a snake, right? Could it also be translated as *lizard?*"

Dr. Cooper paused, and let a moue of annoyance cross his face. Who was this guy, that he wanted to argue about a standard translation, from a language that he undoubtedly knew nothing about? Sometimes the ignorant public could be so exasperating.

"Though Quetzalcoatl, whose name is translated from the Nahuatl as *feathered serpent,* is not mentioned specifically, the box was found beneath his temple. Venus is not mentioned specifically, either. The passage is rather short, actually, describing a serpent who arrived on the wind at dawn from the sky. We naturally assume it speaks of Quetzalcoatl."

"Wasn't Quetzalcoatl prophesied to return? Didn't the Aztecs think that Cortez was–"

"Ah, Wiley!" Dr. Cooper laughed, and if Wiley had been unsure that he was being talked down to before, he was quite certain of it now. "You've seen too many popular culture documentaries passing themselves off as scientific realities. It was the Spanish that invented the *Cortez as Quetzalcoatl* myth. There's no evidence of a pre-conquest belief that Quetzalcoatl would return."

Dr. Cooper shared a *how ignorant are the uneducated masses?* glance with Byron, his fellow initiate into the history of Mesoamerican culture.

You don't know half what you think you do, Doc. Wiley glanced at the bookstore owner and Tom suppressed a smile.

"The markings on the disc are not Aztec glyphs," Dr. Cooper continued, dismissing the wooden box. "They've been studied by several prominent linguists to no avail. Personally," he grasped Byron's elbow, leaned a little closer to him to share his observations *personally,* "I think they're all wasting their time. I don't think it's a language at all, but simple decoration. But, just like everyone else, I'm sure you'd like to see for yourself!"

Dr. Cooper reached for the disc, then stopped within millimeters of it. "I'll need some gloves."

He opened a drawer in the side of the table. There were a few vials of unidentifiable liquids, odd serrated tools that Wiley assumed were used for scraping bones.

"Of course these overpaid taxidermists wouldn't have any gloves."

Vikky opened a drawer on her side of the table and produced a box of latex gloves.

"No dear, not rubber gloves. Inspection gloves. If you'll excuse me for just a moment – I have the proper equipment in my office. I'll be right back."

Dr. Cooper exited the workroom, and the light of conspiracy shown in four pairs of eyes.

"Is this some kind of luck or what?" Tom said.

"It's destiny," Viktoria murmured.

"Make the switch, Wiley!"

Wiley extracted the fake artifact from beneath the bulky sweatshirt he wore and handed it to Byron. He deftly removed the real one from its holder and tucked it out of sight, back under his shirt where the other one had been. Byron placed the fake disc atop the box.

"Now shall the secret be told!" Vikky breathed in a gushing whisper.

"Wait until we return to the bookstore, Viktoria," Byron said. Wiley was surprised to hear a hard edge to his voice.

"No, my brother! The truth burns in me, it longs to be communicated!" She turned feverishly bright eyes upon Tom and Wiley. "Know you now that Byron's tale of Brice and Annett and holy Tyrrel was but a fabrication. Neither Brice nor Annett ever visited this monkey world."

"They were scientists, that much is true," Byron said apologetically. "But I think we should wait, Viktoria—"

"I will wait no longer!" Her gray eyes blazed. "Yes, Brice and Annett were scientists, part of the long line that had worked on turning mermaids into men, through the help of human DNA. At the height of the war, they were kidnapped by the Dinos—"

"Made ready to be appetizers." Tom glanced at Wiley. *What the hell do you suppose is going on now?*

Byron ignored him, and continued this new story, because his sister was suddenly breathless, eyes shining with glee. "The Dinos kept them, and while in their company, this brilliant, forward-thinking couple came to believe that the war was wrong, that Dino and hominid species could and should coexist on Sirius."

Byron waited for another snarky remark from Tom, and he wasn't disappointed: "On Earth, they call that *Stockholm Syndrome,* my son. Where the hostage starts to identify with his captors."

"Or maybe, as Wiley said, they just recognized genocide as wrong."

Wiley was expressionless, surprised into silence. Everything had been going according to plan: Dr. Cooper had fallen for his tender trap and invited young Byron to the museum; here they were. The disc that was supposed to save the planet was even now nestled against Wiley's skin, held in place by a large rubber band he'd worn around his waist, specifically for that purpose.

Then Vikky had suddenly started crowing about secrets like a crazed evangelist, and she and Byron were again talking about the Dino People.

"During their time with the Dinos, Brice and Annett continued their bioengineering work. They realized that even when peace was finally attained, the lizards would never be welcome to live side by side with men. In appearance, they were just too alien."

"Not to mention their diet." Tom elbowed Wiley. "No one wants to live next door to someone whose choice of a midnight snack might be them."

Byron continued as if his cousin had not spoken. "So Brice and Annett devised a method by which Dinos could be genetically transformed, until they appeared almost human. It's almost like a type of mimicry. Like the flies here that pretend to be bees–"

"Are you trying to tell us that you're not human, Byron?" Wiley blurted out.

"Or even Sirian," Tom posited calmly.

"We're as Sirian as you!" Viktoria hissed, her happy smile evaporating.

"But we're not Dinos," Byron said in a softer tone. He held up his left hand. "We really are related to you, Tom. Your sister is our grandmother, just like we've told you."

Viktoria continued angrily, "My point is, even if we were Dinos–"

"Disguised as people–"

Viktoria's lovely face was marred by a hateful sneer. "Even if we were Dinos, we'd be as Sirian as you. It's their planet, too."

"There are cockroaches on this planet, Vikky. That doesn't make it theirs. It doesn't make us hesitate to step on one if we see it. Mankind has tried to wipe them out here, just like we wiped the Dinos out on Sirius."

"You're mistaken about that, Cousin." Viktoria's smile returned. It was smug. Arrogant.

"Let me get this straight," Wiley said. "You're saying that this race of Sleestak-looking lizards is still there, on Sirius? Tom said–"

"Tom was wrong," Byron replied. "The Mermaids didn't wipe them all out. There is a small, rocky continent, far out in the middle of a salty, predator-filled sea–"

"Just get to the point, will ya, my son? I don't really care about the geography of an alien planet."

"You don't really care about Earth geography," Tom told him.

Despite the bizarre mood of menace suddenly coloring the conversation, Wiley smiled, shrugged. It was true. Geography had never interested him. He could find any place he wanted by typing its name into a search box, so he'd never concerned himself with learning where they actually were, in relation to other places.

"There are Dinos on this island. Is that what you're saying?" Tom shook his head. It was ludicrous. "And they've been trying to become human-looking for all these eons? And no one knows they're there? There've been no fly-overs, no sea voyages to this remote place?"

Byron shrugged. "Believe what you want, Tom. I haven't seen the island. Viktoria and I were recruited from our hometown."

His sister took up the tale. "We've been told that the human-like Dinos on this island aren't completely human yet, even after all this time. They're not quite . . . They fear that they couldn't blend in with the hominid populations. They're all right-handed; they always have twins or triplets. Their eyes tend toward greens and browns, not blues and grays. The way they blink . . . It's different than the hybrid mermaid-monkeys."

"The ones that run the planet," Wiley opined.

Now Byron smiled. "For the moment. But that's why we're here."

"Brice was on his deathbed. He and Annett had produced a son during their–"

"Captivity," Tom offered.

Viktoria ignored him. "During their time on the island, Brice perfected the sequencing necessary to make the Dino over into the very picture of the hominid. Left-handed. Blue-eyed. Mammal-like blinks. Single births. They'd of course never be able to breed with true hominids, but breeding with them wouldn't be necessary." Viktoria's smile widened. "The Dinos would simply infiltrate Sirian society, and eventually, they would outnumber–"

"Then why didn't that ever happen?" Tom asked irritably. "You're saying that Brice lived during the war. That was thousands of years ago. When Sirians were still coming en masse to Earth."

"Brice didn't believe that the time was right," Byron said. "He believed that the Dinos would lose the war, as they were, and if they applied his formulas and tried to infiltrate, and then were discovered, the Sirians would just keep importing more monkeys from Earth to combat them, as they were doing to combat the others."

"It wasn't the right time for the Dinos to completely assume hominid characteristics," Viktoria added. "But Brice was dying, so he imbued the formulas onto a golden disc, and gave the secret to his son. Annett and Tyrrel left the island, rejoined Sirian society. His mother taught Tyrrel how to behave to fit in–"

Wiley barked laughter. "Did you find an old book in the store, Vikky? With a yellow cover and black stripes? *Cliff's Notes?* You must've, because this is the plot to *Brave New World.* John, born outside of his mother's society, is returned to it–"

"How beauteous mankind is! O brave new world that has such people in't." Byron's grin widened. He and Wiley had read *The Tempest* just a few days before.

Tom sighed as though bored, and consulted an imaginary watch on his wrist. "Is there a point to this melodramatic fairytale?"

"Here's the point, monkey," Viktoria spat. "Like his mother and father had, Tyrrel felt a kinship with the Dinos. He came to Earth aboard the next Sirian transport. He hid his father's secret in Mexico, in the pyramid, until such time as it would be rediscovered. The eons would've passed by then – the war would be long over. The Sirians would be relaxed–"

"Because the Dino Menace was long ago wiped out."

Byron clapped Wiley on the shoulder. "How astute you are, my friend! I think that I'll–"

"He'll eat you last." Tom didn't smile. "So you're here to retrieve the formulas from the artifact, return to Sirius, proliferate human-looking Dino hybrids, and take over the planet."

Again Viktoria smirked. "You're mostly right. After we get back home and give the knowledge to–"

"Your Dino overlords . . ."

Viktoria ignored Wiley's remark. "After a sufficient, perfected population has been established on the island, then we'll all return *here.* There's always the possibility of detection on Sirius, but the hybrids will blend perfectly on Earth."

"Well, I'll be a son of a bitch," Tom said in amazement. "One of Dionne's conspiracy theories finally turns out to be on the mark."

He explained the gist of the *Alien Archives* episode he'd watched, wherein it was purported that a race of alien lizard-hybrids that sought to masquerade as people existed somewhere in the cosmos.

154

"But this show said they're already here. *Walking amongst us.*"

Byron smiled. "Anticipatory. It'll be true soon enough."

Tom giggled. "I don't know which one of your stories is more far-fetched, kiddies. First, you're here to save the Earth. Now, you're here to retrieve a genetic code that will allow reconstituted, human-looking Dinos to *invade* the Earth. Either way, it's all bullshit."

Wiley saw that Tom was refusing to believe his cousins' story. Yet he'd said it himself: *Byron isn't here for fun. He's here for a purpose.* Well, Byron had just explained exactly what his purpose was, and Tom wasn't –

"Why are you telling us all this? Surely you don't think that Wiley and I are gonna help you."

"Byron believed that you'd be amenable to our cause," Viktoria stated with a sigh. "After all, you're an outcast. Perhaps the only one in history."

Tom's eyebrows went up. "Really?"

"No one has ever been denied return to the homeworld from here. Except for you."

"Really?" Tom repeated. "Because I wanted to bring Liz back with me?"

"I understand that you were rather insistent about it." Byron put on an expression of embarrassment at his cousin's actions.

"Violently so," Viktoria added. "We understand that you commandeered a transport device, but through your ineptitude, were unable to use it."

"They would've slain you upon arrival, had you succeeded," Byron said darkly. "It's forbidden."

Tom shrugged. He didn't believe that it was *forbidden;* he believed that had he asked nicely, offered logical reasons . . . But he'd been desperate, and he had indeed been insistent. Violent.

"I knew I wasn't really welcome back, but I didn't know it was that big a deal. I thought it'd all probably blown over by now, but I've never really given it much thought. I like it here.

"But persona non grata or not, I don't know why that would make you guys think that I'd be willing to betray my entire race for a bunch of . . ." Tom's grin bloomed and he winked at Wiley. "For, literally, a bunch of snakes in the grass."

Viktoria sighed again. "That's what Byron believed. He thought you'd help us. I always thought that it was unlikely, so I only agreed to contact you for this reason: you're established here. You know their ways, and I thought that you'd be able to help us to come into contact with the artifact. And so you have."

"You've helped immensely," Byron added. "And for that we're grateful."

"We require your assistance no longer, however, and what you believe is of no consequence to us." Vikky smiled haughtily. "You're banned on Sirius, Tom. If you try to contact them and warn them in some way, who would believe such a ridiculous story? It would appear to be merely an outcast's second frantic attempt to return home. They'd put it down as the Earth-bred insanity of a too-many-decades' expatriate."

"Janae already thinks you're a lunatic." Byron smiled.

Tom did not. "You've helped her along with that."

Byron shrugged. "It seemed a useful course of action. Since Wiley has been termed *your sheep,* I thought it prudent to cultivate another . . . *connection* here, in case . . . Well, in case what's happening now happened. In case you and I had a – what is the idiom?"

"A falling out," Wiley supplied.

"These days, if you ask Janae who she's more likely to believe, her lover or her crazy grandfather, I think you'll find that she's become *my* sheep." Byron made a petting gesture in the air.

Wiley laid a restraining hand on Tom's shoulder. "You're wrong, Byron. I know Janae. She'd never choose a random piece of ass over Tom."

Byron's detachment was palpable. He could not possibly care less. "What conceivable difference could it make to me now? She might've been useful had I needed to discredit Tom, but regardless, she was amusing." He again made that petting gesture. "I'm afraid she's going to miss me terribly when we return to the home–"

"Here we go!" Dr. Cooper swept into the workroom, and they all jumped. Five pairs of white cotton gloves flapped silently in his hand. He gave a pair to Viktoria and her brother. When Tom reached for his set, Wiley's phone rang stridently.

"Sorry, gang, that's the Bat Phone. I gotta take this one." He stepped to the end of the room.

"Here, Byron. Allow me." Dr. Cooper gingerly removed the phony disk from its holder and reverently handed it to the equally as phony grad student. "As you can see, the *language* is just some circles, some lines of varying length, some squiggles. It's merely ornamentation, don't you agree?"

156

Before Byron could agree, Wiley said, "I'm sorry, Doug. My father-in-law's had a heart attack." At their stunned expressions, he continued, "It's just a mild one. He's not at death's door or anything, but I have to take my wife to the hospital right away. Tom, could you watch Bo for the afternoon?"

"But of course, Wiley."

"I know this is a rare and exciting opportunity for Byron, something not to be passed up. I wouldn't want to take him away . . . Hell, he doesn't even know my father-in-law. After you're done touring the exhibit, would it be possible for you to give them a lift back to Riverside, Doug?"

"It would be my pleasure, Wiley. I hope your father-in-law'll be all right."

"I'm sure he will be. It was great meeting you."

"Likewise. Just go out the way we came in. The door'll lock behind you."

Dr. Cooper shook Wiley's hand, and Wiley would've bet the farm that he was thinking, *Two down, one to go. Now, how can I get rid of the sister?*

FORTY-THREE

Tom and Wiley left without a backward glance. They quick-walked down the stairs and out of the museum, then sprinted to the car.

"Jesus, Wiley! You *did* steal it!"

"Will you stop saying that?" They leapt into the car and Wiley squealed out of the parking lot. "I'm only borrowing it. I've got to keep it away from—"

"Oh, for Christ's sake! You didn't really believe all that claptrap about Dinos bioengineered to look like people?"

"You said it yourself, Tom. Byron came here for a reason. It seems to go without saying that this must be it. I've gone along with all this bullshit, that you people are from another planet. Okay, if that's true, then how do I know this other shit's not true, also? How do *you* know it's not?"

Tom started to speak, but Wiley cut him off. "Look at it this way. Byron and Viktoria obviously believe it. They came all the way across a billion parsecs or whatever, because they wanted to help the Dinos to come to Earth. Even if that's just some myth . . . I dunno, Tom. I gotta think about all this before they start downloading data off this thing. I've gotta get some perspective."

Tom nodded silently. He recalled what Viktoria had said, that he was an outcast, that no one on Sirius would believe him. A line from an old movie occurred to him: *The greatest trick the devil ever pulled was convincing the world he didn't exist . . .*

"Can you get me a satellite dish, Wiley?"

"You mean, like a DirecTV dish?"

Tom was looking at his phone. He nodded.

"Yeah. I think there's one in the store room. Why do you want a—"

"Do you remember your mythology? Cassandra?"

"I'm not sure. Something about prophecy? What does that have to do with—"

"Cassandra could accurately foretell the future, but she was cursed. Her curse was that no one would believe her. I was just thinking about what Vikky said, that if I tried to warn Sirius, no one would believe me. So maybe . . . What could it hurt to send a message? Ask someone if there's a ring of weird-blinking people around, all in a hurry to take a vacation?"

"You noticed that, too?"

"Maybe it has something to do with the company they've been keeping."

"ET phone home."

Tom's face was unreadable. "Something like that."

FORTY-FOUR

"You call this a schematic?" Wiley squinted doubtfully at the big monitor in the office of *Morry's Books*. It showed an enlargement of a picture from Tom's phone of a very old, hand drawn diagram. "What are those things supposed to be?"

Tom was opening and closing desk and file cabinet drawers. "Those are metal spikes. Like railroad spikes, only thinner." He set an old telephone book from a bottom drawer onto the floor. It had obscured what he sought: two rusty pieces of cylindrical metal about eight inches long. Each had a head and point on it.

"What is that?"

"These are the spikes."

"Those are big nails. I meant, what is that book?"

Tom looked at the floor. "That's a telephone book, my son. The *White Pages*. Once upon a time, you could look up the land line numbers of all your friends and neighbors. If you didn't want to be looked up, you had to pay. It was called being *unlisted*. The one for businesses was called the *Yellow Pages.*"

"How quaint." Wiley was unimpressed. "Be sure to recycle it." He looked at the diagram again. "Is that a *sundial?*"

"No, it's an old-fashioned cake timer."

"Analog, like some kind of clock? With springs and hands and you had to wind it?"

Tom shook his head. "You have no appreciation for small machines, Wiley. A mechanical watch is a fascinating balance of tiny components–"

"My phone sets itself, Tom. And it's never wrong."

"Unless the battery goes dead."

"Then I'll look at your phone." Wiley pointed uncertainly at the screen. "Is that an oscilloscope? And *a typewriter?*"

Tom nodded.

"And two car batteries. How exactly is this device supposed to function, Tom?"

"You're the electronics wizard, my son. You tell me."

"It's not electronic . . . It's barely electric."

"I don't know what to tell you, Wiley. I don't know how it works, but I know it *does* work. Morry drew this diagram for me, in case I ever needed to phone home, as you so eloquently put it. Martin had the same set-up in Mapimi. The transport device–"

"What happened to the spaceships again?"

"They were composted. It's a long story, Wiley. After the war, Sirius wasn't interested in interstellar travel anymore. They had an entire, newly Dino-free world to tame, so they let the spaceships rot. They were done with your planet.

"But a couple of veterans, who had spent time on Earth, missed it, so they invented a method by which one person at a time could return. And we've been visiting ever since. The device they developed is based on the same principles as the communication device."

"Only more complicated."

Tom shrugged. "More car batteries. A bigger satellite dish. I don't really know. The transport device is beyond me, but I know that between the two of us, we can build this thing. When he decided that he wanted to go home, I watched Morry cobble one of these together and send a message to Sirius, Wiley. He didn't even use a satellite dish then. It was an–"

"An umbrella." Wiley pointed to it on the diagram.

"A week or so later, I watched him receive a response."

"Where do you receive the response?"

Now Tom pointed at the picture. "Sound comes out of the car stereo speaker. Right there." He grinned. "It's alien technology, Wiley. I can't expect you to understand how it–"

"You don't even understand how it works! And it's car batteries and big nails! It's neither alien nor technology!"

"I am endeavoring, ma'am, to construct a mnemonic memory circuit using stone knives and bearskins. Trust me, Wiley. If we hook it up just like it looks, it'll work. We'll be able to send a message to Sirius."

"Wait till Nate sees this."

"Where is Nate, anyway?"

"He went with Dionne and the girls to the mountains, remember?"

"But it's Monday. Shouldn't they be at work?"

"Is there Alzheimer's on Sirius? It's Veteran's Day. That's why the museum was closed. Brendee and Denny and Nate took the whole week off."

"So they took the monthly pilgrimage to the prepper compound without us?"

161

"I told them we'd be along after the tour." Wiley paused. "I'm missing the nature hike because–"

"You're trying to save the Earth from an invasion from another world. Like Santa Claus – *Wiley Royce Versus the Martians.*"

"It was *Santa Claus Conquers the Martians.*" Wiley didn't smile. "And I'm not sure it's all such a terrible catastrophe after all, now that I've been thinking about it. Mankind surely hasn't done anything great with this planet, so maybe another species . . ."

Wiley wasn't a Nazi, but he had read *Mein Kampf,* because he'd wanted to understand the philosophy. Similarly, he wasn't religious in the least, but he'd read the Bible, in order that he might speak to those that were devout about their beliefs. So he knew that there had been a snake in the Garden of Eden, and that the knowledge he had disseminated had precipitated mankind's expulsion from it. Wiley didn't think it was the knowledge of sin that had doomed his species, however. It was the Industrial Revolution.

Maybe these invaders from another world would found a new religion. These new snakes, who were from their own Garden of Eden . . . Maybe they could turn back the centuries, make Earth a paradise again, like their homeworld was. Maybe a new species could *compel* the ignorant sheep to see how they were destroying this planet, maybe they could *make* them stop . . .

"You can't be serious, Wiley. If what Byron and Viktoria say is even remotely true . . ."

"I don't know, Tom. Byron and Viktoria seem all right. Why shouldn't their friends be allowed to come here? Maybe they're just like us–"

"Their friends are aliens, Wiley!"

"You're an alien."

"But . . . All right. Bryon's also a son of a bitch, Wiley. You heard the way he talked about Janae–"

"I've been called a son of a bitch, Tom, and for the umpteenth time, Janae's a big girl. I'm sure she'll get over it. Have you ever known her not to get over it?"

Wiley paused, frowned. He had bigger things to think about than Janae's hurt feelings. A new, brighter future might be at hand. "Maybe we're a little bit more egalitarian here on Earth than the people are on Sirius. Why couldn't we share this planet with–"

"Let's just say, for the sake of argument, that all of this bullshit that Byron and Viktoria believe is true. If it is – these new Dinos don't wanna share, Wiley. Why do you refuse to see that? If what my race-traitor relatives say is correct, they've wanted to be us for centuries, and they've almost made it. Don't suddenly go all hippie social worker on me. If what Byron and Viktoria say is true, the future of our species is at stake, here."

"*Our* species?"

"I've told you before. I'm no different than you, DNA-wise."

"So you say."

Tom shook his head. Some things just couldn't be proven.

"If this Dino island really does exist, the lizards know that if they come out of hiding, they'll never be able to pass on Sirius, so they want to try to take over here. If they just wanted to share a planet, they would've stayed looking like lizards. But they chose to mimic the dominant species . . ." Tom consulted his phone. "Are you familiar with the concept of a brood parasite? In the animal kingdom?"

Wiley shook his head.

Tom smiled grimly. "I'm disappointed."

"I'm not much into the animal kingdom, Tom. Just like you."

It was true. Sirius was green and beautiful, and being a tourist, Tom was much more concerned with art and movies and literature, with history and architecture, all the products of his adopted culture, so different from his homeworld. His appreciation for these things had made him friends with Wiley. Nature bored them both.

"The behavior is unknown on Sirius, so I read up on it." Tom gestured with his phone.

"Proceed, therefore."

"Brood parasitism is where an animal places its young in the nest of another. The dupe then raises the baby as its own. It would be as if Denny and Nate put Eric in Bo's room, for you to raise, and then kicked Bo to the curb."

"We would know—"

"Of course you'd know. You're not a bird or bug. Apparently some of the birds and bugs know, too, but they raise the foreign young anyway, out of fear of reprisal from the adults of the parasitic species."

"You're making that up."

Tom again gestured with his phone. "It's all right here. But suppose Byron and Viktoria slipped you one of these little Dino-hybrid babies, how could you tell?"

"Now you're going all *Invasion of the Body Snatchers* on me, Tom." Wiley laughed. "They can't make babies that look like existing babies . . ."

"And even if they could, you'd know because they'd probably blink funny, just like Byron and Viktoria do." Tom smiled. Wiley did not. "Anyway, back to the animals. The dupe raises the parasitic offspring, taking resources from its own young. Sometimes, its own young are killed. Of course, there's no breeding later. The parasitic offspring goes back to its own kind once it's grown, and the cycle starts all over again."

Tom paused. Wiley waited for him to get to the point.

"I'm not saying that Byron and Viktoria are gonna steal human babies and replace them with Dino babies, although that's certainly a possibility."

"They seem civilized enough, Tom. Their friends just want to blend here. Just like you did."

"But they can't blend, Wiley. And that's why they can't be allowed to come here. Byron has told you about the *genocide* of the Dino People on Sirius. He's made them out to be human-like; he's touched the sense of fairness in your soul.

"Now that you believe that they weren't wiped out, you want to welcome them, as if they were downtrodden, mistreated refugees. *Give me your tired, your poor, your huddled masses yearning to breathe free. The wretched refuse of your teeming shore,* and all that. You figure that refugees are good for wherever they settle. They're grateful to be freed from the troubles back home; they work, and eventually, they assimilate.

"Don't make me out to be a racist, Wiley. I'm not trying to keep out a culture that's alien to mine, because I want to maintain the status quo. If they're allowed to come here, Byron and Viktoria's *friends* will eventually blend, like you say. They'll become Americans, or they'll become members of whatever culture in which they decide to immerse themselves. As individuals, they will indeed assimilate.

"But there's a difference here that you seem to be purposefully ignoring, my son. This isn't about a poor, oppressed people fleeing injustice. This is every science fiction, alien invasion horror scenario that you've ever seen. Like that one *Twilight Zone – To Serve Man –* they eat their enemies, Wiley. Like in *Independence Day – What is it you want us to do? Die.*

"If there really is a magical genetic formula on that disc, it still won't make them human. It'll only make them *look* human. This isn't immigration, Wiley. This is invasion.

"They've endeavored to look like us, in order to push us out. They aim to take the place of the native species, like brood parasites in the nest. You and Nate have one child each; Viktoria said her *friends* never have less than twins. They live longer. If it's true – we can't let it happen, Wiley. They want to colonize? They can go somewhere else. This planet already has a dominant species."

"They live longer, too?"

"Any species from Sirius is gonna live longer. It's a completely natural place. No plastics, no burnt fossil fuels, no food additives. No chemicals at all in the environment. No *diseases of affluence.* So Sirians are stronger, healthier. We live longer than the natives, here. These genetically re-engineered Dinos would, too.

"This wouldn't be like *The War of the Worlds,* Wiley. They won't land in spaceships and start shooting up the place. It would be subtle. They wouldn't even let us know they were here. It wouldn't take long for them to simply outlive humanity. And no one would even realize it's happening. One day, all the monkeys would be gone, replaced by lizards that just look like monkeys."

"Maybe we should let 'em," Wiley said stubbornly. "Like I say, *Homo sapiens* hasn't done a whole lot of good to this planet." He spoke aloud the hope he'd been thinking. "Maybe a new species will return it to a paradise, like it once was. Like Sirius is."

Tom shook his head. "Who are you, and what have you done with Wiley Royce?"

"I'm just saying, if we know they're coming, they wouldn't be able to push us out. Maybe we could share. Maybe they could help us make things better here, natural again . . ."

"You really are becoming a hippie, and it's really starting to piss me off. Allow me to knock some sense into you. That romanticized idea of the ignorant native living in equality and bliss with nature – that's all bullshit here on Earth. It's hard being an ignorant native here. It's absolutely no fun at all. It's too hot, or it's too cold. You're always hungry, or you're always thirsty. Roughing it out there with nature is a bitch, my son.

"Just because things turned out well for the natives on Sirius . . . Somebody famous once said that the third world will climb over you and your copy of *50 Simple Things You Can Do to Save the Earth* to get to your air conditioning and your big screen TV. Your fast food.

"And the third world – at least they're people. Why do you think the lizards want to come here? Because it has everything they don't have. They want someplace different. Maybe they're tired of all of Nature's bounty. Maybe they want to smoke a cigarette."

"They want to escape persecution–"

"They want to invade."

When Wiley still seemed unconvinced, Tom called up a picture of Bo on his phone. "This is the only new species this planet needs, right here, Wiley. Because of you and me and Denny, your son and her son will be as environmentally-conscious as they can be, I'm sure. Maybe their generation will start the healing. Personally, I'm not so sure the Earth is ailing that much. I think we just have to be smarter than the average sheep, and our little corner of the world can be its own natural paradise. Like you say, the prepper compound in the mountains is our clean corner."

"You're not a hippie," Wiley said darkly.

"Either are you, my son. Not really. You don't care about how the rest of the population poisons themselves, as long as your family knows the dangers and avoids them. And if any of this is true, it's an unprecedented danger. It's an invasive species on a global scale, a brood parasite that'll push out all the human chicks to oblivion. We don't need a return of the dinosaurs. They lost the evolutionary battle once already, here and on Sirius."

Tom tilted his head, studied his friend for a heartbeat. He smiled. "As soon as we get this thing put together, I'm gonna send that message home. Who knows? Maybe it's really going on. Maybe an infiltration *has* begun there, and if it has, maybe my people will come back here and start abducting your people, like in ancient times. Press-ganging them to fight a new Dino War."

Tom was kidding – he didn't seem to believe a Dinos-masquerading-as-humans-invasion could actually occur – but still Wiley's dark mood remained, and he expressed it.

"We're quite a magnificent race here on Earth – isn't that what you always say? And we're a little more advanced now than in Aztec times. We're not gonna bow down and imagine you as gods anymore. Maybe we'd agree to fight the Dinos willingly. The chance to go somewhere else . . . Maybe we'll like it there on your all-natural planet. You know how big eco-tourism is among the hippies.

"But I'm sure we'll want to make some modifications. There's all that unspoiled nature – but why can't I call Mavis and tell her about it? What Sirius needs is some cellphone towers, some artificial satellites. Improve those communications. Import some metal and plastic, and Christ, couldn't ya'll use some concrete? Maybe we'll pollute Sirius, just like we polluted Earth. Will it be worth it to save you from the Dino Menace a second time?"

Wiley remained unsure, and that made him out of sorts. He loathed indecision, especially in himself. Maybe it *was* true, and if it was, was it really so bad? It seemed pretty bad, but on the other hand, Tom's type had already infiltrated here, and the world hadn't been made any worse by a bunch of former mermaids running round. Or had it? Wiley frowned warily at the bookstore owner. Maybe all Sirians were the enemy.

Tom caught Wiley's sudden distrust and it cut him. The clever monkey was his best friend.

"The Dinos wanted to destroy my people once; they wanted to take over Sirius. If Byron and Vikky are to be believed, now they want to destroy your people, and take over here. They're not going to sanctify the Earth, Wiley. They're not going to make it over in the image of the homeworld. They're not even gonna try to do that. And even if they did, it wouldn't be for you or me or Bo.

"I don't think that you can rationalize away the obvious, Wiley. I don't think that you can–"

Wiley's phone rang, and his frown deepened. "It's Byron. Hello?"

"Say hello to your daddy, Bo."

"Hi, Daddy! When you be here?"

"In a little while, Bo. Give the phone back to Byron." Wiley clicked his onto speaker and set it down on the desk.

"This is not unlike the plot from one of your movies, Wiley. A crime drama perhaps? You have something we want, and we have . . . Well, we have everything."

"Where are you?"

"We're at your little community in the mountains, Cousin. Remember? You described it to me. All the Tribes are here."

"But how did you know how to find it?" Wiley looked at Tom and he shook his head.

"Janae told me."

"Is Janae there now?" Tom asked.

"No. But everyone else is. We were all playing charades, then Bo saw a bluebird on the deck railing. I brought him outside for a closer look, and so I could call you in private.

"Your *loved ones* have no idea of the peril they're in, my friends. I'm afraid Viktoria became quite incensed when Wiley absconded with the artifact. I suggested that we simply return to the bookstore and ask him for it, but Viktoria decided on this perhaps more persuasive means. Dr. Cooper wanted to see *Morry's,* but Viktoria told him that we had to leave the museum immediately. I'm afraid the cab fare up here made quite a dent in the family fortune.

"So here we are, one big, happy family. At this time, there won't be any – what did you call it? Stockholm Syndrome? No one will want to side with the captors because they have no idea that they're captive yet. Bring us the disc, Wiley, and everything will be fine."

Tom said to himself, *Will my next words be a lie or the truth? It's all up to Wiley.*

"He was just waiting for you to show up, Byron. I'm afraid he's ready to welcome your Dino overlords. He thinks maybe they'll do a better job with his planet."

"Is that so, Wiley?"

Wiley's feeling of being adrift in a sea of question marks remained, and he didn't look at Tom. "Why not? We've surely made a mess of things."

Byron paused for so long that Wiley was about to ask to talk to his son again. Finally the young Sirian spoke. "You *have* seemed sympathetic to the inhumane treatment of the Dinos, Wiley. You're a humanitarian–"

"A hippie," Tom said bitterly.

"But you'll pardon me if I hesitate. You're Tom's sheep, after all. So perhaps you're willing to concede to a superior species, or perhaps you're not. If you are, we'll have long and in-depth conversations in the future."

Tom typed on his phone, then showed it to Wiley, deadpan: *I'll show u lovin' like u never knew.* Wiley remained expressionless.

"Viktoria admires you as a keeper of the knowledge, and she has–"

"A what?"

"A keeper of the knowledge. You are an initiate into how the technology works here."

"That I am, my son."

"Viktoria believes that you'll be quite useful to the cause in the future."

"And I thought she just had a crush on me."

Byron laughed. "And because you do know all about the intricacies of terrestrial communications . . . All hail the internet! Please don't try to contact anyone here, Wiley. Just bring us the disk. If there are any warning texts, if anyone starts behaving as if they're anything other than having a pleasant day in the country . . . I'm afraid Viktoria is quite adamant. She'll kill them."

"With what? Some kind of Sirian death ray?"

"It hardly matters, does it? The element of surprise is on our side. Something as innocuous as a kitchen knife . . ."

Tom's growled, "Do Dinos bleed red, Byron? I know you will."

Wiley shook his head. "There's no need for these melodramatic threats. Like Tom said, I was gonna give the thing to you anyway."

"Then we're in agreement. When can I expect you?"

"It takes about two hours, depending on traffic."

"We'll see you then."

FORTY-FIVE

When they got into the car, Tom put his phone to his ear. "Where are you, Janae?"

"I'm about halfway to Big Bear. Byron said something about going up to see you guys, so I thought I'd join you."

"We're not there."

"But Byron said—"

"Everyone else is there. We're on our way. I need you to listen carefully to me, Janae. There's a Sheriff's Station in Big Bear. You know where it is?"

"Yes," Janae replied slowly. Guardedly.

"I want you to stop there, take a couple of them to the compound with you."

Janae laughed uneasily. "Dionne's not gonna like that, Tommy. You know how she feels about The Man."

"I'm not fucking around, Janae. Byron and Viktoria are holding everyone hostage. I want you to take a couple cops over there. Wiley's gonna give them what they want, but—"

"Wiley's with you? Put me on speaker."

Tom complied, set his phone on his knee.

"Wiley?"

"Yes, Janae."

Christ! Tommy's finally snapped and I'm gonna have to depend on Wiley! Why couldn't it have been someone else? Even Dionne would've seen that he's gone around the bend. But it was what it was.

"You've gotta get him some help, Wiley. Take him to the hospital. Tell them . . . Tell them he's violent or something. They'll take him then. They'll talk to him, make him all right again!" Janae sobbed and hated herself for it. Wiley was the type to disparage any show of weakness. But it couldn't be helped. "Dad was right—"

"Tom's lying, Janae. He *is* fucking with you. You know, Byron and Vikky are foreigners and all, so he thought it might be funny to pretend that they were really—"

"Terrorists?" Janae's voice cracked from outrage. "You guys think that's *funny?"*

Wiley chuckled believably. "Well, Tom's not too happy with you dating Byron, so–"

"I'm hanging up now, Wiley."

"Okay, Janae. We'll see you soon. Only – do me a favor, will ya?"

"I doubt it sincerely, Wiley."

"Don't tell Byron about our little joke."

"I wouldn't dream of it. It isn't even remotely funny, and he already thinks Tom's crazy."

"Thanks, Janae. Tell everyone that we'll be there in a–"

Tom's phone beeped. Janae had hung up.

"Why did you do that, Wiley? The cops would've at least kept them from hurting anybody until we got there!"

"I think you *are* crazy, you know that? I thought this was all bullshit?"

"Like you say, *they* believe it. And they threatened to hurt–"

"They're not gonna hurt anybody unless I don't give 'em what they want. The cops – Jesus, Tom! The cops would've taken *you* in. I can see Byron, all wide-eyed: *I don't know what you're talking about, officer. We were just about to take a hike. My cousin . . . We've had inklings that he's delusional for quite some time. He thinks he's from another planet.*

"And what are you gonna say? *They threatened to kill our family if we didn't give them this priceless Mesoamerican treasure that we just stole from the San Bernardino County Museum?* They'd lock me up, too!" Wiley blanched white at that thought.

Tom said slowly, "You wanna see what's on it, don't you?"

Wiley's color returned, and with it, his familiar toothy smile. "You said it yourself. It's been under that temple for a long time. Maybe it's a dud by now. Unimbued. But we'll give it to 'em. You've got a laptop at the cabin, and if Byron starts dictating the Syrian equivalent of Watson and Crick onto it – you'll be able to tell, right?"

"I think so."

"If he does – Google this for me, my son. *Temperature gold melts.*"

Tom typed on his phone and after a moment, he smiled. "We got a propane torch?"

Wiley shook his head. "But we got a Home Depot on the way."

Tom read from his phone. *"The gold is placed into a crucible, which is a container that can withstand temperatures above the melting point of gold. Crucibles that are used to melt gold are usually made of graphite. The crucible is placed upon a fireproof surface and a propane torch is directed at the gold within the crucible. The gold should melt within a few minutes."*

"The hell with all that. We've got a fire pit, and we'll pick up a torch. We'll let Byron have the disk, let him transfer the information. It's not like he's gonna be able to remember it, right? I'll set the laptop to self-destruct, as they say in the spy game, for a few hours from now. I'm a Keeper of the Knowledge, am I not? It'll be as worthless as Hal singing *Daisy,* long before he can put together one of those message things and send the data to Sirius.

"And before that happens, we'll say we have to send the disc back to the museum, and put it to the torch."

"What if they've decided they want to keep it?"

"They can't take it with them, can they?"

Tom shook his head. "Too much metal. But they might want to keep it anyway, as a symbol of the New World Order. Something for the invaders to bow down to, the formulas that had made them what they are—"

"Dionne has a pistol, right?"

Tom nodded. "Under the bed. I was amazed when she told me. She said that sometimes, before we met, when she was feeling that the end was particularly near, she slept with it next to her. Right on the other pillow."

"If they won't give the disc to us, we'll take it from them."

"You gonna shoot 'em, Wiley?"

"You know me, my son. Byron couldn't've been more wrong. I'm no humanitarian."

Tom considered Wiley silently for a long time.

"What?"

"I was sincerely unsure of you, my son. *Why shouldn't the Dinos be allowed to come here? Maybe they're just like us . . .*"

"I was a little unsure of you for a minute, too. You're as alien as they are, really, and all this talk of invasion . . . It's enough *to mark the full-fraught man and best indued with some suspicion."* Wiley paused, smiled humorlessly. "Call it a hippie fugue. A momentary lapse of reason. I thought that maybe someone else, from *somewhere else* – maybe they might make things better. Who'd care if they're different, then, if they fix things? I thought . . . You're right – who wouldn't wanna help save the world? *Without a thought of the consequence, I gave in to my decadence."*

"A small regret, you won't forget . . ."

"Whatever I considered, even for a moment . . . Byron changed my mind. Maybe I would've just given him the disk, just to see what happened next. But once he threatened our family . . . Even if they wouldn't've hurt anybody, just that threat demonstrates that you're right. If any of it's true – what he aims to accomplish . . . It's not immigration. It's invasion. Fuck him and his smarter than average lizards, even if they might've cleaned this place up."

FORTY-SIX

Dionne's cabin in Big Bear was perched on the rim of a short valley. Her property encompassed ridge, valley, and the next ridge over, some one hundred and twenty-five acres.

Her late husband's grandfather had acquired it all for a song, a very long time ago.

After meeting Wiley and Brendee and Bo, and Nate and Deneen – Eric wasn't yet born – Dionne had offered to subdivide off some of this largesse of land for them. Tom offered a no interest loan for construction – he could afford it – and almost before one could say, *Repent, the end is near,* two more cabins had sprouted across the valley. They were a little bit smaller than Dionne's, but each also featured a HEPA-filtered underground bomb shelter. She had insisted upon it.

Wiley and Tom found all the Tribes gathered in Dionne's sprawling living room. Byron and Viktoria sat on the couch and blinked expressionlessly in their strange owlish manner. Eric sat on Vikky's lap, absorbed with watching Bo scoot a wooden car back and forth on the floor at Byron's feet.

Janae frowned at the latecomers and said to Brendee, "Do you still wanna take that hike? I think I need some air."

Brendee shared a glance of mild shock with Denny and Dionne. Janae wanted to escape her beloved Tommy's company? The apocalypse must indeed be upon them.

"But they just got here, Janae."

There was a split-second of uncomfortable silence while Tom pointedly avoided looking at his adopted grandchild, then Denny broke it. "We'll go with you, Janae. We just have to stop at our place and get Eric's wrap." It was a sling for carrying the little boy.

As Denny reached for her son, Vikky made eye contact with Wiley. He nodded slowly, and only he and Tom noticed Vikky's slight hesitation before handing Eric to his mother.

"Do you wanna go, Nate?" Denny asked, and waited while her husband looked at Wiley.

It would forever irk her that, if Wiley was present, Nate always wanted to know what he was considering before answering her. It was either a spoken question or it was a questioning glance, like now. Denny sighed. Wiley would do the same thing if Brendee asked him something. They were best friends, and were inseparable, like brothers. She and Brendee were only their wives, the mothers of their children.

In answer to Nate's silent query, Wiley nodded toward the door. "You guys go ahead." In one quick, graceful, fluid motion, he snatched Bo off the floor. He kissed the surprised boy.

"My car, Daddy!"

Wiley picked up the wooden toy and kissed Bo again, then handed him to Brendee. "All you guys go. Tom and I have to have a few words with Byron, then we'll all catch up with you."

Nate was pretty sure that he knew all of Wiley's secrets, and Brendee knew that he had secrets that he'd never reveal to her. Dionne suspected the same about Tom. But both women had been with their *mates* long enough to understand the expressions in their blue eyes: for some reason, Wiley and Tom wanted them *to go,* and not stand around discussing it. Nate knew it, too.

"All right, Wiley," he said slowly.

"Text me when you're on your way," his wife added.

Wiley kissed her for her cooperation, but studiously avoided hugging her, she noticed. Whatever was going on, Brendee figured that he'd tell her all about it later. Unless he didn't.

FORTY-SEVEN

After the Tribes left to take a walk in the clean mountain air, Wiley removed the disk from beneath his shirt and set it on the coffee table. The ancient gold glinted brightly.

"You said something about needing a computer? To dictate the . . . results?"

Viktoria's eyes flashed with fervent joy, as they had at the museum. She stared at the artifact and murmured, "Yes, Keeper. You are about to see interplanetary history being made."

"Get your HP, Tom," the Keeper instructed. "It's got the best mike."

Tom disappeared down the hall for several moments. Suspicious of subterfuge, Viktoria was just about to arise and go after him when he returned with a dark blue laptop.

"I'm afraid I'll have to plug it in," he said, handing it to Wiley. "The battery's dead. I found the power cord under the bed where we thought it might be."

Wiley nodded and when the laptop was receiving power, he opened it and began typing. After a minute he instructed Byron, "Okay, when you're ready, just click on the mike icon right here, and start speaking."

Byron familiarized himself with the interface, then paused. "I want to thank you again for all your help, Wiley. As Viktoria has mentioned, there'll definitely be a place of high esteem for you in the new–"

"Whatever," Wiley replied neutrally. "Let's get this show on the road."

Byron took a deep breath, then grasped the disc with both hands and closed his eyes. He leaned back on the couch. His eyelids fluttered, then opened wide. He gasped, then fainted.

"The wonders unman you, my brother!" Viktoria, beside him on the couch, took the artifact from his limp hands. Its effect was the same; her eyes widened, then she fell back against the cushions in a swoon.

Tom and Wiley shared a glance of astonishment.

"I don't think this is what they were expecting." Tom took the opportunity of his cousins' inexplicable unconsciousness to remove

Dionne's pistol from the waistband of his jeans and hide it beside him between the cushion and the arm of the couch.

Wiley stood, retrieved the disk from Vikky. "Are they dead? Did it electrocute them?" He'd carried the disk against his skin and hadn't felt as much as a tingle, but now he quickly set it back down on the coffee table just in case.

"Sirians have never been too big on electricity, Wiley. There's no way it's electrified." Tom also arose, shook Vikky's shoulder, none too gently.

She sat up with a start, then looked at her surroundings as if unsure exactly where she was. Her eye fell upon the elder Sirian. "Tom! The vision! We've nearly betrayed our race!" She shook her brother. "Wake up, Byron!"

Byron slowly came to.

"Did you see?"

Her brother nodded and buried his handsome face in his hands; the tears streamed silently down Viktoria's face.

"What are you talking about? You *intend* to betray your race." Tom looked at Wiley. *"Our race."*

"No!" Viktoria sobbed.

Byron's face convulsed in guilty pain and he sneered at Tom. "There's more monkey than mermaid about you if you didn't see."

Again Tom repeated, "What are you talking about?"

"You haven't touched it?"

"I guess not, I haven't had the chance—"

Viktoria snatched up the disc and thrust it into Tom's hands. He gripped it, closed his eyes. But he didn't faint; he laughed. He continued to laugh heartily; his own tears – tears of mirth – squirted from his eyes. Wiley began to suspect that it was some new trick on Byron and Viktoria's part, that the alien artifact had somehow driven his friend insane.

Tom grabbed Viktoria by the elbow, pulled her to her feet and hugged her. "I see now!"

Wiley took a step back. "Tom—"

Tom saw the alarm, the fear in Wiley's eyes. "It's okay, my son. I'm not going over to the enemy." He slapped Byron playfully on the top of the head. "They're not the enemy anymore, either."

"What are you—"

"The disc tells a tale, Wiley. The truth. It's not about saving mankind, but it's not about genetic formulas to ensure that Dinos can pass as humans, either. Its purpose is essentially the opposite of what Byron and Viktoria were led to believe."

"We're no longer under the Dino spell," Viktoria whispered with awe.

"What the fuck, Tom?" Wiley was still confused, wary. "First we're gonna have to save the world from reptile invaders, and now you're telling me it's all okey-dokey? How do I know that this isn't some other alien bullshit?"

Tom set the disc on the coffee table again and plopped down beside Wiley on the couch. He nodded at the laptop. "Call off the countdown. We're not gonna need to dictate anything."

Wiley remained motionless. "What's going on, Tom? Is this some kind of trick?"

"No trick, my son." He ran his hand lightly over the disk. "Here's what it says.

"Brice was indeed a hero, but not to the Dinos. They took him and Annett and Tyrrel captive, and threatened the boy's life if Mom and Dad didn't work on the manipulations to make them look human. Brice strung them along, all his long life, giving them little helps with this hybrid thing, but never enough to enable these freaks to truly pass. Brice wasn't a traitor to his race.

"But his son . . . Brice saw that Tyrrel was fond of their lizard captors. He didn't see them as a threat to his species; he'd never seen another member of his species besides his parents. Just as my cousins have been brainwashed to believe–"

"That's it!" Viktoria exclaimed. "It had to've been some kind of hypnosis or something!"

"Brice realized that Tyrrel was sympathetic to the Dino cause. There wasn't anything he could do about that – the kid had been raised with them, after all. Brice had pretended to help the Dinos, so that they wouldn't eat his son – but he couldn't stop them from influencing the young man.

"So Brice came up with the fairytale that Viktoria and Byron have been told, that the secret to the hybridization was on this artifact. Brice bid Tyrrel hide it on Earth, awaiting the day when the Dinos would be strong enough to retrieve it and begin their final transformation . . . But it's all bullshit, Wiley."

"Why didn't Tyrrel figure it out? He had to've touched it to bring it here."

"Brice knew that his son would believe all this once and future king bullshit, that the secret to make the Dinos at last appear human was safely hidden on the imbued disk. He sealed it in the box – it was probably a souvenir someone had brought back from Earth. Tyrrel felt no need to take it out and touch it. The formulas wouldn't mean anything to him anyway; he didn't know anything about bioengineering."

"But Brice couldn't know for sure that Tyrrel wouldn't touch it. To keep the truth hidden, just in case – it has to be magic!" Viktoria gushed.

"No wonder they picked you," Tom said, not entirely unkindly. "You're so gullible."

"Who picked them, Tom?"

"I'm not sure. All I know is that Brice imbued this disk with the real story – when a Sirian touches it, all is revealed to him. The spell's broken and the Sirian realizes that he's been tricked.

"Brice instructed Tyrrel to go to Earth, to hide the artifact. When he returned to Sirius, his parents were dead, and he couldn't continue their genetic research.

"Brice was brilliant. Once he was gone, he knew that the Dinos had no further use for his son. He wasn't a geneticist, and it might be in their best interest to get rid of him. But because of this disk and the mysterious secret it contained – they would let him live, because he and they believed that the day would someday arrive when the secret could be revealed, and the plan could again be set in motion. Because he was human, Tyrrel would be able to leave Sirius and retrieve the disk. If the time wasn't right for that, he would still be able to pass the story along to any Sirian sympathetic to the Dino cause." Tom looked significantly at his cousins.

"We weren't *sympathetic to the Dino cause,*" Byron retorted. "We'd never heard of *the Dino cause* until we were . . . tricked. Hypnotized."

"That's the other part of the story. Brice realized that Tyrrel was sympathetic to his captors but he figured that perhaps that sympathy would wane, once he got back among his own kind. But Brice knew that the Dinos believed in the myth of the formulas, so he imagined that, when they deemed the time was right, they would employ trickery to send a Sirian after it. Hypnosis."

"You're making this up," Wiley stated in flat disbelief.

Tom shrugged. "I'm speculating. Brice put the disc in the box, and Tyrrel didn't touch it. That much is obvious. And when a Sirian arrived to retrieve it . . .." He looked at his cousins. "The vision broke the conditioning they'd received."

"How did Brice know a Dino wouldn't come for it?"

"Maybe he figured that they'd never be able to pass as human enough to come here, and thereby a monkey would have to retrieve it. Maybe the story wouldn't pass to a lizard if he did touch it. I dunno.

"Brice probably didn't realize that it would take all these centuries for someone to come for it. He probably thought that the Dino Menace would always exist, that they'd always be around, like guerillas, kidnapping people and forcing them to do their bidding. He couldn't predict that eventually, the only ones left would be harmless servants."

"The regular ones must still exist," Wiley opined. "The island must be real, and Tyrrel's story has been passed down for all these centuries there."

"I don't believe there's a Dino island," Tom insisted. "It's just another fairytale about a conquered civilization, about a return to a vanished former glory."

"But who's been repeating this fairytale for all these centuries?"

Tom shook his head. "There are no Dinos, Wiley. Only Grays."

"Maybe . . ." Wiley's eyes grew wide and round. "Maybe all that alien shit we've always heard about is true! The Grays . . . All those people that say they've been abducted! Experimented on! Christ, Tom, maybe it's all fucking true! The Grays have been snatching people and taking their tissues, trying to recreate Brice's lost formulas, so they can pass as human!"

Tom tried unsuccessfully to disguise his mirth. "Did you know *gullible's* not in the dictionary, Wiley?"

Viktoria picked up her phone from the coffee table to assure him that it was, but Tom took it from her and set it back down again. "Just think for a second, Vikky. It's a joke. Don't become one of those people that let their phones think for them." He grinned. "The Keeper calls such people *sheep.*"

The Keeper was not amused. "Maybe they've been coming here for all these years—"

"The Grays couldn't pilot a spacecraft, Wiley. There are no spacecraft anymore. Like I told you, they were all composted, centuries ago."

"How do you know? Maybe on the island—"

"The Dinos never had any spacecraft, and there is no island."

"Well, *somebody* knew that this disc existed on Earth; they knew Tyrrel's story about an artifact that contained the formula to allow Dinos to masquerade as people–"

"And they hypnotized us to come get it!" Vikky said. "They brain . . . ?"

"Brainwashed. I guess that's possible. Some servant – like I said, the Dinos supposedly possessed a type of telepathy, just like the mermaids. It was said that Dino warriors in close combat could hypnotize their opponent, like the cobra's supposed to be able to do here."

"I heard that's a myth," Wiley remarked absently. He was thinking about Sleestaks on hidden islands, and alien abductions.

Tom shrugged. "I don't really know. You'll understand when I say that I've never been too big on a study of herpetology. My roots, don't you know." He smiled.

Wiley did not. "There still must be some full-blooded Dinos around, Tom! Someone had to recruit–"

Tom shook his head. "I don't believe it. They were wiped out."

"Someone prepared Byron and Viktoria to come here and retrieve what they'd been led to believe was on the disc," Wiley reiterated emphatically. "Somebody knew Brice's fiction, all these centuries later."

Tom asked his cousin, "Who were you supposed to contact once you got the info?"

"Truxten. He is the servant of the elder Isaac–"

"A Gray," Tom smiled at Wiley. "You were right, my son. Servants tell tall tales of former dominance when the boss is away. *The South shall rise again.*"

Viktoria shook her head. "Elders were involved. They believed the Dinos deserved another chance. Truxten was only a messenger. It was Isaac who was the leader."

"Or that's what Truxten conned you into believing. Did you ever talk to this elder?"

Byron shook his head. "Victoria and I were afield one day. I was about nineteen, she seventeen."

"How old are you now?" Wiley asked suddenly.

"I'm thirty–"

"No way!" Wiley was amazed. "You don't look a second older than twenty-three! You're twenty-eight?"

Vikky nodded.

"It's all that clean living, Wiley," Tom said.

"We were gathering triticum–"

"What?"

"Wheat, Wiley."

"How am I supposed to know what you call wheat on Sirius, Tom?"

"Triticum is what you call it here." An edge of Viktoria's superiority returned.

"We call it *wheat* here, Vikky, so–"

"Anyway . . ." Tom interrupted. "I'd like to hear this before everyone gets back."

Vikky's smugness faded. She recalled that she'd been willing to hurt the Earth children to achieve her goals . . . She put her face in her hands to avoid Wiley's gaze.

"We were afield, gathering wheat. I was newly emancipated–"

"Had your first place, eh?"

Byron ignored Wiley. "And Viktoria was visiting from the center. We were going to make bread. There were also servants in the fields. Truxten . . . Viktoria dropped her bag, and he retrieved it for her."

"His hand touched mine. And then he said, *You will believe.*"

"He touched me, too. I felt light-headed . . . He said, *Consider this crystal,* and showed me a clear cylindrical object in his palm. A bluish light seemed to emanate from it."

"You're making this up," Wiley repeated. He looked at Tom in disbelief. "What next? *You're getting very sleepy? When I snap my fingers, you'll awaken and have no memory that I turned you into a traitor to your race?* Come on, Tom! This is bullshit!"

"*There are more things in heaven and earth than are dreamt of in your philosophy,* Wiley." Byron smiled fondly at him; it had been Wiley who had exposed him to the poetic brilliance of Shakespeare.

"I cannot *as a stranger welcome* this, Byron. It's bullshit."

Byron shrugged at Wiley's disbelief, uncaring, and continued his story. "For the next decade, we met Truxten in the wheat field, about once a month. He told us about the Dino island, about Brice and Annett and Tyrell. He told us that the river of mercury had already been discovered on Earth."

Vikky continued, "He told us that there was a large group, led by his employer, Isaac, and that they were secretly aligned with the Dinos on the island. They wished to see them succeed on Earth. As in the millennia gone by, the time was not yet right for the retrieval of the formulas, but it would be soon . . ."

"You listened to this crap for ten years? Yet you never saw any other Sirians? No one else from this supposed league of traitors?"

"Truxten is a Sirian, Tom."

"We've been over this, Vikky. Truxten is a cockroach."

Byron continued. "Then late last spring, Truxten asked us to describe our lineage. We told him our father's name and our mother's—"

"Isaac tells me your grandmother is called Alba, he said. *Isaac recalls that she had a brother, Thomas. This is your lineage?"*

"Hot damn, Tom!" Wiley slapped him on the back. "The fucking Dinos know you by name!"

Tom said nothing.

Bryon went on. "When we told him that was indeed our lineage, he smiled. His big eyes sparkled. *You have been chosen to fulfill the prophecy!* He told us that Isaac would prepare the way for us to visit Earth—"

"They jumped you to the top of the list. Because you had a relative here. That's what happened for me."

"King Nepot rules all," Wiley mused. "Even on Sirius."

"Once we achieved the formulas and dictated them to a computer, we were supposed to construct a communication device and relay the data to Isaac."

"Via Truxten, of course."

"We were told that the coordinates would intersect a receiver at Isaac's abode."

"You can hook up a computer to that thing?" Wiley said in astonishment. "The thing with the nails and the cake timer?"

"Cake timer?" Vikky said in confusion. "What's a—"

"You obviously haven't seen the new schematics, *Keeper,*" Byron said. "Current plans allow for an interface with your electronic devices. The oscilloscope is upgraded to a more modern model, and—"

"A digital storage oscilloscope."

"Of course, a Keeper would know these things!" Vikky declared.

"Sirius has gone digital." Now it was Tom's turn to be amazed.

Wiley showed his shark's grin. "Or at least the Dinos have."

Vicky shook her head. "The elder was supposed to simply *listen* to the formulas, and imbue another disk with them, for dissemination to the proper individuals on the Dino island. You said *I* was gullible? We still have no machinery, Tom, digital or otherwise—"

"After transmitting the knowledge," Byron continued as if his sister had not spoken, "we were supposed to return to Mapimi and then to Sirius."

"We were promised a hero's welcome," Vikky recalled softly. She put her head in her hands again.

"Does Martin have one of these new communication devices? Maybe we should let him do the calling. He was always directly in touch with the powers that be. We don't want to be contacting whoever it was that you were supposed to–"

"Martin died, Tom. His granddaughter–"

"Thank Christ. At least she grew up in the first world. I'm sure she's got the newest equipment."

"It'll still take a week or so for a return message."

"They must be warned immediately," Vikky's voice rose. "The Dino Menace has returned, it's alive and well! They must be warned!"

Tom smiled patronizingly at her. "I don't think there's as much danger as you do, honey."

Wiley was surprised at his unconcerned, laissez-faire attitude. There was obviously *something* going on behind the scenes on Sirius, and even if it wasn't an imminent invasion of Earth . . . *Mighty oaks from little acorns grow.* "She's right, Tom. We gotta make that call."

"They're not full-blooded carnivorous monsters anymore, Wiley. They're puny, little, big-headed nobodies. They've been engineered to be nothing more than that. Harmless servants."

"We cook your meals, we haul your trash, we connect your calls, we drive your ambulances. We guard you while you sleep. Do not fuck with us."

"They're not so indispensable as all that, Wiley. Just the help. It's not like they're mistreated . . ."

"Because they're created," Byron said suddenly. "They don't reproduce on their own. They're sterile."

"Really?"

"Yes," Vikky said. "They're bioengineered. A highly sophisticated form of what you primitively call cloning. They're genderless."

"That's awful." Wiley was appalled.

"Oh, Christ, here we go with the social work again! Who *are* you?" Tom didn't smile. "What's so awful about it? None of them are unwanted. There's never been an unemployed surfeit of them. If someone needs the help . . ."

"What? They just order one?"

"They're part of the family, damn it!"

"You said you don't have families."

"They're *the help*, Wiley. They help at the childcare centers; with the elderly. They help individuals–"

"You just call up and order one? Like a fucking pizza?"

"They live with us," Vikky said.

Wiley shook his head. "I'm starting to believe those abduction stories again. Maybe they want to have families."

"For Christ's sake, Wiley. There are no Grays coming to Earth, mutilating cattle and stealing reproductive material from your hapless fellow man. It is not possible." Wiley opened his mouth to speak, but Tom said firmly, "It's not possible, my son, regardless of what's dreamt of in my philosophy."

Wiley looked at Byron and Vikky and they nodded in agreement. It was not possible for any Grays to come to Earth.

"That's why they sent you guys. They want to reproduce. They want this genetic-formulas-to-pass-as-human myth to be true." When none of the Sirians spoke, Wiley said, *"I am Spartacus.* That was a slave rebellion, right?"

"They're not gladiators, Wiley!" Tom insisted.

"A famous military man said, *All men dream* . . . Hold on." Wiley consulted his phone. "It was Lawrence of Arabia. *All men dream, but not equally. Those who dream by night in the dusty recesses of their minds, wake in the day to find that it was vanity. But the dreamers of the day are dangerous men, for they may act on their dreams with open eyes, to make them possible."*

"You're a poet, Wiley," Viktoria marveled.

Tom smirked. "Ah, he's just quick on a Google search. At least a perfunctory one. I'm not dismissing this, Wiley. We'll send a message. But I don't think it's comparable to–"

"Okay, how about, *When you ain't got nothing, you got nothing to lose?* The Grays are dreaming of reproduction, of world domination, and even if you think they're harmless . . . This could be a lot bigger than you think, Tom. I don't care if they *are* only servants – they must have some kind of network. This whole formulas-to-make-'em-look-human story has been passed down for a long time, and they were counting on it being true. What are they gonna do when they find out it's nothing but a myth?"

"Give up, maybe?"

"Or maybe they'll start poisoning their masters. This . . . this *movement* has to be fairly entrenched, Tom. They had the resources to hypnotize Byron and Viktoria, send 'em here. They had the pull to jump them to the head of the line."

"One servant. Playing on his boss's name." Tom affected an old-timey gangster accent. *"I hear a lot of talk, but all I see here is you and a couple of your boys. I don't see no Federation. I only saw three guys in that ship. Maybe there ain't no more."*

Wiley responded immediately. *"There's over four hundred guys there."*

"That's your story, buster."

Byron frowned. "You know, the whole movie-quoting phenomenon? It gets to be annoying."

"It's kind of our thing," Tom objected. He remembered all the endless hours he'd spent watching *Star Trek* with Wiley, and was suddenly almost overwhelmed with a quite maudlin sense of gratitude for the clever monkey's friendship.

They had basically the same taste in old movies, surely, although Tom tended toward more classic cinema, whilst Wiley enjoyed the good, the bad, the ugly; the whole smorgasbord of the popular culture of yesteryear. But *Star Trek* had always been their shared favorite. Like Mrs. Lucas's grandmother, some relative of Wiley's had left behind a boxed set in the attic where he'd convalesced as a teenager, and Liz had showed it to Tom on Netflix. Enjoying it with Wiley reminded Tom of her sometimes; if he couldn't have Liz's companionship anymore, he was thankful that he had Wiley's.

"It's rather exclusionary," Vikky observed.

Wiley smiled at his friend. "We can't help it if you guys are Philistines, and alien ones at that."

Vikky frowned, typed on her phone. "We are not *hostile or indifferent to culture and the arts."*

Wiley looked up the word himself. "But you do *have no understanding of them."*

Byron sighed. "We spent the better part of the last decade preparing for this *mission.* We didn't devote a great deal of time to–"

"Studying the culture here? Why should you? The aim of invaders is to invade–"

"So it's not just a clever name?"

Tom paused long enough to wonder again what he'd do without Wiley's quick, caustic, irreverent wit, then he turned on Byron again and said bitterly, "Invaders don't want to assimilate. If you want the gold nugget all to yourself, you're not gonna share it with the nearest monkey in the nearest tree, even if it was his first. He's dumb; he doesn't know that it's gold, doesn't know its value. You don't care about his traditions about its use, or–"

"They've seen the light, Tom," Wiley said quickly, before the old Sirian could start on another anti-invasion tirade. "But we need to make that call. I don't want to get abducted so I can help fight little, big-headed guys."

"Okay, my son. We'll make the call, Sirius will quell the sedition of its servants . . . All will be well."

"If only we can forgive ourselves." Anguish colored Byron's voice.

"The new Dino threat to Earth'll be averted," Wiley soothed. "No harm, no foul on your part, as the saying goes."

"How could you ever trust us again, Wiley?" Vikky wailed.

"It's like this, kiddies. I've been a student of the sheep with whom I share this planet, all my life. I've watched–"

"The girls. Mostly he's watched the girls." Tom smiled.

"My point is this. I saw your reactions when you absorbed the true story. It was so shocking to you that it knocked you out. Then when you woke up, you were appalled, ashamed at what you'd been about to do. You guys haven't assimilated that well in the time you've been here. I don't think you could've faked that guilt." Wiley glanced at Tom, and he nodded reluctantly.

"And you're not blinking like owls anymore. Like Tom said, when you touched the disc, your conditioning was broken. I think your reactions were genuine. I think I'm seeing the real you now."

Wiley paused. "Wait till Nate hears about this."

FORTY-EIGHT

Brendee's text said: *Are u coming, or what?*
I'm not even breathing hard. But we'll b along in a minute.

"The Tribes beckon," Wiley informed Tom. "But before we go . . . Do you have a big envelope? Padded maybe?" He nodded at the disc. "We need to get rid that, ASAP."

"Post Office's closed, Wiley. It's Veteran's Day."

"All the better. I'm sure they've got a big box out front. So all the locals can mail pinecones to their relatives."

"I know what a pinecone is, Keep – Wiley, but what's *to mail?*"

"When we have to transport small items, we take them to a centralized depot. It's called a *Post Office;* the action's called *mailing.*" Tom was rooting around in a cabinet by the door, looking for a shipping envelope. "The Keeper doesn't know much about that, however. He never mails anything.

"You're sure you want to mail it, Wiley? That seems a little . . . careless. What if it gets lost? Shouldn't we . . . I dunno, leave it on the doorstep of the museum?"

"That *would* be careless. They've got cameras at the museum, and I doubt if they've got any at the lil' ol' Big Bear Post Office."

"Although Tom's right, Vikky. I've never been to the post office, Big Bear or otherwise. I've never had to *mail* anything. But I'm sure . . . We'll just drop it in the box. It'll be fine." Wiley leapt up lithely from the couch to help look for an envelope.

"Here's one." Tom reached for it.

"Don't touch it! Fingerprints, my son. You got any *inspection gloves?*"

Tom opened the bottom drawer and produced a pair of gardening gloves.

"Bulky, but they'll do."

Wiley called up the museum's website on his phone, donned the gloves and retrieved the envelope. Tom handed him a pen.

"You're not worried that they'll try to analyze your handwriting?"

"Now you're just being ridiculous." He addressed the envelope and gingerly crammed the artifact into it. He pulled the tab and folded the flap over. "But you know what else we're not gonna do?"

"What?"

"Lick the stamps."

Byron's black eyebrows rose.

"The price paid for the mailing," Tom explained.

"You have to lick something to transport it?"

"Not at all." He told Wiley, "Now you're the Philistine, my son. You don't lick stamps anymore." He dug around in the drawer until he found a sheet of them. "They been self-adhesive for as long as I can remember."

"I don't think I've ever even *seen* a stamp, Tom," Wiley said defensively. "Nonetheless, used . . . How many should I put on?"

Tom bent the card at the bottom of the sheet back, and deftly stuck all eight stamps onto the envelope without touching them. He smoothed them over with the sleeve of his shirt. "If that's not enough, the museum will just be stuck paying the extra postage."

FORTY-NINE

Wiley arrived back at the valley below Dionne's cabin just as the Tribes were returning from their hike.

"I was detained," he told his wife, and took their sleeping son from her. "Tomorrow is another day."

Brendee knew better than to question him about something as inconsequential as why he'd missed a nature walk. She leaned in and whispered into his ear, "If you observe closely, I think you'll get the answer to your question."

"About?"

Brendee nodded over her shoulder, and Wiley observed, as he'd been bid. Vikky was first, carrying Eric, also asleep, in his wrap; next came Tom and Dionne, Nate and Denny, and last, but certainly not least, Byron and Janae; each couple was holding hands.

"That doesn't mean that they're—"

"Look at her face, Wiley. She looks at him . . . Why, just like I look at you!" Brendee kissed him quickly on the cheek, then skipped on up the hill.

Wiley squinted merrily at Janae. *Aren't you guys just adorable?*

Janae dropped Byron's hand, frowned. "Where ya been, Funny Guy?"

"I was detained," Wiley repeated. "Take Bo on up for me, will ya? I need to have a word with your boyfriend." He handed his son to her before she could object. "I'll see you guys in a minute."

He put his arm around Byron's shoulders and steered him back down the path.

"What is it, Wiley?"

"About this Janae thing, my son."

Byron remained expressionless.

"You are assimilating after all," Wiley said in admiration. "That blank look's perfectly fitting at this moment, because I'm about to give you a variation of what my dad used to call *The Talk*. You know, if you're gonna be hanging around here, Tom's gonna expect you to make an honest woman out of Janae."

"An honest —?"

"Pardon *my idiom*. Let me try again. If you're gonna be hanging around here, with Janae, Tom's gonna expect you to embrace that quaint Earth custom, the bane of the drinking class, so to speak. Monogamy."

"But I've got a date all lined up with Dr. Cooper, Wiley! Something about showing me his pool . . ."

"It's November, Byron."

"I understand it's heated." Byron made Wiley wait for a heartbeat, then grinned. "Dr. Cooper's a bit too . . ."

"Gullible?"

Byron nodded. "You, on the other hand . . ."

"It ain't gonna happen, my son."

"Your people are secretive about such things. One does not know if one does not ask." Byron paused. "When we get back from Mexico – you're right. Viktoria and I do plan to *hang around*. Your world is fascinating, as Tom says, and if, in order to assimilate, I must embrace monogamy, well, I guess I can give it a try. Janae will do as well as anyone . . . This custom worked for Tom, and I like Janae very much."

"But you don't love her."

"*I come most carefully upon my hour,* Wiley. Give me a little time. As I say, I like her very much. I'm sorry about the cruel remarks I made at the museum. She's no sheep."

"Well, maybe a little bit. I saw how she's looking at you these days."

"It is not unexpected." Byron shrugged with just a shade of ego. "I find that she intrigues me. She's beautiful, intelligent. She reminds me a great deal of you, actually."

"You can pay her no higher compliment than that, my brother. Allow me to make you a drink. After the day we've had, I think we deserve one."

FIFTY

Tom and Nate already had the barbeque fired up on the deck. When they got to the top of the stairs, Tom poured Wiley and Byron a gin and tonic from a waiting glass pitcher.

"I think you Sirians really are telepathic, my son. I was just telling your cousin that I needed a drink."

"I just know you, Wiley. I can't read you mind."

"Why would you want to?" Nate studied his friend for a moment. "So Tom tells me that the world teetered on the brink of invasion while I was out frolicking in the forest."

"You should've come to the museum with us."

Nate shook his head. "I knew you were gonna steal that thing. I can't believe you just dropped it in the mail. It's priceless."

"You and Tom have no faith in the U.S. Postal System. They mailed the Hope Diamond to the Smithsonian, once upon a time, so I'm sure that one little piece of gold from another planet will be fine."

"They're gonna know who took it."

"Probably. The young man to whom their eminent archeologist has been sending slightly and some more than slightly risqué texts for the last week. The young man he invited to the museum when it was closed, whom he allowed to be alone with the treasure, whom he allowed to touch it. All these activities, I'm sure, are against museum protocols for the handling of priceless artifacts."

"Dougie'll be so goddamn glad to get it back, he's not gonna tell anyone. Besides, the methods by which I communicated with him are untraceable. Byron's phony Facebook presence has *been* gone, and my phone . . . My phone's a ghost. All the good doctor has left of Byron are his fond memories, and the relief that we didn't steal the thing outright."

The sliding glass door opened and Bo, fresh from his brief nap, bounded outside. Brendee paused in the doorway. She'd been a little annoyed that Wiley had sent them out and then had failed to join them, but watching her husband with their boy, she couldn't stay mad at him for long. He was a good man, the sexiest one she'd ever known, and if that wasn't enough, he was a great father, too.

Wiley set his drink on the railing in time to catch Bo and toss him into the air. Brendee smiled at the delight on both their faces.

"How goes the world with you, my son?"

"Well, Daddy! You missed the hike."

"We'll go again tomorrow."

Brendee knew it would be so. Wiley might prevaricate with her on occasion, but he kept his promises to Bo. He turned his happy smile toward her. "Have a drink, Brendee!"

"All right." She walked out onto the deck and accepted a glass. "Are we celebrating something?"

"But of course. Your husband's just saved the world."

Brendee laughed at Tom. "What from this time? The plastics apocalypse?"

"Alien invasion," Nate said over the rim of his glass.

"This time?" Byron said in surprise. "You mean there've been other times?"

"Just an attempt, my son."

"You haven't heard that story yet?" Brendee asked archly. "About how Wiley tried to warn the first world that our food is poisoned?"

"I was shot down," Wiley explained. "The media said nobody cares."

"I told you nobody cares, Wiley," Tom said gently.

"Bo cares. What don't we eat, Bo?"

"Things that come from ending machines."

"Vending machines, son. What else?"

"Things that come in cans. Or boxes." He looked at his mother. "'Cept cereal. And sgetti. They're forty-fied."

"And what does fortified mean?"

"That it's good for me."

"Out of the mouths of babes, just like I told you, Wiley," Tom said. "Go get your Auntie Janae, Bo. Tell her she's missing the party."

Wiley set him down and he scampered into the cabin.

"I don't know if Janae can teach you anything you don't already know about . . . *other things,* Byron." Wiley closed one eye and squinted at Tom. "But not unlike your cousin, here – he pretty much taught me, and she can teach you."

"About . . ."

"Drinking, my son."

FIFTY-ONE

The Tribes barbequed steaks and ate vegetables freshly picked from the garden in the valley below. Because the idea amused him, Wiley insisted that they watch an ancient copy of *The Little Mermaid* that he materialized off the internet and played on the big TV over the equally big fireplace. He said it was for the kids' benefit, but soon found the entire clan enrapt by the old cartoon: none of them had ever seen it before, not even Tom.

Except that Dionne had seen it, and proclaimed it another piece of patriarchal propaganda. "Her father thinks he owns her!"

"Hush, Dionne." Wiley nodded at Nate and Deneen, curled up together on a big chair, at Janae and Byron, again holding hands on one end of the couch, at Brendee waiting for him on the other. "It's a love story. Go sit with your lover."

The boys fell asleep in the playpen long before Ariel got to get married and be *a part of our world*, and Nate and Wiley gingerly picked the whole thing up and took it down the hall to Tom and Dionne's bedroom, so the noise from further movies wouldn't disturb them.

The grown-ups drank and laughed, watched old movies, watched new movies and drank some more. Viktoria passed out facedown on the couch, and Dionne covered her up with a blanket. During an intermission, Bryon had a discreet word with Wiley in the kitchen, and when the lights dimmed for the next feature, he and Janae slipped out. Wiley had lent them the spare bedroom in his cabin for the night.

Nate and Denny retrieved their son and also went across the valley. Brendee and Wiley and Bo curled up on the floor in front of the fireplace amid many soft blankets and pillows. Soon the prepper compound was wreathed in silence.

FIFTY-TWO

Again Wiley Royce dreamed.

He found himself seated on a wooden bench beside a pebbled path in an unfamiliar forest. The wood felt warm, alive; he looked down and discovered that he was naked, and thinking that dreams about being naked in a public place were supposed to indicate a sense of vulnerability or unpreparedness, he laughed. Wiley had never felt vulnerable, nor had he ever been unprepared in his entire life.

He arose and traced the path through the forest. At last he came to a beach, the shore of a small lake. Some kind of seal smiled at him from the shallows, barked happily. It approached him with its odd, rocking gate, and he bent over and patted its head. The seal barked again, again smiled, then returned to the water.

Wiley noticed the pristine cleanliness of the beach. There was not a single piece of litter; no bleached plastic bottles, no smudges of rusted metal, no garish, out of place shards of clouded green or blue or brown glass. Neither were there masses of seagulls, rooting through such seedy treasures. And there were no signs, no parking lots, no cars.

Neither was there any kind of wharf, no marina with gas pumps, no smoking restaurant. Yet he saw boats: a couple waved at him from something that resembled a wooden canoe. The man raised a paddle that seemed to consist of only a sturdy branch with a stiffened, concave leaf at the end. Wiley waved back.

And there were boats propelled by some kind of power; flat, they held four or five people with one manning a tiller at the stern. Yet Wiley heard no engine whine, neither smelled nor saw any exhaust.

Across the lake, he saw dwellings, constructed of some dark wood. They reminded him vaguely of pictures he'd seen of Mesa Verde, the ancient Pueblo site. But there was neither sheltering cliff above, nor primitive ladders between levels. Here the apartments were connected by sweeping walkways and ramps, their balustrades of intricately woven, viney plant material. The whole complex was o'ertopped with a leafy canopy. Purple mountains, majestic and snowless, rose in the distance.

Wiley walked down the beach; he arrived at an apple orchard. He saw trim, attractive men and women picking the large, luscious fruits – he thought that they might be Red Delicious apples based on their size. One of the pickers was partially hidden behind a tree trunk. Wiley thought he might've been a child as his (or her) legs and torso were smaller and slighter than the rest. But when the kid ducked from behind the tree and Wiley saw the bulbous head and black, almond shaped eyes – the creature didn't look exactly like the ones he'd seen in pictures all his life, and on Dionne's alien conspiracy shows – but the vision was close enough. This one was in the flesh, expressionless, pale and greenish, not forty feet from him, blinking owlishly in the slightly hazy overcast daylight. It was a Gray.

Wiley knew then where he was, and it was just as incredibly awesome as he'd imagined it.

He felt a tap on his shoulder and turned. Vikky was there, smiling, lovelier than he'd found her to be in real life. Her dark hair was down, impossibly lustrous and shining like something out of a shampoo commercial. She was wearing a pale mauve gown that brought out the sparkle in her gray eyes and accentuated curves that Wiley had not noticed before.

"Welcome to Sirius, Keeper," she said with a breathless little laugh. "Apparently Tom was right." She looked him up and down and giggled again. "You're even unclothed, as if you'd just arrived."

"This is a dream, Vikky. I sleep unclothed."

"But you're sleeping across the room from me. Surely, you're not–"

"Sometimes one appears in dreams as will be most useful," he replied philosophically.

Another man might be asking a million questions: *What's going on, Vikky? Why am I naked and you're not? Am I really feeling vulnerable? Unprepared?*

But Wiley always adopted a wait-and-see attitude in his dreams. If he had a pocket from which to extract his phone, he could've found Freud's exact quote: *Dreams completely satisfy wishes excited during the day which remain unrealized. They are simply and undisguisedly realizations of wishes.* Wiley's subconscious mind figured that asking too many questions would obstruct whatever wish might be about to be fulfilled.

In the waking world, he considered himself to be master of all he surveyed. He had very few wishes that remained unrealized there.

He'd recently hoped that collaboration with men from an alien world – this one – might've cleansed his own world, might've returned it to its pre-industrial glory. He'd clung to that hope, even after he'd been told that Byron's first story, of Sirian formulas to cure all mankind's self-inflicted wounds, was all just a fantasy. Still, he'd thought that even lizards masquerading as monkeys might've cleaned things up. But when Wiley's family was threatened, he'd realized that collaboration with an invasive species such as the Dinos would've amounted to treason, even if they might've helped the sheep.

These events explained why Wiley's dreaming mind had put him on Sirius.

And as far as his nakedness was concerned, Wiley was not unaware of actions that played through his waking mind that he would never actually attempt. But he considered them, nonetheless. Freud also said, *The dream is the liberation of the spirit from the pressure of external nature, a detachment of the soul from the fetters of matter,* so to Wiley, his dreams were like that brilliant old saw created by the Las Vegas Chamber of Commerce: what his subconscious whimsically presented to him stayed within his mind only.

Besides, he was sure that, in her sleep, his beloved wife still took the occasional moonlight stroll through the Elysian Fields with Wes Thomerville and his black guitar.

What one's subconscious mind played with was of no consequence; only one's concrete actions mattered in the real world. He would never cheat on Brendee, nor she on him, so even a little harmless flirting in the real world was okay with Wiley. He'd learned his lesson on that score, however, and had refrained from it since that little misunderstanding with Janae. Some women just couldn't take a joke.

But this was only a dream, for his eyes only, so to speak, so when Vikky put her soft, warm hand in his and led him back into the secluded forest, Wiley enjoyed it guiltlessly.

They sat on one of the wooden benches again and Vikky smiled at him in what he took as invitation, the same admiring, unwavering stare she gave him in real life.

"Maybe I'm naked because you want me to be."

But when Wiley moved closer, to kiss this gray-eyed vision of Sirian pulchritude, Vikky laughed. She guffawed. She slapped her knee.

Wiley opened his eyes. Above him was the peaked, rough-beamed ceiling of Dionne's cabin. Beside him was his son, awake, rolling his wooden car over a pillow. Beside Bo, Brendee slept on.

"How goes the world with you, Daddy?"

"Curiouser and curiouser, Bo."

Wiley sat up and looked around him. Red embers glowed amid white ashes in the fireplace. Vikky slept, face down on the couch, in the same position she'd been in the night before when Dionne had covered her.

Wiley stood, stretched. "Let's make some breakfast, Bo. What would you like?"

"Pancakes!"

"Why do you want pancakes?"

"Because they're forty-fied!"

"Go on out to the kitchen and see if you can find Grandma Dionne's big mixing bowl. But be quiet. Everyone's still sleeping."

"Where you goin', Daddy?"

Wiley glanced over at Vikky's sleeping form, grinned to himself. "I have to visit the facilities, son. I'll be with you in a minute and we'll whip up those pancakes."

FIFTY-THREE

That afternoon, Wiley sat on Dionne's deck with Tom and Byron and Nate. The women and children were in the valley below, again tossing a Frisbee. Wiley watched Vikky throw it clumsily; she was holding Eric. He reflected that, while he'd had many wild adventures in his dreams, none of which he'd pursue in real life, he'd be goddamned if he'd ever been laughed at before. How bizarre it was that his own subconscious would make a fool of him . . .

"Wiley."

He turned and looked at Tom

"You seem distracted today, my son."

Nate looked over the railing. "He's just doing what he does, Tom. Watching the women."

Tom arose. "I see Persephone and some Oceanids, and there's gray-eyed Athene." He turned and winked at Wiley. "Frolicking. Are you worried that Hades is going to burst from the ground and harass them?"

Byron blinked blankly, but not owlishly. Nate rolled his eyes. Tom might as well have been speaking in a foreign language sometimes, for as much sense as he made. But Wiley understood. "I think they're safe for the moment. Bo'll defend 'em."

"Indeed." Tom sat back down. "You didn't answer Byron's question, my son."

"I'm sorry, I must've missed it. Watching the Oceanids and all."

"I asked if you wanted to go to Mexico with us. To send our message."

Wiley sighed. "Christ, that's such a long way! Why can't we do it from here? I know I can scare up the car batteries."

"Better to let the professionals handle it."

"Professionals? Professional what? You said yourself, Tom, it's the third world down there."

"Martin's family's been helping us for a long time, Wiley. Since the U.S. was the third world. That makes them professionals."

Vikky ran up the steps and collapsed breathlessly into a chair beside her brother. "I've been sent for water."

"Under the sink in the kitchen," Tom instructed, and Byron arose to fetch refreshments for his panting sister and the thirsty women below.

Wiley frowned, still considering the question put to him. "I don't wanna go to Mexico, Tom. I don't speak the language–"

"We speak the language, Keeper," Vikky said with her superior smile. "We'll assist you." She stared at him for several seconds, then at last asked, "What did you think of Sirius?"

Wiley's eyebrows rose, but he remained silent.

"I discovered that it's true what you told us, Tom. The monkeys can see, can enter into our dreams. Last night, I must've been feeling a little – what's the idiom? When one misses *where one is from?*"

Byron returned, his arms laden with plastic. "The word is *homesick.*"

The bottles bounced onto the table with familiar thumps, and Wiley picked one of them up, considered it thoughtfully. *"Aqua vitae,"* he murmured to himself.

Vikky uncapped one, drank half of it off, then continued. "I must've been feeling *homesick,* because I dreamt of the lake and the fields. Then who should I see, but the Keeper–"

"Please stop calling him that, Vikky," Nate requested. "It makes me think of an insane asylum. The keeper and the inmates."

Viktoria ignored him and grinned at Wiley. "So what did you think?"

"It was . . ." The words came out as a croak, so he cleared his throat and began again. "It was beautiful. I looked up, but the sky was overcast. Would I have seen two suns?"

"You'll have to Google that, my son." Tom winked at his cousins. "See what your scientists think. We have to keep some secrets."

As usual, Nate was suspicious. "So you're saying you *saw* Sirius?"

"To be completely accurate, Vikky saw it," Tom explained. "She remembered it, was dreaming about it. Wiley saw her dream, dreamt it along with her. It happened to Liz once. She dreamed she was in Mapimi, with Martin, because I was dreaming of the day I arrived here."

"Really," Nate stated flatly. He was surprised that Wiley wouldn't meet his eye, so he asked, "What else did you and Vikky do in this dream?"

Wiley didn't directly answer his friend's question. "It was very real. I patted a seal on the head, and I could feel his fur. I could feel the pebbles under my feet. The air – it seemed like it was perfumed somehow."

"Not perfumed, Wiley. Just unpolluted. Even here, in the mountains, there are unburned hydrocarbons in the air, maybe some carbon monoxide floating around."

"I've never smelt air like that," Wiley mused, mostly to himself.

"No. Even the cleanest place on Earth has residue of industrialization."

"But what did you think of it?" Vikky insisted.

"Like I say, it was beautiful, awesome. I felt like some kind of explorer, landed on the unspoiled shores of some never-before-seen continent. The carefree natives, unconcerned with the kind of messes we have here, playing on the water . . ."

Tom's eyebrows went up at Wiley's poesy, as it was completely without irony. He sang, *"Conquistador, your stallion stands in need of company. And like some angel's haloed brow, you reek of purity."*

Wiley shrugged, feeling self-conscious. Perhaps he was coming off as a little awestruck. It was only a dream, after all. But it had seemed so real; when he breathed, he thought he could still taste that untainted air.

He ceased his contemplation of the water bottle in his hand and addressed the other aspect of the vision. "Well, seeing as how it was only a dream after all, I was hoping for a happier ending than being laughed at. I kinda thought, what with me being . . ." Now Wiley offered her the full glint of his shark's smile. "I thought you liked me, Vikky."

If Wiley expected her to stammer and blush and ask, *Whatever do you mean?* it was because he'd forgotten that he was talking to a Sirian woman. Unable to contain her mirth, Vikky laughed as she had in their dream, again slapped her knee.

"I *do* like you, Keep – Wiley! Only not in the way in which you apparently desire me to!"

"It was only a dream," Wiley said with a trace of defensiveness. "So, I thought, hey, why not–"

"Oh, Wiley!" Vikky burst out laughing again. "If I were to accede to such a thing, you would undoubtedly expect me to also be monogamous!" She wiped a tear of merriment from her eye and giggled again. "Besides, you're not, as my friend Denny terms it, my *type*. You too much resemble my brother."

Vikky gave Byron a playfully shove, then in the ensuing silence, she wondered if she had perhaps offended Wiley by laughing at him, so she said quickly, "But still my admiration for you is enormous! You are a Keeper of the Knowledge of How Things Work, and thus my respect for you goes well beyond any passing physical attraction. How brilliant you are!"

"Stop, Vikky," Nate said, now with an air of mock pleading. "If we don't believe Wiley's brilliant, all we have to do is ask him. We don't need to hear it from you, too."

"But I never expected to meet such a one as him!"

"The *knowledge of how things work* is not some mystical secret, Vikky. Everything you want to know about . . . about anything, it's right there on your phone."

"But how does my phone itself *work?* It's all so effortless to you!"

"That's because it interests me."

"It also interests me. I would give anything to learn these things!" The fervent glow was back in her eyes.

Wiley glanced at Tom to see if he was witnessing all this, to see if he thought that Vikky was for real in her fervor; it was only electronics, just zeros and ones. Tom shrugged.

"I'll tell you whatever you want to know, Vikky. We'll start with a basic electrical circuit. Once you understand that, well, the sky, as they say, is the limit. As for my payment . . ." Wiley paused, then leaned forward and set the plastic water bottle on the table. "I don't wanna go to Mexico. I wanna go to Sirius."

There was a heartbeat of silence, then Byron shook his head. "It's forbidden."

"Here's what I figure, my son. You guys toddle on down there to Mapimi and get on the cake timer to the homeworld. You tell them that I was a key player in uncovering the imminent Gray Uprising."

His dream of Sirius had left Wiley still feeling philosophical. "If I may paraphrase – *is it not meet for them to know how much I love them? They are not wood, they are not stones, but men, and being men, hearing about this dangerous treason lurking in their midst, it will inflame them, it will make them mad.*"

Tom smiled at Wiley's amalgam of Shakespeare's immortal words. "But Wiley Royce on Sirius? *O, what would come of it?*"

"Seriously, though. What if we hadn't uncovered this plot, my son? *O, what a fall was there, my countrymen! Then I, and you, and all of us fell down, whilst bloody treason flourish'd over us.*"

Tom shook his head. He remained unconvinced that the Grays could truly be a threat. But Wiley was right. It would be best to nip the thing in the oft-mentioned bud. It would be best to make that call.

Wiley went on, still addressing Byron. "You can tell 'em that, in return for my unprecedented Earthling heroism, I'd like to pay a little visit. I can't do a goddamned thing for my own planet, but I just saved theirs."

The savage flash of bitterness in Wiley's voice lasted only the tiniest portion of a second, but it surprised Tom, as had his earlier, wistfully lyrical description of Sirius from his dream. *He really is a hippie,* Tom thought with a trace of pity. *He can't save anything but his own family, no matter how much he'd like to.*

"Tell them, I don't want to *emigrate,*" Wiley continued. "I'm not gonna tell anybody about it – I just want to visit for a few days. Breathe that incredible air. Pat a seal on the head. Tell 'em that I'll make sure that the one outcast in history returns to this backwater rock with me." He slapped Tom on the back.

"It's forbidden."

Now Wiley dismissed Byron and concentrated his killer smile on the older Sirian. "What d'ya think, Tom? I'm sure you'd like to see the *auld sod* again. Visit your sister, maybe?"

Tom thought that he *would* enjoy it. Wiley was right: he'd like to breathe that incomparable air again, *touch the green, green grass of home.*

"I know you could talk 'em into it, my son."

"I dunno, Wiley. *For I have neither wit, nor words, nor worth, action, nor utterance, nor the power of speech, to stir men's blood.*"

"Not so, Tom. I know of no man on any planet as eloquent as you."

Tom was flattered by the clever monkey's praise. "I guess I could give it a try."

"*I am glad that my weak words have struck but thus much show of fire from you.*"

Tom was instantly fascinated by Wiley's sudden desire to visit Sirius. What did the technological man think he wanted to do in a place with no electronics, amongst a people with no technology at all except for a knack for biologically molding their environment to suit them? Did Wiley think he'd be able to teach 'em how to grow cellphones, as they'd once grown interstellar craft?

Or was it just the latent hippie in him that cried out to experience a world with no landfills, that had never seen an internal combustion engine or an oil spill, an aluminum can or a discarded plastic bag? *Simplicity is the most difficult thing to secure in this world. It is the last limit of experience and the last effort of genius.* All Wiley sought was his own clean corner, so of course he'd long to encounter a world he saw as untainted.

Divorced from the dirt and seeds and water and sunshine that were the source of his food, there was still a sense of romantic mystery and amazement to the growing of things to Wiley. He was as delighted and surprised as was his son when the flowers first appeared on this years' tomato and cucumber vines.

When the garden began to take off in the spring, Wiley's self-proclaimed *childlike wonder* never failed to amuse Tom. For someone who had spent some of his formative years on a farm, Wiley was still always amazed when the things they planted actually germinated, sprouted, grew, produced. *As if he can't quite believe it's actually gonna happen,* Tom thought, *that this little sprig of nothing will grow to feed his family.*

But if Wiley expected nature lovers on Sirius, revering nature, Tom knew he was in for a shock. The bounty of the harvest was no more compelling or miraculous to them than turning on his car was to Wiley; perhaps less, because they understood how to grow things, whereas Wiley wasn't so sure about how his car worked. Food came out of the ground on Sirius, right nearby, not from the market in a box or out of a can or bag. They would only be surprised if the plants *didn't* grow.

Tom thought that perhaps Wiley was as unprepared for Sirius as Sirius was for him. Not only were things expected to grow, and along any useful ways the Sirians wanted them to: not only as food but also as medicine and houses and clothes, and once upon a time, as spaceships – there was also the whole polygamy thing. Tom knew that Wiley was devoted to his wife; how would he deal with a bunch of curious and straightforward young Sirian women showing him interest?

But on the other hand, this was the inimitable Wiley Royce that he was considering. Whatever he encountered on the homeworld, Tom was confident that Wiley would just roll with it, and effortlessly.

"If you wanna go to Sirius, my brother and only friend, you gotta go to Mexico, first."

"Apparently they can't just beam you up from Riverside, Wiley," Nate said.

Wiley sighed expansively. "Allow me to acquire a passport then. And make a few adjustments to our cellphone plans. What about you, Nate? I'm sure that if Tom can convince them to allow one monkey to see the sights, he can convince them to let two."

Nate shook his head. "You can tell me all about it when you get back, Wiley. I wouldn't want you embarrassing me in front of the aliens. You're kind of an asshole, after all."

"Better men than you have said so, my son."

Nate peeped at his friend. "You *will* come back?" He still pretty much believed it was all bullshit. *Pretty much.*

Of course he'll come back, Tom said to himself. *He's got his adoring wife and his beautiful boy. He's master of all he surveys here.*

Wiley echoed Tom's thoughts. "Of course I'll come back, Nate." But then he paused, offered them all his toothy, shark's grin. "Or see if I can run the place."

"O brave new world that has such people in't," Byron recited drily.

Wiley shrugged. "Somebody famous said, *The only limit to our realization of tomorrow will be our doubts of today.*"

Vikky typed quickly on her phone, scrolled. "That was Franklin D. Roosevelt."

Wiley's smile persisted. "It's always been my philosophy on life."

*****

Also by LM Foster

A Passing Resemblance
Contrariwise – A Tale of Twins
Corvino
Crypsis
Duck Feet
Peter's Sisters

Two Green Keys:
Two Green Keys
Adapted for the Screen

One Wilde Ride Trilogy:
Part One: It Might Have Been
Part Two: An Exceptional Boy
Part Three: What Should Never Be

Stars and Guitars:
Talk To a Movie Star
Where The Guitars Play

Tom and Wiley:
This Carnival of Strange
Wiley Royce
Generally Recognized as Safe
Wiley Royce Versus The Martians

www.ingramcontent.com/pod-product-compliance
Lightning Source LLC
Chambersburg PA
CBHW071713140626
46557CB00011B/125